HEARTWOOD
BOX

ALSO BY ANN AGUIRRE

Enclave
Outpost
Horde
Vanguard
Mortal Danger
Public Enemies
Infinite Risk
The Queen of Bright and Shiny Things
Like Never and Always

WITH RACHEL CAINE

Honor Among Thieves
Honor Bound

HEARTWOOD BOX

ANN AGUIRRE

A TOM DOHERTY ASSOCIATES BOOK

NEW YORK

HEARTWOOD BOX

Copyright © 2019 by Ann Aguirre

A Tor Teen Book
Published by Tom Doherty Associates
120 Broadway
New York, NY 10271

www.tor-forge.com

Tor® is a registered trademark of Macmillan Publishing Group, LLC.

The Library of Congress Cataloging-in-Publication Data
is available upon request.

ISBN 978-0-7653-9764-5 (hardcover)
ISBN 978-0-7653-9765-2 (ebook)

Our books may be purchased in bulk for promotional,
educational, or business use. Please contact your local bookseller
or the Macmillan Corporate and Premium Sales Department
at 1-800-221-7945, extension 5442, or by email at
MacmillanSpecialMarkets@macmillan.com.

First Edition: July 2019

Printed in the United States of America

0 9 8 7 6 5 4 3 2 1

For my son, Alek, who always knows what to say

HEARTWOOD BOX

1

This is where hope goes to die.

That's what I'm thinking as I step off the train onto the sparse platform. There's absolutely nothing here, not even a ticket machine, let alone someone I can ask for directions. Few people were left on the LIRR when I got off here, though one woman did flash me a glance like she was asking if I was sure.

I'm really not.

The area gives off a strange vibe, rural but also industrial, with green fields interspersed with machinery and equipment. It's a bit too far to walk to my great-aunt's house where I'll be staying for the next year, but I planned to get a cab when I arrived. I assured my parents I'd be fine—they could proceed to Venezuela without worrying about me—but now I'm having second thoughts.

It's not late, just past four, but there's nobody in sight. A shiver crawls over me, nerves and exhaustion. I've had a long-ass day, beginning with a tearful parting from my folks in front of an OXXO at Benito Juarez Airport in Mexico City, then a six-hour flight to JFK, immigration, customs, baggage claim, then two more hours on two different trains. I'm so tired, and the quiet here is eerie. I'm so not used to being alone.

As I walk along the platform, MISSING posters flutter in the breeze, drawing my eye. The way I understand it, this is a small town. Why are there so many flyers up? It's not just children either. Grown men and women, teenagers, little kids as well. I stop to read one of them at random. *Ronell Leon Salazar, age 11, last seen* . . .

The chill doesn't go away as the wind kicks up. I've been warned about international data usage, but I have to turn it on long enough to use a ride-sharing app. There's a driver ten minutes away who can pick me up, and I wait on the platform without seeing another soul, just the flutter of those MISSING posters to keep me company.

It's funny how technology has changed the caution our parents tried to instill in us as little kids. *Don't get in the car with strangers!* But I'm doing that as my driver rolls up and I ID him based on data from the app. He doesn't say much, only takes me past a lumberyard and a lot where police vehicles are repaired. By car, I'm only fifteen minutes from my great-aunt's place, but it would've taken me forever to walk.

The town isn't much to look at, and it gives off a strange, old-fashioned air, like time stopped here fifty years ago and they'd rather keep it that way. The driver lets me out in front of a ramshackle Victorian monster house that stares me down with its dirty windows. I gaze up at the peeling violet paint and the chipped stained-glass windows, the overgrown ivy digging into the walls.

This is the kind of neighborhood where I shouldn't loiter. There's not much space between these historic houses, and a curtain is fluttering next door, a sign I'm being watched. Soon, somebody will ask what my business is here. To avoid that on my first day, I gather my courage, hoist my belongings, and mount the four steps to the sagging porch.

Before I can knock, the door flies open, and an old woman stands staring at me. I never cared for Charles Dickens, but this woman could've stepped straight out of *Great Expectations*.

I almost say, "Miss Havisham?" but there's no reason to piss off my guardian first thing.

"Um, hi," I start, but she cuts me off with a Venus flytrap of a hug, just all snap and here I am, against her bony bosom, breathing in talcum powder and lilac.

She's a tall woman, thin and gristly, with papery skin and lipstick bleeding into the cracks around her mouth.

"No introductions are necessary," she says, pushing me back to arm's length for deeper scrutiny. "You can only be Araceli, dear Simone's daughter. You're quite like your mother in your features, but you've got your father's coloring."

None of that is wrong, but it sounds strange, and I don't know if it's supposed to be a compliment. Still, I say, "Thank you," just in case it is.

"Did you have any trouble getting here?" she asks, ushering me into the house that time forgot.

I don't mean it in a cruel way, but everything is just so faded and dated that it feels as if I've stepped back in time. Not even to the fifties like I thought about the rest of the town, more like 1917, when the Victorians gasped their last breaths and ladies cut off their hair and learned to smoke cigarettes. I take in the worn carpet and the peeling wallpaper in discreet glances, hoping she won't realize how creeped out I already am.

This is such a tall, *narrow* house, and the old wood has a distinctive, musty smell. I'm not used to that. We always lived in small two-bedroom places, whatever we could find for rent closest to the town center. The walls were usually solid, cement or block, built to stand against earthquakes or bombardment. I can't remember ever living in a freestanding house. There will be no rooftop garden parties here, no barbeques that draw out the neighbors so that we grill whatever's on hand and I take beer from the cooler without anyone asking how old I am.

"No. I took the train from the airport." More than one, but she probably knows that, if she's ever visited NYC.

That's the most appealing aspect of living here. This hamlet has less than six thousand people, most of them white, but after a couple hours on the train, I can be in New York City. There will probably be all kinds of fun things to do on weekends, if Great-Aunt Ottilie gives me some latitude.

Now she's staring at my luggage like she wants to hug me again. "Oh dear. Is this all you have?"

I glance at my single suitcase and backpack. Moving once a year is a wonderful way to streamline your worldly goods. "Yeah, that's it. Could you show me where I'll be staying? And thanks for having me."

"It's truly my pleasure. I'm a bit set in my ways, after living alone for so long, but I hope we'll get along well."

I'm curious how long she's been alone—and why. She starts up the stairs slowly, showing signs that she has a bad hip, and I immediately feel guilty. "It's fine, you can just tell me, you don't have to—"

"Nonsense. My room is downstairs, so once I get you settled, I won't be traipsing up here to bother you often. Let's attend to the formalities and then be good housemates, shall we?" Great-Aunt Ottilie flashes a smile over her shoulder.

Okay, maybe I can deal with her.

There's also one other bright spot. Though I've attended six schools in seven years, I've got some awesome online friends, and I'm about to meet one of them for the first time in real life. We first "met," like, six years ago when I was starting junior high, and we were both fans of 7TOG, a K-pop band who debuted around then. I joined a fan forum to connect with people who loved their music. I got close to NotJustAny-Won, which was her forum handle, and just before I moved to the US, our chat convo went like this:

NotJustAnyWon: OMG, that's so wild, you're moving here? That's where I live!

Me: GET OUT, does this mean we'll be at the SAME SCHOOL?!

NJAW: Possibly? Reality is so wild, I can't wait!

If it hadn't been for the prospect of hanging out with NJAW in real life, I might have fought my parents when they suggested the Great American High School Experiment. At least I'll have one friend here when I start over. Again. Belatedly, I realize my great-aunt is staring at me from the stairs, waiting for me to speak or follow, something.

Uh, what were we talking about?

"How long have you been on your own?" I ask, thinking this is a harmless question.

Her thin mouth tightens. "Twenty years. Before you ask, my husband didn't pass away. He simply vanished. And no, I don't wish to discuss it further. This way, please."

Well, shit. That's just enough information to get my imagination going. If ever a house could devour a person and leave no trace, it'd be this one.

Shivering, I follow Great-Aunt Ottilie into the shadows of the upper story.

2

Narrow stairs wind upward, branching off at a dark hallway lined with closed doors. I can only imagine how dusty it must be, with only one old woman taking care of this place. The runner is frayed at the edges, little spiderweb threads creeping across the scuffed hardwood floor.

Great-Aunt Ottilie opens the first door on the left with a flourish.

The room is . . . quaint. I guess that's the right word, not one I use a lot. At least it's spacious. And decorated in vintage style, from the wrought iron bed with an antique quilt to the weathered bookshelves lined with leather-bound volumes like *The Mad Count* and *Ophelia's Ghost*. White lace curtains hang at elongated windows, perfect for fluttering in the middle of the night and making me suspect spirits. The walls are painted pale yellow, a fair contrast to the dark wood trim. Other than the bed and bookshelves, there's just a dressing table with a cloudy mirror and an upholstered bench, where I can picture a woman with fabulous forties hair plotting some intricate revenge.

"It's nice," I say, because she's waiting for my reaction.

"I moved most of the bric-a-brac into the next room. You're free to have a look, see if there's anything you'd like to use."

There's no closet, I notice. Something to do with the age

of the house, probably. The six drawers in the dressing table should be enough for my stuff anyway. "Thank you."

"Let's go over a few rules, and then I'll let you rest. I've never raised any children, but I'll tell you what I can do for you. I won't be making breakfast, but I'll put a hot meal together in the evenings. It's up to you whether you eat or not. I won't have drinking or smoking in my house. You're free to come and go as you please, but I expect the courtesy of being informed of your plans. That's common sense too. People disappear all the time, even without those precautions."

Like your husband, apparently. It's impossible not to wonder if he took off and is living a good life somewhere else, under a new name. But maybe not. I recall all those MISSING posters at the deserted train station.

"I don't have a problem with any of that," I tell her.

"Then I suspect we'll muddle on together well enough. I took care of your school registration, though they're still waiting on some of your records. You can walk to Central from here. I can draw you a little map if you like."

"That would be good." It's such a cute, low-tech offer.

Even Ma and Papi met online back when it was divided up in newsgroups and bulletin boards. They met on something called CompuServe. Otherwise my mother, who was from a tiny town in Kentucky, and my father, who was born and raised in Monterrey, Mexico, would never have even met, let alone fallen in love, gotten married, and had me.

"All right, then. Final order of business, I'm sorry to say there's only one bathroom and it's downstairs, closer to my room. I take my baths at night, so if you can work around that, I don't think we'll have any conflict."

Already I'm not looking forward to creeping through this house late at night to find the downstairs bathroom she mentioned. On the other hand, I'll have all the space and privacy I could want around here. Maybe that's not such a good thing since I've mostly been raised in bustling cities, where I could walk to the zócalo to get hot coffee and fresh pastries or buy hand-squeezed juice from a bicycle cart.

"I'll try not to bother you," I promise.

"That's not at all what I meant," Great-Aunt Ottilie grumbles. "Anyway, I'll leave you to rest and unpack. Come down in about an hour. I've got a pot roast on."

So, that's what I'm smelling; it doesn't get more American than that. My mom never made stuff like that. Wherever we were living, she'd always learn new dishes from the locals and sometimes her food was terrible, but it was never boring.

"I'm looking forward to it."

"Good." She moves to the doorway and pauses only long enough to say, "I really am glad to have you here."

That sounds sincere enough that I feel bad about how reluctant I've been to come. It must suck to get old and feel forgotten. Great-Aunt Ottilie shuts the door behind her with the delicacy of someone who has crept through life, never causing a fuss. With a soft sigh, I leave my suitcase on the floor and plop my backpack on the bed, then head over to the window to survey my new world. From here, I can see a tangle of trees in the yard and the rooftops of shorter, newer houses across the road.

I miss the tiered houses built into hillsides, buildings painted in bright hues, and terra-cotta roof tiles shining in the sun. Today, it's the green and yellow of a fading summer. Whatever, even if I can't get used to living here, it doesn't matter. I'll just put in my time, study hard, and lock in the college fund my parents promised.

Unpacking takes five minutes because I truly don't own much, and suddenly, I'm worried about that. At other schools, half the time I was wearing a uniform, but I don't think that will be the case here. People will judge me based on what I wear (or don't), what brand of stuff I use. Or at least, I suspect that might be true. Most of what I know about living in America, I'm basing on old Disney shows.

The full-sized bed beckons, so I stretch out on it for half an hour and fiddle with my phone. There's no Wi-Fi in this house, just faint signals that must belong to the neighbors. I might be able to use the internet at school, but there will probably be blocks. Music it is. I listen to a few songs until it's time to eat dinner.

Really, I just want a shower and to crawl in bed, but the sooner I fall asleep, the sooner tomorrow will come. It would be a lie if I said I'm not nervous.

A creaky floor and squeaky steps announce my arrival, so Great-Aunt Ottilie is already pouring me a glass of water as I step into the kitchen. It's not an expansive room either, barely space for the table tucked beside the window. Wearing over-sized oven mitts, she brings the pot roast to the table with wobbly arms. Probably I should've offered to help, but I'm walking that awkward line between family and guest, so I don't know what she expects.

Clearly, she's not a big talker. She eats silently, and I do the same, staring at the gravy trickling toward the edge of my plate. I block it with a scoop of potato. This isn't bad, but I'm already homesick—for my parents, if not for the last place we lived together. A building isn't your home anyway; that's wherever the people you love most are.

Once she's done, I carry my dishes to the sink. "I can wash up."

Ottilie shakes her head. "Not on your first day, sweetheart. If you want to do it starting tomorrow, I can allow that since I'm cooking, but you deserve one day off at least."

She might look stern, but it seems like she's nice. I try a smile. "Then I guess I'll go up, if that's okay?"

"No problem at all. I won't see you off when you leave to-morrow. It takes me a while to get up and around these days, but I'll leave the map I promised on the table. I don't think you'll have any problem finding the high school. But if you're worried, there's a neighbor boy who goes to Central. I could call his mother—"

"No, thank you," I cut in quickly.

The last thing I want is for some rand-bro to think he should keep an eye on me because we live on the same street. I'd rather slide in quietly on my own. Besides, I've taken the subway in Bueno Aires (much simpler than the buses), so how hard can it be to navigate a few blocks here? Ottilie studies me for a few seconds before apparently concluding that I'm trustworthy.

"Then make sure you leave by half past seven. I'm told school starts promptly at eight. I'd drop you off if I hadn't lost my driver's license last year. It wasn't my fault at *all*. That pig never should've been in the street." She tips her head, visibly curious. "Do you drive, by any chance? I have a perfectly good car in the garage, gathering dust."

"Sorry, I never needed to learn."

"Then perhaps you should ask at school if they still offer driver's education."

"Ah, sure." I'm the last person who would know if that's still a thing in American school, but with budget cuts, I predict probably not.

And I don't much want to dedicate my time to learning that anyway—*oh*. Maybe she could use the help for running errands or for transportation to doctor's appointments. Apart from the train station that runs an extended service to NYC, there's no public transportation out here. If that's the case, I guess I'll get a driver's license. Somehow.

"Good night, sleep tight," Great-Aunt Ottilie says, patting my shoulder. "Don't let the bedbugs bite."

Yeah, I've seen bedbugs. I may never sleep again.

3

I might have gone to bed if not for the noise coming from the room where only unwanted junk is stored.

Frozen, I stare at the closed door, listening for the sound. It doesn't come again, but it's the quick scrape of something bumping into the furniture. The hallway suddenly feels cold, though it's late summer, and I put my hand on the dull brass knob, cold as ice beneath my palm. Part of me wants to scramble back to my room, back to brighter lights, and crawl under the quilt.

None of that.

I open the door in an aggressive move, my fist upraised, like I'm going to fight a raccoon or whatever might be scurrying around, only to find I'm facing a dark, empty room. The window is open, though, and filmy curtains billow in the breeze. Despite the night air, the room smells musty, and in the moonlight, I can make out odd stacks of things, boxes and books, vinyl records so old that my parents probably haven't heard of the singers, and furniture covered in white sheets.

Maybe a small animal went out just before I came in. I heard something, but there's only a lingering chill now. Cautious, I step into the room, rubbing at the goose bumps rising on my bare arms. Every instinct is telling me to get the hell out, but I have to live in this creepy specter ranch for the next nine months at least. If I'm defeated on my first night, I'll spend that time cowering in my room, afraid to go downstairs to pee.

Deliberately I flick on the light, which illuminates the space for two seconds, then the bulb winks out. I'm starting to feel unwanted, house. Just then, the light shifts; I'm not entirely sure why, but a moonbeam shines through the window to spotlight a box on top of the chest of drawers. It's roughly the size of a regular notebook, rectangular, and about six inches deep. Even in this light, I can tell it's old, and I like the tree carved into the top, all stylized; it reminds me of the tree of life I've seen depicted elsewhere.

On impulse, I pick it up and carry it back to my room. I'm claiming a prize for my bravery, and Great-Aunt Ottilie did say I could use whatever I wanted from in here. In better light, the wood shines with a surprising warmth. I've already decided this is the perfect hiding spot for all my little mementos, treasures I didn't discard when we moved because they were tiny and could be tucked away. Inside, the box is lined with red velvet, worn in spots, and I breathe in the faint hint of cedar.

When I tip the box over to examine the initials etched in the bottom, the liner shifts. I tug at it, revealing a false bottom, and a yellowed letter tumbles out. The paper is incredibly old, and I've never seen stamps like the ones on the outside of the envelope. I can't make out who the letter is addressed to, but it's been opened, so someone must've read it at some point.

This feels like something I shouldn't dig into. What if the missing husband had a secret lover? No, he's only been gone twenty years, and the postmark is much older. Since this might be the most interesting thing that happens the entire time I'm here, I shut the door behind me and carry the box over to the bed and switch on the lamp. It takes careful handling to unfold the page, and soon I'm reading someone else's mail.

Dear Lucy,

I'm writing because I promised I would. You're the only one who might care if I come back, and I'm sorry for what I said before I got on the train. You don't have to forgive me. Don't wait for me either. Just receive my letters and maybe reply if you get to feeling nostalgic.

The camp is nothing like I expected, and they work us hard. None of the guys I came in with have any soldiering experience. They're pushing us through route marches, physical drills, and I'm learning how to tie knots. Most of us are from the city, and the officers think we're all a bunch of pinheads. They scream at us a lot, and I'm always tired or hungry or both.

I hear the group that came in before us will be sent across soon. Can you imagine? I'll be going next. You were right, you know. I was acting big that night, and I am sorry. Please watch over Lester for me. He's not half as clever as he thinks.

Still thinking of you,
Oliver

Whoa. Judging by the date on the faded postmark, Oliver must be writing to Lucy right before World War I. I haven't studied that much American history, but they entered the war in April of 1917. This is dated a few months before, and the writer speaks of training and waiting to be sent across. On a whim, I pull out my phone to do a little internet sleuthing, but then I remember there's no Wi-Fi, and I don't have a local data plan yet. My parents will disown me if I run up the bill with international rates. This probably isn't something most people would worry about, but I've moved so much that they drilled it into my head early on.

With careful hands, I fold the letter, put it away, and replace it in the hiding spot beneath the box's false bottom. I'm not sure why I'm being so careful when Oliver and Lucy are long gone. That makes me a little sad as I slide under the covers. After I set the alarm on my phone, I realize it will be tough to sleep in this new bed with sheets that smell faintly of old-lady potpourri, so I read until my eyelids feel heavy.

. . .

I'm not awake; I know that. I can't be.

The town looks different, and it's daytime. The women are wearing long dresses with pinned curls, and the men have their hair slicked back, old-fashioned caps pulled down. They're all hurrying, as if something big is about to happen. It's strange because I'm there and not there. When I glance down, I can't see myself. It's like watching a show on TV.

I follow the excitement and find an old-fashioned station like you'd see in period movies. Girls are stretching up on their tiptoes for a look at the train chugging toward the platform, and when it arrives, the car disgorges a bunch of disheveled young men of various races, all looking tired and or scared. Nearby, an older man spits.

"These draftees will ruin our armed forces," he says. "Just look at them. They look like they're used to eating out of trash barrels. Half of them probably can't read or write."

I'd like to call him a pendejo, but I'm not allowed a speaking role in this dream. I've had "unseen observer" dreams before, but never anything this detailed. The air even smells different, much cleaner, but I can also detect manure, and the people around me could all use a shower.

A boy with dark hair, light brown skin, and riveting eyes swivels his head toward the older man, who takes a step back.

His wife grabs his arm. "Stanley, be quiet. I'm president of the Ladies' Auxiliary, and this doesn't look good."

At home, she'll probably let him bad-mouth the troops as much as he wants. I'm already mad because it seems like this dream is about how poor people always get stuck fighting other people's wars. The boy is wearing torn pants, suspenders, and a stained shirt that's too big for him. Unlike many of the town men, he doesn't have a cap to shield him from the wind. By the size of the leaves, I'm guessing it's early spring, but there's still a nip in the air. With such scared eyes, he doesn't look old enough to go to war. Just thinking about it freaks me out, and thanks to my parents, I've seen some shit.

"This way, fall in!" someone shouts.

I'm still watching the boy, who can't see me—of course he can't—as he falls into ragged formation with the other conscripts. I can't shake the worry sweeping over me, as if something terrible is going to happen. Dread creeps up on me like a fat, furry spider crawling down a wall. Suddenly he glances back, and we lock eyes, though this isn't real, and in this weird dream, I'm not even here. Still, he raises his hand halfway and gives a sad, wry smile. It's the look of someone who knows he's bound for a duty that doesn't end well, but he keeps walking.

My chest hurts, and I can't breathe.

When I wake, I'm covered in sweat, and my alarm won't go off for ten minutes. Shakily, I gather up my toiletries and make a run for the downstairs bath. I'm used to taking three-minute showers because sometimes the hot water heater in our rental wasn't very big, or sometimes there were water rations. Ottilie has been kind so far, but I still feel weird about staying here. I can't even remember if I've ever met her before. I'm conscious that water costs money the whole time I scrub myself and that taking care of me might feel like a burden to an old lady on a fixed income.

That discomfort drives in the nail of certainty so clearly— this is not my home and never will be.

4

Getting ready takes all of ten minutes since I wear my hair in a choppy bob. I do lips and eyes for my first day at the new school, a bright red matte paired with black negative-space eyeliner, then I scramble into leggings and a sweatshirt. It's not cold enough for me to need a coat; I guess I'll have to get one when winter comes. It's been ten years since I saw snow.

As promised, a crude map drawn on yellow paper waits for me on the table. I feel strange rummaging in Ottilie's fridge, where I find various mysterious plastic containers. Since I don't know how old any of this food is, I make a peanut butter sandwich and wash it down with milk one day ahead of the expiration date.

Letting myself out quietly is depressing. The streets are silent, shadowed with trees, and I count the cracks in the sidewalk as I follow the map. After ten minutes of walking, I end up at the high school, which looks more like a hospital with its blocky build and plain yellow bricks. I've been educated in a tent before, and in Argentina, the secondary school I attended was more like a small university, complete with ivy-covered brick buildings.

I wish I could message NJAW, or any of my friends, really, but I'm still disconnected, reinforcing the feeling that I've traveled back in time. Glancing around, I decide I must be early because I don't see anyone else, and when I cross the parking lot, the front doors are locked. It's 7:30, so teachers should be here by now, right? The sky is gray, different than my dream, and I'm standing there staring up when tires scrape over the pavement. A boy with laughing eyes is astride a bike, ten feet away.

"You're really dedicated," he says.

"Excuse me?"

"It's Labor Day. The school's closed. But here you are, waiting to get in."

Dammit.

"You're here too," I point out.

"I use the parking lot to practice bike tricks."

The smooth pavement must be excellent for twirling on one tire or whatever stunt he's trying to perfect. Sighing, I spin away from the door. Why didn't the old lady tell me? If she's hazing me, it doesn't bode well for our future cohabitation.

Offering a nod, I jog down the steps. "Thanks for the tip. Apparently I don't remember American holidays well."

For me, the conversation is over, but he falls in step with me, walking the bike. "You're not from here?"

That's an open question with a complicated answer. I settle for saying, "I'm American, but I've been raised abroad, mostly."

"Abroad?" He tries to copy my accent, but he draws out the vowels, and I want to punch him because that's not cool.

Besides, with the way I've been raised, nobody sounds like me anyway. "If you wanted more info, that wasn't the way to make it happen. Bye, random stranger."

Thankfully, he takes the hint, leaps onto the bike, and zooms away with a celerity that I admire, even if he's kind of a dick. It occurs to me that I have the entire day free, so I could catch a train to the city. Part of me is tempted, but

I only have so much money, and that's the perfect way to burn through it.

Instead, I wander around town for a couple of hours. There isn't much to see, other than closed shops and rundown buildings. I find a post office near the library, along with a few open businesses, like a real estate office and a seedy bar. I'm only interested in the library.

Sadly, it's closed along with the school. It's kind of funny that Labor Day is celebrated by giving everyone the day off. Dammit, I wanted to get a library card and some new books, but at least the weather has brightened from the gray morning. I do have something to read on my phone, so I decide to chill in the park until I get hungry. I enjoy people watching, and there was plenty of opportunity for it in Rio, my favorite place of everywhere I've lived. Here, not so much; just a few elderly folks who throw seeds at the birds and wander off.

Around noon, my stomach starts growling, and I explore a little more. Joe's Deli, a recreation center called Great Escapes—they seem to have laser tag, snacks, Skee-Ball, and some old arcade games, among other things—Pizza Inn, Quik-Mart. On a holiday like this, I expect to find more people out, enjoying the good weather, but the town reinforces my impression of isolation. I pass only a few people as I roam around. Joe's Deli has free Wi-Fi, at least, so I get their cheapest sandwich and some water, settling in to check messages.

I eat slowly, replying to my parents, my family in Monterrey, and all my online friends. NJAW has sent me five messages, each more impatient than the last.

Are you here?

I thought you were arriving last night?

What's up with you? You're never quiet this long.

Are you mad at me? Did your plane crash?

Answer, OMG, did something happen for real?

She can't imagine life without internet, I guess. It's not awesome for me either.

I'm here! I'm fine, not mad. Sorry if I worried you. Just trying to get settled. I don't have a local SIM yet. I'll see you tomorrow at school.

Whew. You seriously scared me. This . . . never mind. I can't wait to see you!

Same.

Much as I'd like to talk more, I need to buy a SIM at the QuikMart. I wrap the other half of my sandwich and ask for a bag to go. "Be careful out there," the dude says.

That seems like overkill in such a small town, but I nod in thanks and head out. The QuikMart is a few blocks over, and on the way, I nearly run into an old man with abnormally red hands and ears. He's stumbling, slurring his words, and I step back to get out of his way. Only he doesn't pass by. He grabs my arm, and I expect him to reek of liquor, but he doesn't. There's another smell, something I can't place, but sharp and chemical and strange. The whites of his eyes are yellow, dotted with blood specks, and he can't get the breath to speak.

Finally, he wheezes, "Out. Get. Out. It . . . got out."

I yank away from him and scramble back, torn between fear and pity. He's clearly not okay, but before I can decide if he's an actual threat, a squad car pulls up with a siren chirp, lights flashing, and a middle-aged man gets out. He's tall and square-jawed with padding across his stomach, and short, buzzed hair beneath his sheriff's hat.

"I'll take care of this," he tells me curtly.

He doesn't ask if I'm all right. Instead, he shoves the man toward the car, and the homeless guy, if that's what he is, struggles wildly, thrashing arms and legs, but the sheriff is just too strong. I watch as he forces the man into the car, and a creepy feeling drifts over me. It's not like I was hurt or even threatened, per se. This seems like an overreaction, if he's been arrested for rambling at me. Maybe drunk and disorderly? But I didn't smell alcohol . . .

That strange feeling persists as I continue to the QuikMart I passed on the way to the park. The door is framed by MISS-ING posters, some of the same faces I saw at the station yesterday, but others are new, and I study them for a few seconds before going inside. I'm in luck and the clerk sells me a 3-in-1 SIM, the smallest of which will fit my phone. I buy a top-up card there too so I can add some data when I call to activate the service.

"Do you have a pay phone?" I ask.

The clerk shakes his head, but he lets me use the store phone to call the cell company's 800 number. Ten minutes later, I have a local number and enough data for a month, if I'm careful. I tuck my old SIM in the coin section of my wallet and dispose of the other stuff on my way out. It's close to two o'clock now, so I figure I should head back to the weird old house where Ottilie is waiting.

She's watching out the front window, and I wish I could say that makes me feel more at home, but it gives me the shivers instead.

"You're early," she says.

"More like I'm late. There's no school on Labor Day."

Her expression flickers from surprise to chagrin. "I'm so sorry. I completely forgot. It's been so many years since I needed to mind the calendar."

"It's fine," I lie. "I'll have my first day tomorrow."

In all honesty, I feel abandoned. My parents have only messaged me a little; maybe they're still in transit with no data or Wi-Fi, but it's tough not to feel like I've been dumped. Add that to this strange town and what happened with the homeless guy, and I'm pretty messed up emotionally. None of that is Ottilie's fault, so I'm trying not to take it out on her, but really, I just want to go upstairs and cry. I retreat to the room I've been given, though it doesn't feel remotely like home, shut the door, and curl up on the bed like a little kid. I cry silently, tears trickling into the pillow I'm clutching.

By dinnertime, I have myself together and I go downstairs when she calls. She's decided to pretend everything is good and that she doesn't notice my swollen, red eyes. That's fine by me.

"I made beef vegetable soup. Help yourself." She's already gotten her bowl and is eating without me.

I scoop some out and sit, trying not to imagine how many awkward meals we'll eat in silence, but Ottilie surprises me. "I suppose you're wondering about my husband," she says, out of nowhere.

I'm not, because she told me not to ask the night before, and I have problems of my own. So I eye her warily, wondering if this is one of those occasions where she says, "don't ask," but she really wants me to, and the longer I don't, the more it will aggravate her.

"Not really," I finally respond.

"Ah. Then you're the kind of girl who does as she's told. Docile."

Nobody wants that word applied to them as a descriptor, so now I'm low-key pissed, which is better than feeling sorry for myself. Two points to my great-aunt for levering me out of the pool of self-pity I'm wallowing in.

"Did you want to talk about it?"

"It's more that I want to warn you."

"About what?" I'm eating my soup because it's there, as bland as I expected. My mouth waters when I think about spicy carne empanadas and crispy milanesa. Of all the places I've lived, Argentina has the food I love most.

"This is a strange town, Araceli. If you see lights in the woods, don't go looking for them. And if you hear noises upstairs in the night, ignore them too."

"Excuse me?" That's basically all I can come up with because I'm so shocked.

I've heard creepy stories, of course. Whenever we move, it seems like there's always someone who wants to freak me out with local legends, but my great-aunt doesn't look like she's about to crack a smile. In fact, her eyes are somber, her brows drawn.

"I've heard about ghost lights," I say. "Isn't that usually swamp gas or something?"

"Or something." Her mouth pulls tight, and she lowers her gaze to her soup bowl, leaving me to shiver over a draft that creeps along my bare arms, raising goose bumps that won't go away no matter how much I rub.

Ottilie probably thought warning me against the weird sounds would dissuade me from checking them out, but I've always been stubborn. As soon as I finish dinner and wash the dishes, I rush upstairs to inspect the third floor, but there's a door blocking the staircase and it's solidly locked. It occurs to me that Great-Aunt Ottilie might have killed her husband and hidden the body in the attic. Maybe his mummified corpse is sitting in a rocking chair upstairs, his ghost walking the floor in search of freedom. Or possibly she confined him, Rochester-style, and he's been locked away for decades. I want to know what's up here, but I'll need to get the keys first, and I have no idea where they might be hidden.

Grumpy as hell, I retreat to my room to finish the book I read in the park earlier. As I settle onto my bed, something thumps hard overhead. I freeze. It's so cold in this room, a direct contrast to the bright sunshine I can see but not feel through the smudged windowpane. Though I strain my ears,

I don't catch anything else, but it's like ten minutes before I move a muscle.

It could be something else, I try to tell myself. An animal rummaging in the attic? But then I should hear some follow-up noises, like little feet scurrying around, more rustles, but there's nothing else. And it doesn't explain this unnatural chill; I can actually *see* my breath. In the dead of night, it seems like there's only one explanation.

I've experienced some shit in my life, but I can't say I ever lived in a haunted house.

Until now.

5

Day one, take two.

The parking lot looks entirely different from the day before. People hang around in clusters, apparently in no hurry to get inside. School's been going on for a few weeks now, I suspect, but in a town this size, the cliques have been in place for years. I've started over so often that I'm good at making friends, but I don't know if I have the energy. Part of me thinks it's pointless since I'll be moving on as soon as possible, and I already know how it goes when new friends promise to keep in touch. Probably better not to go in with that attitude, though.

I messaged NJAW before I left this morning, and she says she'll be wearing a black hoodie and a T-shirt with the faces of JaeY, Moonie, QT, Jungmin, X, Ghost, and K-Dream emblazoned on her chest. Since 7TOG isn't wildly successful in the US, I doubt I'll have any trouble spotting her. Keeping an eye out, I head straight to the main office and give them the paperwork my great-aunt provided. In exchange I get a printout of my schedule and a green pencil bag with WELCOME printed in yellow and below that, GO LIONS! and a stylized leonine face captured mid-roar. That must be the school mascot.

Inside the bag, I find two unsharpened pencils, a ballpoint pen imprinted with the school logo, and a folded piece of paper that tells me what's for lunch over the next month. I mumble my thanks to the secretary and join the trickle of students in the hallway. It's early, so nobody's running yet. I have time to meander around and locate my first class. There are a couple of people by the door, no teacher yet, and I don't know what desks are available, so I go into the room, prop myself by the window, and pull out my phone.

My parents still haven't responded to my most recent message and my cousins in Monterrey must be busy. *This is me, pretending I have someone to talk to.*

"Did you get the Wi-Fi password?" It's the boy from yesterday, dressed in baggy shorts and a gray T-shirt that says CLOWN SCHOOL DROPOUT.

His brown eyes sparkle like he knows a funny story, and his black hair falls in messy waves. He's kind of cute in a puppyish way, all awkward arms and legs and shoulders that are broad but bony. I notice he's got a fresh scab on his right knee. Maybe the bike tricks didn't go well yesterday.

"Not yet."

"Here." He grabs my phone and inputs the code, and while I don't love that he did it without asking, it feels good to check messages without thinking about how much it costs.

I don't know if it's a coincidence, but when I change networks, four messages from my parents come in, two in the group chat we share and a private one from each parent. They've settled into the little apartment they're renting in Caracas, so they'll have a front row seat to the riots and civil unrest. I won't read the news or else I won't be able to stop worrying about them. The fear lingers in the back of my head; one day, they will become casualties of the atrocities they report, and I will be left alone.

My hands are shaking as I reply. Everything is fine here. I'm at school. More later.

When I glance up, he's staring at my face, brows drawn together in concern. "Are you okay?"

"Yeah. Do you know what seats are empty?"

His hesitation says he doesn't believe me, but he's nice enough to pretend. "The one behind me is available. Over here."

I follow him away from the window and set my stuff on the desk he indicates. It's near the back, which I like. "Thanks."

"No problem. What's your name, anyway?"

"Araceli Flores Harper."

I expect some dumb question about why I have two last names, but instead, he brightens up like he's won a prize. Until he smiled, I wouldn't have given him a second look, but that grin is breathtaking. "Wow, seriously? Your name is Araceli? I've only heard that name once before. Sorry, getting ahead of myself. I'm Logan Reed. My middle name comes from my great-grandfather, and he's related to that, so—"

Before he can finish, the teacher strides in. He's all business with a briefcase beneath one arm. "I see a new face. You can stay there behind Reed; that seat is available. You probably know from your schedule, but I'm Mr. Timmons, your English teacher. If you don't have a copy of Bram Stoker's *Dracula*, get one as soon as possible and read the first ten chapters."

"On it," I say.

I download a copy from a site that offers free novels in the public domain and open the book on my phone. Meanwhile, the class discusses the themes of the novel, which I've already read. If the teacher knew that, he'd make me contribute, so I keep my mouth shut. Logan of the gangly limbs is an eager arm-waver, always blurting something strange. From the way the others react, it seems like he's the class cutup.

Mr. Timmons quiets the room. "Don't think I've forgotten about the composition component of the course, and since this is an epistolary novel, I want you to write a letter and bring it in for critique tomorrow."

"Nobody writes letters anymore," a red-haired girl complains.

"To who?" That question comes from the front of the room.

"I don't care. A fictional character, a historical figure, your late grandpa. Whomever you choose, it needs to be at least three hundred words."

The bell rings before anyone can whine more. Just as well; writing a one-page letter isn't too tough an assignment. If the rest of the day goes this well, I won't be drowning in work. Everyone files out while I pack my stuff slowly. In my previous schools, I usually didn't have a locker, and if I did, I rarely used it, so I don't need to head there between classes. My backpack contains everything I need.

None of my morning classes seem that hard, but there are a lot of pale faces in this town. The Black and Brown kids sit together at one table during lunch along with a few white kids. As I'm trying to decide where I belong, I catch sight of a Korean American girl wearing a black hoodie, and when she leaves the cafeteria line, I identify the 7TOG shirt. She's slender and a couple of inches shorter than me with light brown eyes, delicate features, and shoulder-length black hair.

I hurry toward her, noting that she's heading *out* of the lunchroom, back toward the hall that leads to the auditorium. Crap, I'm going to be so embarrassed if I'm wrong and she's a random 7TOG fan, but what are the odds?

"Hey, NotJustAnyWon!" I call.

She spins, nearly dropping her food. "NomadtotheBone?"

Shit, that's embarrassing. I thought it was clever when I was twelve. "Yep."

"Finally! I've been looking for you all day." She rushes me, and I get a one-armed strangle-hug.

We're jumping and squealing, drawing some looks, then she says, "Crap, I have a lunch meeting today. You can come if you want."

I shake my head. "It's fine. We'll catch up online, or tomorrow in person. I'll be here all year." Since I say it like a punchline, she laughs.

"Since we're real-world friends now, my name's Eunsoo. Park Eunsoo!"

"Araceli Flores Harper."

Giving me a wave, she hurries off to her meeting. For now, I head to the courtyard, where a few picnic tables have been set up, probably for students who bring lunch from home. This will be fine through late summer and fall, but when winter rolls in, I'll have to eat inside. Hopefully, I can sit with NJAW— I mean, Eunsoo. A few other kids wander out while I'm eating, but they pay me no attention. I'm cool staying low for a while. Once I get a feel for this place, I'll join a club or something. Along with hanging out with Eunsoo, that should open enough social doors to make this situation bearable until I graduate.

Another bell tells me it's time to wrap it up. I make it through repeated introductions and "tell us a little about yourself" requests. At least Mr. Timmons didn't do that. I get the feeling he's a book guy lacking in people skills, but that disinterest spares me from the other end of the spectrum, where people try way too hard. Currently I'm slumped in my economics class, after revealing as little as possible about myself.

When classes finally end for the day, I have some idea what life will be like here. I can stick it out long enough to graduate. Everyone is in a hurry, heading out for extracurriculars or part-time jobs. I feel like the only person in the world with nothing to do and nobody particularly waiting for me. It's embarrassing to admit, but I've never been separated from my parents this long before, and I miss them. Their quirks got on my nerves, but now that they're just words on a messenger app, I want to see their faces.

I'm the last one to leave the classroom, slower than the teacher, even, and I amble toward the front doors, pausing when a bright notice on the bulletin board catches my eye. The dance team is holding auditions next week. This isn't as cool as swing club in Buenos Aires, but it's something to do besides study. Well, assuming I make the cut.

I take a picture of the flyer describing the date, time, and tryout requirements. I'll need to choreograph a one-minute performance and then learn one of their dance routines and execute it with other hopefuls. I should be able to manage that. While I'm not talented enough to become a professional, I'm pretty good and I love to dance for fun.

Feeling more cheerful, I head out of the school into the afternoon sunlight. Walking back takes fifteen minutes or so, and I don't expect much, but Ottilie is waiting by the front door when I get in, and the smell of something delicious wafts from the kitchen. She greets me with a tentative smile.

"Hope your first day was good. I wasn't sure what kids eat after school, so I made some bread. To my mind, there's nothing better than fresh bread with butter and jam." She pours me a glass of milk to go with it.

I don't see a bread machine either, which means she did this by hand. She may not be great at expressing herself, but I guess I'm welcome.

"Wow. I wasn't expecting a snack. Thank you." It's kind of cute that she thinks of me like an elementary school kid.

Still, I'm not turning down fresh bread; I've only had that from bakeries, never at home, and this is delicious. I tell her a little about how school went because she's wearing a hopeful expression. She listens and nods with more interest than I would've expected.

"You'll make friends, don't worry."

I finish the milk and wash up my dishes, then set them in the drainer. "Thanks again. I have some homework already. Is it okay if I go up?"

"Of course. I'll see you at dinner."

6

Normally, I'd type this assignment, but I don't have a printer and I'm not sure I'll have time to visit the computer lab before first period. There's something fun about breaking in a new notebook anyway. Ma says I get that from her, and since she's a writer, that's probably true. English teacher Timmons doesn't care who I address my letter to, and the natural choice would be my parents, but that message would be full of too much emotional honesty for something that might be read aloud in class. I open the wooden box on my dresser and pull out the yellowed letter from the stranger named Oliver. I'll write to him like he's my pen pal. That should be good enough, right? I unfold the brittle page and reread it to respond.

Dear Oliver,

I can't imagine how you're feeling, but scared and trapped? I understand those feelings well. It's normal to be scared, considering what you're about to face. I mean, I've only seen pictures, but that's some heavy stuff. It also must feel like you're entering another world, comparing where you are now to where you came from. I'm guessing, though, because I don't know anything about you.

It seems like Lucy was special, and I'm wondering who Lester is. I'm curious about you too. I'm sure you're wondering about me as well, so what can I tell you? My name is Araceli, and I turned eighteen a few weeks ago. I speak English and Spanish fluently, conversational levels of Portuguese, and I'm learning Korean and Mandarin in my spare time. Since I've traveled a lot, I think I want to major in languages. I have a knack for them, and it would be awesome to work as a translator, or maybe I could go into foreign service as a diplomat or something. My skill at languages would come in handy for that, and I'd get to travel.

Even though I complain about being constantly uprooted by my parents, the truth is, I'm not completely sorry that we lived like we did. My folks are doing important work and a lot of news wouldn't have gotten out, if not for them. We lived in a lot of places where there was unrest. One time, my dad was uploading photos and my mom's article using a sat link while we were in a bunker and the signal was so spotty. There were soldiers looking for us and trying to stop my folks from telling the truth about what was happening. We could've died that day, but that's true of anywhere, anytime. I know some places are higher risk than others, but sometimes the risk is worth the reward, you know?

Most of all, I'm sorry they left me behind this time. Now that I'm old enough not to get in their way, maybe I could help. Anyway, wish me luck getting acclimated here. This town has a seriously strange vibe. Take care of yourself, whenever, wherever you are.

Regards,
Araceli

Counting the words, I've written 340 or so, more than the minimum required. There's no benefit to overwork, so I stash the letter in the box along with Oliver's for safekeeping. I'll proofread it later; if I put it in my backpack before I'm 100 percent done, I might forget to get it out again.

I decide to take a study break, so I pull out my phone and start an otome game that rewards you for making the right choices. Before I know it, it's dinnertime and I'm eating quiche Lorraine with my great-aunt, who's asking about the car again. "Did you find out about driver's education?"

"They don't have that anymore." Not a lie. I checked the school website during lunch, and while there were, like, twenty after-school clubs, nowhere did I find any mention of driving classes.

"Then I'll look into finding an instructor for you. Living here, it will be *much* better if you can drive."

Maybe she doesn't mean for her tone to sound like that, but it rings ominous, like something dire could go down if I can't drive out of this town with my own two hands. I stir uneasily, setting my spoon down to study my great-aunt. "Like, you mean in case you get sick or there's terrible weather, or . . . ? Level with me, Tía, what kind of emergency do you foresee in my future?"

She doesn't hold my gaze long, glancing down at her plate. The tines of her fork scrape against the surface, almost as bad as nails on a chalkboard. "Oh, I don't know," she says. "It's just better to be prepared, isn't it?"

"I guess. If you're willing to help, I'll get my license."

Looks like I'll be studying the rules of the road along with my senior classes. I'll download a guide from the DMV website at school tomorrow.

She nods. "I'll renew the insurance. I can afford the bump of adding a new driver."

"Thank you."

"It's my pleasure." Her gaze goes distant, telling me she's thinking of something else. "You may not know this, but your mother often stayed with me during the summer when she was growing up."

Huh. That was quite a topic change, but I go with it since I don't want to keep talking about the driving. "I had no idea. Didn't Grandma Irene move to Kentucky a long time ago?" I'm asking because it seems strange that Ma would have stayed at her aunt's house for an entire summer, unless there was some family drama I don't know about. Maybe Ma didn't get along with her own mother and they both needed a break?

I've spent very little time with my mother's family. My grandpa died when Ma was a baby, and my grandmother moved from upstate New York to a small farm in Kentucky. Before, I had no idea why she wanted to cut ties, but now that I'm seeing the town for myself, I get why Grandma Irene left. Of course, my mother was no happier with Kentucky than I am with this place, which is why she took off as soon as she could.

The deepest roots I have are planted in Monterrey, Mexico, as I've spent a few weeks a year visiting with la familia on my dad's side. There, I have an abuelo and abuela, two uncles, three aunts, and countless cousins. I stifle a wave of bitterness over not being allowed to stay with them, but no, I had to have a "typical American experience" instead.

Ottilie nods. "It's been more than forty years now. When was it, 1976, I think, just before the bicentennial . . ." She tells a rambling story about fireworks and commemorative coins, and I never am sure what that has to do with Grandma Irene.

It takes me half an hour to clean up the kitchen and put away the leftovers. Under Tía's watchful eye, I wipe everything down and I'm about to start on the floor, when she says, "It's fine. I only do that once a week."

Whew. I did not want to sweep and mop.

"Noted. By the way, is there anywhere in the house with a lot of floor space? I'd like to work on a routine for the dance team, but my room . . ." I trail off, not wanting to say it's too small, because it's not for most things. Just not sizable enough for choreography.

Really, I'm also angling to get access to the third floor. The noises I heard were no joke, and a complete inspection of the premises might make me feel less creeped out. Though I concluded this place is haunted in the middle of the night, in the daylight, I can't make that surety stick. I'm looking for logical explanations here. I wait with wide and hopeful eyes, a look that works on Papi half the time, almost never on Ma. Ottilie is susceptible, it looks like, because she's nodding.

"The attic has plenty of space, if you move some of the junk and clean up a bit. I wouldn't wish that dust on my worst enemy, but I suspect it could be turned into a decent dance studio."

"I won't bother you if I'm up there?"

"The house isn't soundproofed, so I'd appreciate if you didn't tap dance after midnight, but otherwise, it's fine."

"Awesome, thank you! Is it okay if I check the attic out tonight? I probably won't start cleaning until this weekend."

She smiles, her eyes genuinely warm. "Please do. The keys are in the drawer by the stove."

"I'm heading to the top floor, then," I tell her.

"You don't have to keep me *that* informed." The fact that she has a sense of humor will probably help us get along for the next nine or ten months. "There's a flashlight in the drawer by the fridge. Take it with you. I'm not sure if the bulbs are still good up there."

After grabbing the light and testing it, I leave her sitting at the kitchen table, staring out the window at the empty yard while a cup of tea cools before her. If someone painted her like this, it could be *Portrait of Loneliness,* and I feel slightly guilty for going to rummage in the attic instead of hanging out longer. Not enough to keep me from jogging up the stairs, eager to see my practice space.

And to figure out what might be making those strange noises.

7

The attic stairs wind up and around, opening into a wide, dusty space with a ceiling like an inverted V. I shine the flashlight around, and it's good that I have it, or I'd probably break my neck on the boxes and trunks piled around. I'm half expecting moth-eaten furs, a dressmaker's dummy, and a rocking chair that will creepily move when nobody's in it. So far, I'm only seeing cardboard and vintage hatboxes, though.

Tiny, smeared windows don't let in much light, and it's nearly full dark, so I fumble around, looking for the switch. Then I realize there likely isn't one. This floor hasn't been used in years, so there may just be a pull switch and a simple bulb for lighting. Marshaling my courage, I move deeper into the junk maze, sweeping the flashlight up and down like I'm scanning for enemies. I can hear my heart in my ears, and there's no rational reason for why I'm this scared, but my skin is crawling, as if someone's watching me. Chills spill over me, bumps prickling my arms even beneath my sweatshirt sleeves.

Since I enjoy ghost stories, but I don't really believe in that stuff, I square my shoulders and search until I spot the swaying string in the middle of the room. Even that detail bothers me, though. Why is it moving? There's no breeze up here; it's musty and airless. Before I get to the pull cord, it's tugged by an invisible hand until the distinctive click, and the light flares on.

This house is so damn haunted.

For a few seconds, I'm frozen, and then logic kicks in. There must be some reasonable explanation for this shit. Right now, I can't come up with anything, but I refuse to believe there's a spirit with nothing better to do than turn on lights. And honestly, if that's all it does, I could categorize this thing as helpful, right?

Yeah, that pep talk didn't work for crap. My heart is still racing, and I want to sprint out of the attic. Instead, I walk over to the bulb and stretch up on my tiptoes to pointedly turn it off again. Then I make my way downstairs, all while trying not to be terrified, and half expecting a push that will leave me a broken wreck at the bottom of the stairs.

By the time I get back to my room, I'm shaking.

It's fine. This is fine.

I can't even message my parents or my cousins in Monterrey. The only thing I can do is go downstairs and ask Great-Aunt Ottilie about the weirdness. Since I need to shower anyway, I gather up my bath supplies and do just that. She's sitting in the front parlor with a cup of tea, and when I tell her what happened, she averts her eyes.

"It's an old house, Araceli. Of course there will be some . . . vagaries."

"That's not just an oddity. It's an anomaly."

Finally, she lifts her pale eyes to meet mine, and to my surprise, there are actual tears shining in them. "You don't have to believe me, but I have always thought these events signify that my dear Archibald didn't desert me entirely. I take comfort when small, strange things occur in the house. It means I'm not alone."

Whoa.

"Does that mean you think he passed away?" *And you never*

found the body is the natural extension of that question, but I can't bring myself to go that far.

She gives me a helpless look. "I don't like to think so, but what else can I imagine?"

"This is pretty far outside my comfort zone." Hesitantly, I pat her shoulder in an attempt at consolation, knowing it's awkward, but she puts a cool hand atop mine.

"You're sweet. Thank you."

"No problem. I guess if it happens again, I'll just take it as a greeting from Great-Uncle Archibald." I'm not sure I can be as cool as I'm pretending, but right now, I don't have anywhere else to go.

To get the college fund my parents promised, I need to graduate from Central and take all the necessary tests to start my own life. I can't follow my parents around forever, and I think that's why they made a move now, so it will be easier for me to get into an American university. Cheaper, too, if I establish residency in New York first; there are a lot of great schools here. Vassar is an impossible dream, as there's no way my parents have that much socked away. I'll need to choose a public university, maybe Binghamton or Stony Brook. My parents don't want me to take out loans to pay for my education, and I agree with them. I'm lucky they can help me, but I'll still need to work while I study.

"Please do. I really am glad you're here," Ottilie says.

Since that's not the first time she's stated it, it must be true. She might say it once to be polite, not repeatedly, though. Still, I can't bring myself to hug her freely yet. Maybe closeness will come in time. Mumbling a vague response, I head for the bathroom. After my shower, I wrap up in two towels, one for my body, and one for my hair, then make a run for my room. The parlor lights are off, so Tía must be in her room, but she's left the stairway lamp on dim, so I can get to my room. Small kindnesses like this send a message. Maybe I'll feel more at home here in time. I dry my hair on low so it doesn't end up poufy in the morning and then crawl into bed. It's been such a bizarre day that I think I won't be able to sleep, but I wink out almost as soon as my head hits the pillow.

In the morning, I wake late and scramble to get ready in time. At home Ma would be yelling at me, but there's only silence in this old house. The floor creaks as I run back up to my room to snag my backpack. In my rush, I almost left my homework behind . . . and I forgot to proofread it last night. Too late for that. I open the wooden box, lift the false bottom, and . . . it's not there. Nor is the original letter from Oliver.

"This shit is not funny," I mutter.

I've read stories about prankster ghosts, who take objects from the house and they're either gone forever or the items reappear later in some weird place, like the freezer or a bathroom cupboard. But I don't have time to play with Great-Uncle Archibald even if he's bored and lonely. Maybe I should be scared, but right now, I'm just pissed. I'm already late, and what is even happening today?

"Let's not do that," I say. "Give me back my homework, or I'll never talk to you again. I can't be late on my second day and show up without my damn assignment."

Nothing.

I guess I was hoping the ultimatum would strike fear into Archibald's spectral heart. No such luck. Aggravated beyond belief, I turn the box upside down and shake it, tapping the bottom for good measure, but only a bit of dust wafts out. Those two letters have vanished, just like Great-Uncle Archibald.

Swearing beneath my breath, I rush down the stairs while slinging my backpack over one shoulder. There's no way I'm getting to school on time at this rate, and I won't have time to scrawl something to get completion credit either. As I shoot out of the front door, Logan is passing on his bike. He brakes suddenly, tires scraping hard against the pavement. He beckons frantically.

"Get on! We can get there before the late bell."

I don't know why I'm running—I hardly know this boy—but I jump on behind him and he stands up, peddling with all his might. The wind blows through my hair, and we're moving at a good clip. We pass a few people sprinting full-out toward the school. The first bell is ringing as he skids up to the bike rack.

"Don't wait for me to lock it up. Run!"

It's like avoiding this late slip is a freaking spy mission. I take him at his word and sprint for the doors. No locker stop, so I skid into the first period classroom just as the final bell rings. I stumble to my desk seconds before Mr. Timmons enters, with Logan creeping behind him doing some weird monster walk.

"Not amused, Reed. Sit down immediately, or I'm marking you late."

"Yes, sir. Sorry, sir." He doesn't sound sorry, and the class is laughing.

Well, I'm not late, but I don't have my homework. Timmons goes around the room checking it personally, and I slouch, avoiding his eyes when he stops by my desk. "Where's your work, Flores Harper?"

He earns instant points for using both my last names, but I hesitate over my answer. Am I really gonna say this? Screw it, I was never gonna be popular anyway.

"I'm, like, seventy percent sure a ghost stole it."

8

The entire class laughs. Not my intention—I'm not trying to establish myself as funny to earn credit with my new classmates.

That ill-advised response wins me a long look from Mr. Timmons. "I must admit, Flores Harper, that's one of the more creative excuses I've heard. Far more interesting than simply admitting you didn't do the assignment. But out of curiosity, what's the other thirty percent?"

"What?" I hadn't expected the teacher to stop class to grill me. If anything, I'd guessed he would make me stay after.

"You said you're seventy percent sure a specter stole your homework, meaning you've left some probability for other outcomes."

Oh. I know what he's driving at. To nip this in the bud, I say, "That I forgot to do my homework. I'm sorry. I'll turn it in tomorrow."

"No need," Timmons says. "You'll get a zero for this assignment, and if this happens again, I need to see your parents."

"Good luck with that. I want to see them too, but they're in Venezuela." I should stop, I know I should, because I'm only making things worse.

By the clench of his jaw, Mr. Timmons already dislikes me profoundly. "Your guardian then. Say one more word, Ms. Flores Harper—"

Just then, Logan spills a bottle of chocolate milk in such a profoundly dramatic way that he must be creating a diversion. The brown liquid spatters all over the teacher's sensible shoes, and then Logan's on the floor, crawling around with tissues while the class laughs some more. I should help, but since he did this to get everyone's eyes off me, I won't ruin a perfectly good distraction. Slouching in my chair, I do my best to become invisible. It mostly works, and then Timmons gets the class back on track while bitching about class time lost forever.

The others read their letters aloud, just as I'd speculated, which is why I didn't write my parents. I check out during the analysis, and after class, I catch Logan in the hallway, stopping him with a tug on his sweatshirt sleeve. "You didn't have to do that for me, but . . . thanks."

"What makes you think it had anything to do with you?"

"You always open your milk during first period and throw it on the floor?"

"If I say you're welcome, will that stop the interrogation?"

"Probably."

"You're welcome, then. Word to the wise, Mr. Timmons doesn't have much of a sense of humor. If you thought he might react better to a joke, and that's why you said the ghost thing, well, don't do that again. He prefers groveling and pleas for mercy."

I really did do the assignment, I consider saying. But there's no point. Logan won't believe me either. Even if I told the absurdly detailed story about putting the letter in the box, I have no proof I wrote anything last night. Sighing, I just nod.

"Noted. Thanks for the tip."

We go our separate ways then, though I'm low-key wondering why he helped me. No chance to ask him, since that's our only class together. At lunch, Eunsoo is waiting for me outside the cafeteria. We don't have any classes together, but it's nice to know someone, at least. She's not wearing any 7TOG memorabilia, and we hug again spontaneously.

"I can't believe you didn't message me at all last night," she says.

"Sorry. I got distracted by some stuff at home."

"I'll forgive you this time. Don't let it happen again."

It's so weird (but cool) to be standing here with someone I've been chatting online with for almost six years. "Did you bring lunch?" I ask.

"Yep. You should eat with us," she answers.

I have a basic lunch packed too, no need to get in line, so I follow her to the table. It's the one I noticed on my first day with the Black and Brown kids clustered together. I smile as I sit next to Eunsoo, making eye contact with the rest of the group: a fit Black boy with medium-brown skin wearing headphones, a pretty brunette with short, wavy hair and light brown skin sporting red glasses, a gorgeous Black girl with rich brown skin, hazel eyes, and long hair in spirals swept back in a colorful scarf, and a skinny white boy with shaggy, sandy hair and blue eyes.

"I'm Araceli."

"We already heard all about you," the girl with the red glasses says. "A ghost stole your homework?" She laughs and shakes her head. "I'm Tamsyn Leon Salazar. That's Derek Washington," the headphone guy, "Kimala Burke-Jones," the gorgeous Black girl, "and Jackson Pruitt," the nerdy white kid at the table. Eunsoo sits across from me, giving me a thumbs-up. "You seem to know Eunsoo already."

I nod. As I memorize their names and faces, I'm startled when Logan plops down at the table. I didn't see him here the day before, but nobody is reacting like this is weird. Maybe this is his normal group? He could be like me, fair enough to pass, but that carries its own problems.

"What're you having?" Logan asks.

"Cheese sandwich, apple, water." Spoken aloud that way, my lunch sounds depressing, even to me.

Everyone at the table has better food. I might as well be carrying a sign that says I'm currently unparented. They offer me some of their lunches, but I decline—mostly out of pride, because Kimala has a layered salad that looks incredible, and I'm dying to try some of Eunsoo's kimchi fried rice and rolled eggs. I can't start out mooching food on the first day. Even if they want to be nice, they'll still talk about me—maybe not in a mean way, but they'll wonder about my situation—and I'm not ready to drop that story.

"Thanks, anyway," I add, so potential new friends don't think I'm rude.

"Are you thinking of joining any clubs?" Eunsoo asks. "I'm in drama—that was the meeting I had yesterday, electing this year's officers—and we could use some help behind the scenes, if that sounds like your thing."

"Actually, I was looking at a flyer for the dance team . . ."

Kimala perks up. "Really? I'm the co-captain, and I'll be glad to answer any questions you have about the squad."

Exactly the kind of connection I'm hoping to make. "Can you give me any tips as to what you're looking for? I have a background in swing dancing, but I can also do hip-hop, salsa, and a little bit of—"

"I can't give you any inside information, but I'll send you a list of songs that I'd pick from if I was putting together a routine," she cuts in.

"That would be fantastic."

"Are you on messenger?" She names a chat program, and I give her my info so she can send me the song titles.

Pretty soon everyone's adding me, which is cool. But it sucks that I have to say, "I'm staying with my great-aunt, and she doesn't have Wi-Fi, so I'm on limited data right now. Messages should be fine, but at home, I won't be able to watch any videos you send."

I like them all more when they accept that without asking a lot of questions. If we click, I'll tell them about my life, but I hate giving personal details for no other reason than to satisfy the curiosity of strangers. Any info I divulge should come by choice.

"Has anyone warned you about the forest lights yet?" Derek asks. He looks like a football player, and the headphones give him away as a music lover as well.

"My great-aunt mentioned them. Told me not to follow them." When I say it out loud, it sounds so absurd that I laugh a little, only the sound dies when I realize nobody else at the table is amused.

"I thought the same thing when we first moved here," Eunsoo says. "I never believed in that stuff."

Part of me wonders if I'm being played, a gentle hazing for the new kid, but it doesn't seem like something she would do. I've heard you can't really know people based on online friends, but she's never struck me as a prankster. "Uh, did something happen?"

Eunsoo glances at Tamsyn, as if seeking permission, and the other girl nods. "We think her little brother saw the lights. That he followed them."

Tamsyn studies the table. "We never found him. My parents are still posting flyers, pressing the police for answers. The cops assume he was taken, but nobody saw anything. No strangers, no vehicles parked where they shouldn't be. In a town like this, newcomers stand out. There should be a witness or a clue about where Ronell went, but he's just gone."

Like Great-Uncle Archibald. A second later, it hits me. I saw this little boy's MISSING poster, first at the station, then at the QuikMart. It must be so hard for his family.

"I'll be careful," I say, because I don't think Tamsyn is telling me this for sympathy.

Logan hasn't said much, quietly eating his lunch, but as the bell rings, he slips a scrap of paper into my hand. I added him on chat; why didn't he text me? I unfold it and read:

I live across the street. If you want, you can borrow our Wi-Fi if the signal is strong enough. Here's the password.

That's nice of him. I glance around, intending to thank him again, but the crowd has swept him up. With a mental shrug, I save the note. I won't abuse the neighbors' bandwidth, but it will be so nice to message my parents anytime I want and do basic fact-checking for homework, worry-free. I can also chat with my cousins in Monterrey and the international friends who still respond to my posts.

The rest of the day goes better than the morning, and I have no more mysteriously missing assignments. After school, I'm happy to find apple slices and cheese cubes waiting for me. My mom stopped making me this sort of thing when I was eleven.

As I eat, I input the password Logan gave me. No need to waste my precious data if I can borrow the Reed home network. I only get two bars, sometimes wavering to one, but when I go to the window, it steadies.

Finally, my American exile is looking up.

9

I'm listening to the playlist Kimala made, and I've narrowed down the song choices to my top five. They're all good picks, but I think an upbeat song suits me best. I should head to the attic to clean before it gets dark.

I hesitate, though, remembering the creepy feeling of being watched and how the light switched on by itself. There are a lot of things I can explain away, but I watched the tug on the pull string. I saw it happen. Come up with a rationale for that, brain.

I can't.

I've been trying.

And it's why I'm not eager to return to the third story, even though there's nowhere else for me to practice. Time is ticking on that audition routine.

"This is all your fault," I say to the wooden box.

I open it up, mostly to reassure myself that I didn't hallucinate this morning. My letter is really gone, right? After pulling out the false bottom, I freeze.

Because the box isn't empty. I find a folded piece of paper, and it looks fresh, but at the same time, it doesn't look like any kind I've seen sold in modern stores. As if it's a snake that might bite me, I pick it up gingerly.

It's a letter. Addressed to me.

Okay, this shit really isn't funny. Did Logan sneak in here

somehow? I know he's a bit of a joker, but I'm not laughing. The weird part is, I didn't tell anyone about the box. I start reading.

Dear Araceli,

    That's a pretty name. I've never heard it before, but now that I have, I'll never forget it. I'd sure like to know how you managed to sneak a note to me. Security inside the camp is tight, and if you're caught wandering, they might think you're a spy or a sympathizer. You write well, better than me, so I guess you don't need me telling you to be careful.

    I'm also wondering how you know who I am. Do you live on our street in the city? You asked about Lucy and Lester, so you've already got a leg up on me. It's not any secret that I was sweet on Lucy when we were kids, but she never felt the same. I got over it, and these days we're good friends. Lester is my younger brother, and I'm worried for him now that I'm going away. I was the one that kept him safe and fed. Not sure what he'll do. Scared he'll fall in with a bad crowd and make some dumb choices. Might be if I survive this dustup, I'll come back to find that nitwit behind bars. Don't know why I'm telling you any of this, except you asked. You're a stranger, but I was happy to find your note in my treasure box.

    I didn't understand everything you said. In fact, some of the words didn't look like anything I ever heard of, but I didn't get much education.

    If it's safe to do so, please write again.

All my best,
Oliver

I stare at the handwriting for a long moment after I read the letter. It matches my memory. How can it match? Though

I'm not an expert or anything, I remember how the cursive looked on that antique note that piqued my curiosity, tucked away in this curio box. And this handwriting is identical, and that letter wasn't written on modern stationery either. It's not cold, but I'm shivering, and I can't stop.

Let's review.

I found a note in this wooden box, and I wrote a reply for a school assignment. Both disappeared, then later, a response was waiting for me. Oliver mentioned having a treasure box—wait, is it this box? To my eyes, there's nothing special about it, but there must be a connection, somehow.

Or someone's pranking me. That's the most logical explanation, and the culprit probably lives across the street. If this is a joke, I'll find out how committed he is to messing with me. I decide to reply, wondering how Logan will respond.

Dear Oliver,

I don't know you, but I found your letter to Lucy. It's a long story, but I wrote a reply for school, and then you answered me. This whole thing is strange, but I'm intrigued. Where did you find my response, exactly?

Thank you for saying I write well. I'm not as good as my mother, but I'm not trying to be a professional, so it's fine. What's it like at camp? I wish there was something I could do for your brother, but that's beyond my power.

Of course I'll keep writing. This is no trouble, no risk to me at all. I'm not a spy, and don't worry about me getting caught sneaking around your camp. That will never happen. Maybe that sounds overconfident, but I'm not sure you'd believe me if I told you how I'm delivering these letters. So let's just preserve the mystery a little longer and get to know each other better. I'm willing to listen to anything you have to say. I'll keep your confidence, no matter what.

Don't work too hard, and look after yourself.

Until next time,

Araceli

There. I've been embarrassingly earnest, so if someone is hoaxing me, they'll feel bad about how seriously I'm taking this.

This time, I don't put Oliver's reply in the box. I only hide my answer in there, and tuck his letter into a shoebox instead. Now, I have to stay sharp and wait. I consider building some booby traps, but I might accidentally injure my great-aunt, so I settle for taping string across my windowsill. If anyone comes in, they'll break it. I do the same at the bottom of my door and leave it open when I head up to the third story with cleaning supplies.

In the daylight, it's not as scary, and I'm ruthless in shoving the junk to the far edges of the room. Good thing I don't have allergies, or dusting this space would kill me. I've just finished mopping the floor when Tía calls me to dinner.

Tonight, it's cheeseburger macaroni and green salad. I eat it dutifully while yearning for more flavorful options.

"Have you ever heard of anyone writing letters across time?" I ask.

Great-Aunt Ottilie tilts her head. "That's an interesting question. You mean in literature? Off the top of my head, I can only think of *The Lake House,* that movie with Sandra Bullock and Keanu Reeves."

"I've heard of it, I think." Haven't seen it. If my great-aunt knows about it, then it's probably pretty old. "Can you tell me about it?"

"From what I remember, they both lived in the same house, at different times, and they sent letters back and forth through the mailbox they shared. It was very romantic, and I seem to recall it had a happy ending." She sips her water, then asks, "Is this for school?"

"Sort of," I say, since my letter assignment started everything.

"Ah. Well, I might have that film on DVD if you're interested. Should I take a look?"

"If you don't mind. But I don't have a player for it."

"Oh, I do, sweetheart. I don't watch the television a lot these days, but I do have one in a cabinet in the parlor."

"Then let me know if you find it. We can watch it this weekend if you want?"

My great-aunt's smile is so bright, you'd think I'd offered her something truly stupendous. "I'll find it. I can make popcorn, and we'll have a movie night."

I realize this might be the bright spot of her month, and I resolve to be warmer and friendlier. She's trying, so I need to do the same.

After dinner, I clean the kitchen and then retreat to the attic, where I set my phone in a cup for better music volume and start choreographing my audition routine. While I'm dancing, I don't worry whether my parents are safe or if I'm losing my mind in this strange town. I fall into the music and live the beat, close as my own pulse. I pause, make notes, revise the steps, until it's later than I realize.

Now I need a shower. Satisfied with my progress, I tiptoe down the stairs in silence, expecting to find my great-aunt already in bed. I'm startled to see her in the dark kitchen, spooning a bit of casserole into a dish. Maybe she feeds stray cats or something? That seems like a normal hobby for an old lady who's lived alone for such a long time.

Only she doesn't set it on the back porch. Great-Aunt Ottilie puts the bowl on the table and whispers, "Please enjoy this. I miss you."

She turns without seeing me and retreats to her bedroom. How am I supposed to take that? To me, it seems like she's leaving food out for her lost husband. I've never seen anything like it before, but what's really freaking me out is . . .

When I get up early, there's never a bowl of crusty food left from the night before.

Which means one of two things. Either Tía gets up in the middle of the night to clean—so no wonder she doesn't feel like seeing me off to school in the morning—or we are living with a hungry ghost that devours the food that's left out for him.

10

I can't sleep for thinking about that bowl of casserole on the kitchen table.

I'm wondering what's happening downstairs.

I lie there ten more minutes before I give up and creep downstairs. This town is making me weird; that's the only explanation for my behavior. I don't know what I expect to find, but I honestly have no idea how to respond to the fact that the bowl is now empty. Not only that, but it's also been washed and left to dry in the dish rack next to the sink.

Did Great-Aunt Ottilie do this?

If she leaves food out, then eats it later and cleans up, I'm not sure she's qualified to act as my legal guardian. My parents must not know anything about her vagaries . . . how would they?

Hurriedly, I rush back upstairs and crawl under the covers. It hasn't even been a week, and I'm already so unsettled. I fall asleep with my head full of strangeness, and I dream of missing people with missing faces. I dream of Tamsyn's lost brother, still endlessly roving the woods and crying to be rescued.

In the morning, I wake even more tired than I was before I went to sleep. It takes all my energy to get my ass to school before the warning bell. Exhausted, I put my head on my desk and wait for the teacher to arrive.

Something is set beside my face. "You want coffee?"

I crack open one eye and find Logan offering me a paper cup. "Yeah, thanks."

"You look tired, and school hasn't even hit the rough patch yet."

"When will that be?" I don't really care; I'm just wondering what he'll say.

"Around November. Have you started working on your college applications yet?"

I don't want to admit that I'm way behind. Instead of worrying about supernatural stuff, I should be focused on my future, researching colleges, and making an appointment to take the SAT. Everyone else took it last year, I'm sure, but since I didn't even know going to university in the US would be an option for me, there was no reason to worry about it then. International schools don't care about it that much; there's other criteria for admission.

I'm in such a weird place right now.

Intellectually, I know I need to buckle down, focus on school, and just let the strange extraneous stuff glide past me. Even if there is something deeply wrong in this town, I'm not the chosen one. It was wrong before I arrived, and shit will still be messed up when I graduate and move on.

Somehow, this mental pep talk doesn't help at all, and Logan is still watching me, wearing a puzzled expression. "What?" I demand.

Before he can answer, Mr. Timmons strides in, briefcase in tow. I down the lukewarm coffee like it's a shot that can get me through the day.

The worst part about all this is there's nobody I can talk to about it. Ma and Papi will worry if I start sending strange messages, and they can't afford to be distracted while they're working.

I sleepwalk through the day and don't perk up until lunch. Logan isn't at the table where I sat yesterday, but everyone greets me with a welcoming smile as I open my bag.

"Are you working on your routine?" Kimala asks.

"Yeah, I started practicing last night."

"I hope you make it," she says. "The squad could use more color."

"The whole town could. It's hard to believe we're so close to New York City when this burg is so . . ." I don't know how to finish that sentence.

Tamsyn nods, leaning forward and lowering her voice. "You know why, right?"

I shake my head.

She answers, "This place has the weirdest history. It was founded by German immigrants and in the twenties it took a dark turn. There used to be a Nazi youth training camp here. Streets were even named after Hitler and Goebbels."

My eyes widen. "No shit?"

Derek is nodding. "She's not kidding. The place looks so perfect . . . it's so clean and well-kept, but when you start digging, some scary shit comes to light."

Kimala adds, "My parents had to sue to buy property here because of some outdated law on the books about how everyone who lives here must be of German descent."

"That . . . is terrifying," I whisper. "Do you mind my asking why your family went through all of that? It seems like a lot to put you through and if it's not safe—"

"Short answer? My mom doesn't let anyone tell her no. She says we're indebted to the ancestors who walked the road ahead of us. Sometimes I wish she'd pick an easier path, but I agree that there shouldn't be anywhere we can't buy property. My dad's ready to move, though."

"I wish my parents hadn't sent me here," I mutter.

But maybe they did for similar reasons, so I can see how far we've come and how much farther there is yet to go.

"But wait, there's more," Eunsoo adds.

"I don't know if I can handle it."

"This isn't as bad as the other stuff, just kind of weird," she says.

"Okay, tell me."

"Before the Nazi stuff, this was just a normal town. There was an army training camp here for soldiers from NYC, and at some point, I'd have to check the dates, they converted that land into a top-secret government research facility. Fairhaven Lab is still open to this day."

"Now you'll tell me that nobody knows what sort of experiments are happening there?" I predict.

Some part of me wonders if they're messing with me, but I doubt it. All these revelations can be checked easily online, and I grab my phone—wow. They weren't kidding about any of it. I even find an article about the lawsuit Kimala mentioned.

Eunsoo laughs. "No, that's not the case. Both my parents are physicists, and they work at the lab. Of course, they've also signed an NDA, so while they know what's being researched—"

"They're not allowed to talk about it," I finish. "That sounds about right."

My head is swimming with all this additional info. Derek taps my arm to get my attention. "Look, the reason we're telling you this stuff . . . well, this town can be tough on people who look like us."

Kimala nods, and I figure I need to take the warning to heart if they're spelling it out this way. The town has such a grim history that I need to be on guard.

"Thanks for the heads-up. I wish my mom had warned me."

Tamsyn says, "Unsurprising. The place looks great on paper, if you don't dig into it."

I'm quiet as I finish my lunch, and my head is a mess for the rest of the day while I process the kind of place I've ended up. Colorism and racism are problems in many of the countries where I've lived, but I've never lived anywhere with this kind of secret stain. Streets that are named Main and Elm now used to have signs honoring Hitler and Goebbels? That . . . that is a lot.

As ever, Tía is waiting for me with a snack. Today, it's tiny sausages and celery sticks.

"You look upset," she says.

"I heard some disturbing stuff at school." I'm trying to be vague, but from her sober expression, she won't be put off.

"About the town?" she guesses.

"Wow, you're good."

"I wish most of that wasn't true, but it is, and there's definitely racism that needs to be rooted out. If anyone gives you a tough time while you're here, tell me immediately. I'll do whatever it takes to make sure you feel safe. I promised your father that I would protect you before he agreed to let you stay with me."

So far, people have mostly ignored me. I haven't seen anything scary yet, unless you count the paranormal activity in this house. If I'm going to ask, this is the time.

"Actually," I start.

"Did something happen?"

"I saw you leaving out a bowl of food last night."

Tía bites her thin lower lip, smearing pink lipstick on her front teeth. "I wish I could explain in a way that makes sense, but sometimes, the best answer is to pretend you don't know. You wouldn't understand or believe me if I told you more, so can you do me this favor, Araceli? Just act like you don't know while you're here. Accept this as something strange I do because I've lived alone for so long."

I'm unclear if she means leaving the food or tidying up afterward. Sighing, I decide I won't get anywhere if I press. She's quite agitated, twisting already knotted hands together.

"I hear you," I say finally. "I won't ask any more about it."

"Thank you. If I can ask one more favor, please don't mention this to your mother. It would only worry her needlessly."

Yeah, I'm already keeping plenty of secrets from my parents for exactly that reason. What's one more?

Just then, a knock sounds at the door. I peek out the window and find Logan on the porch. Well, he does live across the way and I'm bumming his Wi-Fi. I should have seen this visit coming.

I open the door with a smile that I don't have to fake completely. "What's up?"

"Are you down for an adventure?"

11

"That depends on what it is," I say.

Really, I'm not feeling it. I'm tired and confused, and I want to check the box to see if my letter has vanished, if another note is waiting in its place.

How am I supposed to think about college and the SAT with so much wild shit going on? It all seems so strange and random, but part of me thinks there must be a unifying thread, and if I could figure out exactly what that is, all these chaotic elements would coalesce into something that makes sense.

Logan is still standing there, making faces, as if he's daring me to go without getting further information. Nope, that's not happening.

"Look, if you're not giving details, I have stuff to do."

I start to shut the door, but he catches it. "Fine, take all the fun out of the surprise. I want to show you something cool. Just trust me, okay?"

I don't know this boy that well, and I have zero desire to take him on faith, but something about his puppy-earnest eyes are working on me. I sigh.

"Fine." I call over my shoulder, "I'm going out with Logan for a bit. Back later!"

"Is that the nice Reed boy?" Ottilie asks. She comes to the door to scrutinize him, and he beams like it's his job to submit to septuagenarian inspection.

"Yep, that's me, the nice Reed boy. I cut your grass during the summer."

"Where are you going?" she asks.

"Pizza Inn," he says, so promptly that I'm positive it's a lie.

She agrees and heads back inside, and I'm proved right when he beckons me to his bike, currently facing away from the small business district where you can find Pizza Inn, a real estate office, Joe's Deli, a fleet store, Great Escapes, the Quik-Mart, and a moving company.

"We're not getting pizza, are we?" I get on the back of his bike anyway.

"Brilliant deduction. Listen, I heard the group got you up to speed on the town weird, so I figured you'd need a distraction, and this will be top-notch."

What the hell; I go with it. I hang onto his shoulders because we're not in a place where I'd loop my arms around his waist and lean into him. I admit, he's good on the bike, even with my additional weight on the back. We speed out of the neighborhood and a few streets over he veers off to a dirt road leading into the forest, the one place my aunt told me not to go. Presumably, this is also where Tamsyn's little brother disappeared.

"I didn't sign up for this," I call.

Logan makes a placating gesture over one shoulder. "Don't worry, we're not going much farther. You'll like this, I promise."

I'm having serious doubts as the woods swallow us up. Even the dirt path vanishes, and he gets off his bike, pushing it toward a cluster of towering trees. The light is different in here, faint and green-tinged, with a dank-smelling breeze. I'm a city girl, so I'd be getting a creepy vibe even without all the ominous stories.

"Is this the part where you tell me you're the Renfield for

some pitiless antediluvian god and that I've just agreed to be its next meal by following you?"

"How'd you know?" Logan answers, deadpan. "Usually, people don't guess until they see the gaping maw."

I stifle a flicker of surprise. Logan gets points for being sharp and playing along. But just in case he's not kidding, when he steps forward, I scramble back. "Okay, this isn't funny."

He laughs. Asshole. "Sorry, you should see your expression, though. Look up."

At first, I glimpse only the tangle of branches, then I spot what he must want me to see. A tree house, strung with solar lights, and it's seriously freaking nice, like, this is the secret clubhouse all ten-year-olds dream about. A rope ladder leads up, and I follow him because I'm curious about the inside. We're both too old for this kind of thing.

The tree fort interior is even better than I could have guessed, with painted wood and posters of famous magicians on the walls. Simple wooden crates are filled with knit afghans, probably for cold nights, and there are bright cushions and pillows on the floor. Spools that used to hold wire or cable have been repurposed as small tables, currently spilling over with comics in four different languages. I recognize Japanese first, Korean next, and damn, this is way more than I expected. The windows even have mosquito netting stapled over them, so the tree house is free of bugs and leaves.

"It's cool, right?" he asks, waiting for my reaction like it matters a lot.

"Yeah. This is badass. You hide here a lot?"

"As much as the weather lets me. It's not like I can have a fire in here. I don't want to burn the place down."

There's no power, so a space heater is out of the question, and he's right about a normal wood fire. "I'd be more worried about smoke inhalation, but . . ."

"What?"

"We lived in small places a lot. In Buenos Aires, we had a tiny balcony, so my dad got a ceramic pot and put foil and charcoal in it. World's smallest firepit."

"You think that would work in here?"

"Maybe, if you kept it near the window. And you'd need to be careful with the ashes afterward."

"I think we have a super-small grill in the garage, the kind used for tailgate parties . . ."

"What's a tailgate party?"

"How can you not know that?" He doesn't wait for my reply, instead elaborating on the American custom of grilling meat in the parking lot before some sporting event.

"Anyway, is this the adventure you mentioned? Your tree house?"

"Not quite. You'll see when it gets a little darker."

"You want to stay out here until dark?" That sounds like a terrible idea. The woods are scary enough in the daylight; I don't want to be roaming around here past seven p.m. I can see the shadows lengthening already, and when I check my phone, it's past six. Though the sky still has some light left, the horizon is brightening at the edges and gloom is gathering beneath the canopy of autumn-painted leaves, filling me with wordless dread.

"Don't worry. I've done this before, many times. It'll be fine if we stay put."

Wow, talk about not reassuring me. I'm about to argue when the first light appears in the distant trees. He pulls me to the window, and I don't resist, helplessly spellbound by what I'm seeing. What *am* I seeing?

The ghost light or whatever is prettier than I expected, not a simple glowing ball, but swirls of light that look like a slice of the aurora borealis. I'm speechless as more colorful swaths appear. They shimmer and spin, moving in random directions. I can't pick out a pattern, and after a while, the kaleidoscopic display simply fades in the trees, leaving full dark behind.

I blink slowly and glance at Logan, who seems similarly hypnotized. Before, I didn't understand why anyone would follow the lights, but now I get it. There's a deep enchantment about them, capable of overwhelming your good sense. Even now, I'm wondering what the lights mean, what causes them, and where they went.

"Wow," I whisper.

"Incredible, right? I don't know why, but I really wanted you to see them."

"Thanks. You were right. That did feel like an adventure."

"I knew you'd get it." In the glimmer of the solar lights strung outside, his eyes are bright. "Just don't ask me why I thought that."

"Why not?"

"You wouldn't believe me if I told you."

I almost say, "try me," because this town has dumped all kinds of improbable nonsense on me in the brief time since my arrival, but I decide not to push him. It's enough that he shared this private light show with me.

"Do you know why it's so dangerous to follow the lights? My aunt even warned me about it, and I guess the danger is real, given what happened to Tamsyn's little brother."

Logan nods. "The forest gets swampy to the east, something to do with the dam they built in the eighteenth century. There are sudden drops and sinkholes, easy for someone to fall in and never be seen again."

"You think there's a reasonable explanation for the town disappearances?" I don't mention the ghost of my great-uncle. Is it possible he went for a walk and drowned in the bog? And now, his ghost is calmly eating cheeseburger macaroni at home. Sure, that makes sense.

"I'm not sure, but . . ." he says softly, then stops, studying me with somber eyes.

"Tell me. If you said that much, you have to finish it. That's the rule."

"This is probably just paranoia," Logan says finally, "but sometimes I worry that it's *not* the swamp claiming people."

"What are you suggesting?" I demand.

"I wish I knew. Maybe I've been watching too much TV, but doesn't it seem strange that people go missing so often in a town this size? I looked at the MISSING posters in the post office the other day, and . . ." He shakes his head. "It's just weird, that's all."

Since I had the same thought only a little while ago, I can't argue. I just stare into the dark and wonder what might be hiding there.

12

The weekend arrives at the speed of light.

I keep my promise to Great-Aunt Ottilie and watch *The Lake House* on Saturday. It's kind of a romantic movie, even if it doesn't answer any of the questions I have regarding my own situation.

I haven't received a reply from "Oliver" either. Maybe Logan felt bad for messing with me, now that we're hanging out more. My thread remains unbroken on the windowsill. On the door, too, so my great-aunt doesn't even come in my room, which rules out the idea that she's playing an elaborate prank on me—with the letters and the bowl of disappearing food. The more I get to know her, the less I think she's capable of it. She's genuinely trying to make me feel welcome, as far as I can tell.

Sunday night, I have my first video chat with my parents since I arrived, and it's hard to know exactly what to say. They look good, healthy and happy to see me. Ma talks for ten minutes about what they're seeing in Venezuela.

"It's bad," she finishes. "We were right to send you to New York. Are you settling in okay?"

Papi laughs. "You'd know if you gave her a chance to answer."

The conversation starts in English, shifts to Spanish, and then Papi quizzes me to see how much Portuguese I remember. It's all normal and good, and I can't figure out where to begin. I want to tell them, I do, but even I think some of this stuff sounds preposterous.

"You look worried," Ma says. "Are you having a rough time at school? Are the courses—"

"No, it's not too hard. If anything, it feels like this is a review year."

"I'm glad to hear it. Have you checked on when you can take the SAT yet?"

"It looks like the end of September. I'll have to take the train to a bigger school, unless I learn how to drive, which Great-Aunt Ottilie seems to want. She said she'll let me borrow her car."

"That's not a bad idea, peque. Do you need more money for the lessons? Just let us know and we'll take care of your expenses with the AmEx." That's Papi's solution to everything.

Ma is the one who worries about paying off the cards.

"I haven't looked into a driving school yet. There probably isn't one here. I'll have to take the train for that too. This town is really small."

And strange, I add silently.

"It'll be valuable experience later," Ma says. That's her default statement about pretty much any situation I encounter.

I imagine myself telling her, Ma, I'm living in a super-racist town where people disappear, this house might be haunted, and I suspect my great-aunt is at least slightly unhinged. Plus, there are ghost lights in the forest, and I got a letter from someone who might have fought in the First World War.

Wow, Ma would say. That will be valuable life experience one day.

Actually, that's not true. If she or my dad had any suspicion I might be in danger, they'd hop on the next plane. And I know my parents are working on an important story. If they don't document what's happening there, it could be those stories will simply go untold. I can handle this; I can. No need to raise the emergency flag.

"I'm sure."

I let the conversation sweep past my temporary home, and name a few universities I'm considering. We chat a little more and then I hang up because it's getting late here.

The minute I disconnect from the vid chat app, a message from Logan pops up.

Quiet weekend?

Are you watching me or something?

Not really, but I have to do yardwork, and it's hard not to notice you haven't left the house.

You are way too interested in my business, I send back.

Or maybe you're too uninterested in mine. You know you've never asked me a single personal question?

Is that true? I mentally scan back through our interactions, and it might be.

Huh. Okay, did you knit all those afghans in the tree fort?

I'm surprised by the reply. Most of them. Your great-aunt taught me, so she made a couple of them. I did the pillows too.

Honestly, I'm kind of impressed, both by the fact that he's handy that way and that he's not embarrassed by it.

That's pretty cool, I send.

I built the tree house too. Out of scavenged wood and fallen timbers.

There's a secret edging that claim. Isn't that the kind of thing fathers and sons normally do together? But it would make more sense if the fort was in Logan's backyard, not deep in the forest on what is most likely government land. If someone in authority found his secret hideout, they'd probably tear it down.

Which brings me to my next question.

Why do you need a place to hide?

A long silence follows, then he sends an emoji that I have no idea how to interpret, followed by: You went from zero to sixty on personal questions. I'm gonna pass on that answer until we know each other better.

Understood. G'night.

He sends, Night, along with a sleepy face.

I really didn't need to wonder about Logan's secrets. It would be better if he were exactly as he seemed—a nice, slightly awkward boy with a clownish streak—but I don't think that's true anymore.

For what must be the tenth time this weekend, I check the treasure box. This is the last time, I tell myself as I lift out the false bottom.

And this time, there's a folded piece of paper waiting.

My strings are still intact at the door and window. If this is a prank, the perpetrator is a step ahead of me and must have spotted my simple security measures.

With trepidation, I unfold the sheet of paper. I have no idea why, but my heart's beating fast; even I couldn't say if it's nerves or excitement. Really, I should be scared because a joke on this level is more akin to having a stalker—someone who watches me constantly, knew I found an old letter, and can acquire old stationery and forge someone else's handwriting. The only person who pays me that much attention is . . . Logan.

Does he have the skills to pull off a hoax like this? If so, why would he bother?

Yet even with my doubts, I'm reading the letter eagerly.

Dear Araceli,

I told myself not to reply. Tried not to. Because it just doesn't make any sense how you're able to slip in and out of camp without anyone seeing or hearing a thing. I stayed up all night watching for you and dropped off for just a few minutes before dawn. Somehow you managed to find that gap.

I tell myself you're probably a spy, but that doesn't make any sense either. If you were, you'd be stealing intel from the officers, not wasting your time on a nobody like me.

I've reread your second letter about a hundred times, and the guys are joshing me about it. They won't leave it alone and keep asking me about my girl back home. I guess it's better if they think that way because I sure can't explain what's happening.

I keep going back to the line where you say you'll listen to everything and keep it quiet, just between us. I feel like maybe I'll need that later, so I had to reply, no matter who you are or why you're contacting me.

Right now, I'm tired. They work us hard, and I never get exactly enough to eat. I've never been called so many bad names in my life, except by people who accused me of stealing.

I'm scared too. Before last week, I never shot a gun, and they expect me to get on a ship and go kill men over there. I don't know if I can kill a man, Araceli, even if they tell me he's bad and he wants to steal our freedom. I'm even more scared that I can, and that I won't recognize myself anymore if I do like I'm told.

I'm supposed to be sleeping, so that's why this is messy. I'll be punished if I'm caught writing after lights-out, so I better stop before I say something I regret. I appreciate you reading this far, if you stayed with me. I don't know how you found me, but I hope you'll stick around. It's nice having a sweet little secret when everything else is, well, I shouldn't write that word to a lady.

Looking forward to your next letter,
Oliver

This reads so authentic that I'm impressed with the writer's skills. Okay, let's be frank—with *Logan's* skills. He's almost managed to convince me that I'm communicating with a frightened young American soldier who's about to be shipped off to the Western Front. And I'm sure Logan is behind this, somehow. Nobody else in town has this much interest in me, and while I appreciate his creativity, this has to stop. We just said good night by text, but it's not that late. It's rude to show up unannounced, but that's the only way I'll catch him.

Making up my mind, I slip into a sweatshirt and put my shoes on. "Going to Logan's for a minute to get help on an assignment," I call as I come down the stairs.

Great-Aunt Ottilie glances up from *Mysterious Disappearances*, the book she's reading in the parlor. "Thanks for letting me know."

I have my excuse ready for Logan's parents too, but he answers the door personally when I knock. "This is unexpected," he says. "What's up?"

"Your parents aren't home?"

"Why, are you planning to do something they'd disapprove of?"

I give him a look. "Reed."

"Fine, no, they're not. They went out to dinner." He steps back, waving me in.

That makes my life easier. I don't tell him why I've come over because that would alert him. Better if he doesn't realize I've figured it out. I need to search his room. I know I'll find that unusual paper he's using. But how am I going to do that with him watching me?

Okay, one step at a time.

His house is much smaller than my great-aunt's, built later too, a bungalow with a simple two-bedroom layout, plus front room, kitchen, and bath. Though I've never asked, I guess he must be an only child, like me.

The house is decorated in dusty blue and mauve with wallpaper borders, like the family stopped caring in 1995, which seems odd because Logan wouldn't even have been born then. It smells like smoke too, and the curtains have a yellow tinge.

"Sorry, I'm a little stressed about our English assignment. Have you started working on your essay yet?"

"Yeah, I finished it."

"Would it be all right if I read yours? I promise I won't steal any ideas." I try a smile, and he gives me a melting look in response.

"Absolutely. My room is this way."

His room is dark with old paneling, made more so by the pulled shades. He has a single bed, a battered desk, and a very old TV, like, it's a cube. His closet has a curtain, not a door, and he's using plastic crates for storage. This is not the room of a beloved only child.

Logan hands me a few printed sheets of paper, and I perch on the bed. Then I make my next request. "Actually, my throat is a little sore. I know I'm being so high-maintenance tonight, but could I get a cup of tea? Milk and sugar would be great if you have it."

I watch him like a hawk because if he's guilty, he won't want to leave me unattended in his room, but he gets up with cheerful alacrity. "No problem! I'll be back in five minutes."

As soon as he leaves, I scramble to search every square inch of his space. Each drawer I open, I'm convinced I'll find evidence, but there's nothing. No old-fashioned pen and paper, no proof that implicates Logan at all. Hurriedly I take a seat on the bed, picking up his essay as I hear him coming down the hall.

"How is it?" he asks.

"The essay? Way better than mine. Thank you," I add, taking the tea. He clearly spent time on this drink while I was ransacking his room, and I drink every drop while feeling somewhat guilty.

"You can come over anytime," he says. "Actually, I'm glad you asked me for help. I thought you didn't like me."

"That's not true." Rising, I hand over the mug. "I need to finish my essay now that I've seen how it should be done. Thanks again for the sneak peek and the drink. See you tomorrow!"

I bail before Logan reads into this visit and complicates my life even more.

13

When I get back, I have messages waiting from NJAW, I mean, Eunsoo.

Are you busy?

What's with you?

We talked way more before you moved here. Is something up?

Maybe I should confide in her. We've been online friends for a long time, and I hate that my silence is making her feel bad, so I summarize everything that's happened to me since I got here in one long text, starting with the MISSING posters, my great-aunt's weirdness, the food she leaves out, the bulb that switched on by itself, the strange noises upstairs, the ghost lights I saw with Logan, and finally the two letters that appeared in my heartwood box, the security measures I took, and my search of Logan's residence.

Whew. I feel ten pounds lighter with all that off my shoulders. Though I couldn't tell my parents or my cousins in Monterrey, it feels so much better to talk about it. Eunsoo is silent in the chat app for so long that I start to sweat. *She thinks I've lost it, right?*

OMG! No wonder you've been quiet. Like, I knew this town is a mess, but it seems like you're getting the worst of it. What is even happening?! Those letters . . . oh! Bring them to school tomorrow. I want to see.

Okay. We'll talk more then, okay?

Guaranteed. Hang in there. I'm in this with you now.

Relief floods through me. Until she said the words, I had no idea how much I needed to hear that. Everything that's happened . . . it's a lot. And while I've seen my mother investigate things, I've never done it myself.

Fortunately, my essay is done and polished, despite what I said to Logan. I put that in my backpack along with the two letters Eunsoo wants to see, then I go to bed. It's been a long day, and I'm exhausted.

. . .

In the morning, she's waiting for me in front of the school, a good fifteen minutes before the bell. We head for the auditorium and sit in the back, using the lights on our phones so she can read the letters. I don't have the original one to Lucy, but I have the two that have arrived since, and I summarize what the one to Lucy said.

"So the first letter was in the house when you arrived," Eunsoo says, as if thinking aloud. "And it had a postmarked envelope with it?"

I nod.

"Then it definitely wasn't left for you. Do you remember the mailing info, like the sender's full name or the recipient's name or address?"

Reluctantly, I shake my head. "I didn't know it would be important."

"That's too bad. That would've been data we could check."

Eunsoo reads the first, then the second, and then she raises her gaze to mine, somber in the light emanating from her phone. "This . . . reads so legit. Like, I swear this letter came from someone who's about to deploy. I don't think your great-aunt wrote this. Neither did Logan Reed."

"I checked his room last night, and I didn't find a pen or paper that match this."

She rubs the edge of the paper and cants her head. "I don't even know where you'd buy something like this. This seems like a lot of effort for a joke."

"Then what's left? That I'm writing letters across time?"

She thinks about that. "Maybe there's a way you could test him."

"How?"

"I'm not sure yet. Anyway, keep writing. I'll let you know when I figure it out. And you have to keep me in the loop. This is the most exciting thing I've ever been involved in."

I can't resist asking, "Even more than when you went to see 7TOG? I was so jealous! They never come to South America."

Eunsoo makes a face. "No comment."

So, I guess I'll take her advice and act like there's a soldier desperately looking for my next letter. I'll pretend as if this is real, and my letters can help him feel less alone. Like Eunsoo says, I'll keep writing until there's some explanation, one way or another. If it's a joke, the writer will slip up and reveal awareness he shouldn't possess about modern life.

Just then, the first bell rings.

We go our separate ways, and I hand in my essay during first period. "You should buy me a Coke if you get a good grade," Logan says as we pass our papers up.

"Deal." Since he allegedly helped me, I can't argue.

The day passes in a blur because I'm mentally writing my reply in my head all day. With a wave for Eunsoo, I rush home, chat with my great-aunt for a few seconds, then hurry to my room so I can continue this strange correspondence.

Dear Oliver,

I was so glad to get your letter. It's not a stretch to say I was waiting for it. Thank you for that. Stop thinking that I'm a spy! I swear that's not true. I can't pretend to know what you're going through, but the fact that you're worried about how war will change you proves you're a good person. It's going to be so hard for you, I know that, and I'm concerned. That may sound odd coming from someone you've never met, but I mean it. My thoughts will go with you, wherever you are.

You're probably wondering how I'm getting your letters too, if I pick them up when I'm leaving mine. Simply put, don't worry about how this is happening. I read somewhere that belief is required for magic to exist. Once we start questioning how incredible things are possible, the wonder melts away, leaving us with mechanical explanations. I don't want to question our connection out of existence. Just remember that I'm here for you.

Hearing from you has become a bright spot for me. Things are tough right now, though I feel terrible telling you that when I know your situation is worse. Without dropping a complicated story on you, I'll just say I used to travel a lot, and now I'm stuck in one place. Not somewhere I'd ever have chosen on my own either. This town is scary in ways I can't easily describe, and I miss my parents, but I'm also mad at them for leaving me here. I haven't asked that much about your past, but feel free to tell me as much or as little as you want. I'm really curious what your life has been like, but I don't want to pry.

This may sound strange, but I had a dream recently. I was on a train platform watching soldiers arrive in the town where I'm living, and nobody could see me except a dark-haired boy with brown eyes and deep dimples. He was *wearing baggy brown trousers with a torn tan shirt and striped suspenders. Sometimes I imagine it was you, and that I saw you show up for training camp.*

You'll probably guess I'm hinting for you to describe yourself, so I can form a mental picture. If you want, I'll go first. I'm five feet four inches, medium build on the muscular side, and I'm relatively fit because I like to dance. My skin is light, though I tan easily, and I have dark, wavy hair and hazel eyes. Whether I look basic or amazing depends on how well I'm dressed and whether I did a great job on my makeup that day.

Anyway, this is getting long, so I'll close now. I'm wondering how much longer you'll be at camp, and how long it takes for my letters to arrive. Is it an instant drop, or is there a time delay? There's really no way to track it, I suppose. You probably don't get why I wrote that, so I'll stop being cryptic. Take care of yourself until next time.

—Araceli

Intellectually, I know I shouldn't get attached. If this is an elaborate hoax, I'm communicating with a masterful liar. I've decided to respond as if it's real, though. And in that scenario, in my time, Oliver is gone. He's a memory, a historical footnote, not a person I can meet and spend time with.

To be old enough to serve in the First World War, he must've been born in 1899. It's so strange and sobering to do the math. He'd have to be a vampire to be wandering around in my lifetime. He definitely died long before I was born, even assuming he didn't get shot in the trenches. That possibility sends a pang straight through me, strong enough that my chest aches. I rub my sternum as I get up and put his letter in the shoebox I'm using to safeguard the new ones, those addressed to me and not Lucy.

I use an app to scan the letter and send it to Eunsoo, and she replies at once:

Wow, so sincere! If I read this after messing with you, I'd probably confess. Are you sending it now?

Putting it in the box now. It's hard not to check immediately to see if it's still there, but they say a watched pot never boils.

I have an idea! I'm a genius.

Tell me!

You have a laptop, right?

Obviously.

Does it have a webcam?

Yup.

Excellent.

Eunsoo sends me a link to an article that gives step-by-step instructions on "How to Turn your Laptop into a Home Security System." She doesn't need to explain further. Placing my laptop by the window, my borrowed Wi-Fi is strong enough to handle this request. If I angle my laptop toward the box and install this free software, I will know the minute someone steps in my room. It takes me half an hour to finish the installation and setup, but now I'm covered. Eunsoo is messaging me again, impatient.

Did you figure it out?

"Araceli, dinner is done! I made a nice pork roast with rosemary potatoes."

Yep! We'll talk more tomorrow. My great-aunt's calling me to dinner, then I have homework to do.

Same. Later.

I don't take my phone down, as Great-Aunt Ottilie hates when I look at it at mealtimes. That's really weird since Ma and Papi live with their phones in hand, but I'm all about complying with Tía's rules. Tidying up the kitchen after dinner takes half an hour, then I watch some TV with her so she doesn't feel lonely.

Around eight, I say, "I have assignments. I should—"

"Please, go ahead, sweetheart."

I'd be lying if I claimed I got right to my homework. First, I check the laptop—no new files yet—then, I look in the box. My letter is still there.

Somehow I fall asleep doing homework and wake groggy, confused about what day it is. Tuesday, I think? That means tryouts are tomorrow. I need to practice tonight, or I'll have no chance at making the dance team.

As ever, the house is quiet as I leave, but I notice an extra bowl in the dish drainer. Normally I'd assume Tía had a late-night snack, but since I'm aware she leaves food out for a hungry ghost—food that disappears—that sends a little chill down my spine. Sometimes I feel as if someone is watching me in this house, but I don't get that sensation right now. Quickly I eat breakfast and get ready for school, and I'm out the door in plenty of time.

Logan isn't passing by this morning, which is fine because I'm not running late. I take my time walking to school, conscious of the way curtains flutter when I go by. People are clearly staring out their windows at me, but their wariness feels sinister, more than simple curiosity. I try not to mind it, but I'm slightly unnerved by the time I get to school.

I find Kimala waiting outside my classroom. She's beautiful in a bright red sweater and black fitted skirt. Her boots are freaking adorable. "Are you ready for tomorrow?"

"Still perfecting my routine but getting there." That's pretty much a lie. My choreography needs work, and my moves are sloppy.

"Glad to hear it. I'll send you an invite to our group chat now." I'm curious whether she means the dance team, but before I can ask, she clarifies. "It's unrelated to the squad. You'll have to make the cut before I add you to that one."

"So this is a different group?"

"Everyone from the table is in it. I'm sending you some video of last year's performances. It might help." She clicks away, and I receive the notice that I've been added.

"Thanks. I'll watch the first chance I get."

Kimala waves and rushes off as the first bell rings. I dart into the classroom just ahead of the scurrying wave of last-minute students and take my seat. Mr. Timmons already doesn't like me, thanks to the ghost thing, and there's no way I'm making it worse with a garbled explanation. I'll just take the zero and make it up over the rest of the semester.

Without realizing it, I'm watching for Logan, expecting him to race in ahead of the bell or to come creeping in behind the teacher just after it. Mr. Timmons strides in and closes the door, wearing his usual brisk expression. "Good morning, everyone. Let's start with chapter fifteen . . ."

Still no Logan. Huh, seems like he's absent, but I don't know him well enough to be sure if that's strange or not. I just met him, so maybe he's sick a lot or skips school to do bike tricks.

After class, I stare at my phone and hesitate. What the hell, what will it hurt? I send to group chat, Logan's not here today. Anyone know what's up?

He's in the group, so he could explain, if he wants, but he's absent and running silent. A chorus of "nah" and "what?" scrolls down my phone, so I guess the others aren't clued in either. It seems like this group doesn't know him that well, maybe no better than me, even though I just got here. Interesting. Somebody who seems open and lighthearted turns out to have all these layers. I bet they've never been to his secret hideout, either.

Even if I have ten other things going on, I can't let his absence go after he's been so nice. I text him right before lunch. You okay? I send. Didn't see you at school.

Logan doesn't answer, and I put my phone away as Eunsoo grabs my arm. "Did you set the app up to ping you if there's movement at home?"

The others are looking at us, but I don't explain. "I did, but there's nothing yet."

"The wait continues," she mutters.

Tamsyn, who's sitting on my other side, pokes me. "You two have secrets already?"

Before I can answer, Eunsoo does. "We knew each other online, if you can believe that. I've been talking to Araceli since we were twelve."

That's an awesome distraction, and we talk about our mutual love for 7TOG instead of explaining what we were talking about before. Now the group knows I'm obsessed with K-pop, but that's fine since it's true.

Kimala says, "I should've put 'Make You Sorry' on the playlist. I love that song."

"Me too." It's a classic, up-tempo breakup anthem. The title makes it sound a little scary, but it's only about revenge in the sense that success is the best payback.

When lunch is over, I head to class still worried about Logan and wondering how often he misses school. The others don't seem that alarmed so it must happen fairly often, but they probably don't know about his hideout.

I'm adding Logan's secrets to the list of things I need to investigate in this town.

14

After school, I find another snack waiting, Tía's way of showing she's on board as my legal guardian. I eat the carrot sticks and string cheese while reflecting on the letters that even Eunsoo agreed seem legit.

Finally I decide the direct approach is best. "I was wondering if you know anything about World War I," I say around a mouthful of mozzarella.

"I'm not old enough to remember it," she says, with a head cock that might be amusement or annoyance.

"No, I know that, but maybe you heard stories?"

"My grandfather fought," she answers. "Trained right here in town. There are probably some old pictures in the attic, maybe a few letters as well. I hate throwing things away, as you've probably guessed by now."

"Do you mind if I take a look?"

"Is this for school?" Fortunately, she assumes that's the case and goes on, "Well, I don't mind. Just don't include anything deeply personal in your project."

"I won't take your grandma's love letters to class," I promise.

"If you don't find anything useful up there, you could try the library."

"Right, thanks."

I need to watch the videos Kimala sent and practice my

dance routine, and then I'll search for World War I memorabilia. Up in the attic, I sit by the round window that feels like a porthole, because I get better signal, two strong bars of stolen Wi-Fi. Looks like the dance team performs at halftime, and they are good, but she's right: The squad needs more color. They could also use more flair, more creativity, because all this lockstep precision is vaguely unsettling, especially when I'm looking at so many blond girls with bouncy ponytails.

Something is deeply wrong with this town.

No response from Logan yet. I turn on my choice of audition music, put in my earbuds, and tuck my phone in my pocket. Time to move.

An hour later, I'm sweaty and relatively sure I won't embarrass myself at tryouts tomorrow. If I push too hard now, I'll risk an injury that would eliminate me before I even try. Kimala seems to want me on the squad, and I won't let her down.

The boxes are calling me, but I don't find much, just a handful of pictures featuring serious people I don't know and a bundle of letters. Sitting for a portrait was such a somber business back in the day. My great-great-etcetera uncle was a handsome man, and I dig the moustache. As I stare at the envelopes I unearthed, I realize I'm holding a complete love story in my hands, separation and reunion tied up in a faded yellow ribbon.

I shouldn't look, I shouldn't . . . but the writers have been gone a long time, and I do have Tía's permission. Maybe I'll have a look at the handwriting, compare it to the ones I'm getting. Even with a cursory glance, I can see it's different, more polished and graceful. There's an uncertainty that comes through Oliver's pen, like he's not the most experienced correspondent. He probably thinks the same about me since I'm way more used to typing on a keyboard.

I open a letter at random. This one is dated 1918.

Dearest Maude,

It seems the Allies will soon be victorious. Your patience and devotion have carried me when I could barely walk. The trenches were hell. I tried to cushion it, dear, so you wouldn't worry, but the truth is, I had barely a dry night. Rain, so much rain! And nothing clean to change into. We're moving now, but I will carry the shadow of ███ ██████ *with me, even after I return. I hope you can be patient with me. I am not the man who left two years ago, but I love you still. Knowing that you're waiting for me, taking care of Mother, it's all that keeps me on the march some days.*

The others want me to go with them. There's a general store in a village near, but they have nothing much to sell. Still, I'll go and see. The shells have stopped, and we're not seeing zepps anymore. I hope no man can call himself a proud German ever again after what I've seen here, what they've done to France. I'm telling you too much now, but the ruins of France are everywhere, and there are so many orphans, thousands of them. ████████████ ██████████████████████████

ah, let me stop.

My darling, I hate the forest. Let's move to Kansas, shall we? Where it's all golden fields and sunlight. I hope I'll be home soon.

> *All my love,*
> *Thomas*

What's most interesting about this letter is the censored sentences, probably more specific details about troop locations. That means the government was reading all the letters that came back from the front to make sure the enemy didn't get info that way. How freaking wild.

Sadly, Maude and Thomas never did get to Kansas. For whatever reason, they stayed here with the creepy forest. It must have bothered Thomas until the end of his days. With quiet reverence, I pack the letters away, glad that I indulged my curiosity.

It's not dark yet, so I still have time for the library run my great-aunt mentioned. I take a quick shower and tie up my hair, and as I'm getting dressed, I call, "Okay if I head out for some research?"

"Of course," Ottilie answers. "By the way, did you ask at school about driving lessons?"

She's really set on this. "No, was I supposed to?"

"I just thought one of your teachers might have a recommendation for a private academy."

The way she puts that makes me laugh because it's like I'd be attending some ivy-covered institution to learn how to drive. I think I probably need to download a manual from the state website and then find someone to teach me. In a town this small, it seems unlikely there's a driving school. Ironically, I'd probably have to drive somewhere to get lessons from a professional teacher.

"Can't we just use a ride share app when we need to?" I mumble.

"What's an app?" she asks.

So much for that.

"Never mind. It's on my list, okay? I'll be back by eight or so."

"Learn a lot!"

Sure, I'm on it. Not for the reasons she imagines, but acquiring knowledge is never bad, right?

I'm planning to stop by Logan's house and see how he is, but the sheriff who dragged the homeless man off earlier pulls into the Reeds' driveway. Holy shit, is Logan in serious trouble? But no, the man stalks from the car and slams into the house. So maybe it's even worse; this scary asshole lives with Logan? Either his dad or his stepdad, I don't know which. Since he left the door open, I can hear him yelling at his wife.

"Where the hell is he? I told him to come straight home from school and look after the fucking yard!"

I can't hear what Mrs. Reed says in response, but I've learned that Logan's not home, so it won't do me any good to stop by. With a shiver of thanks that my situation is better than that, I head for the library, which I found my first day wandering around town. It was closed then due to Labor Day. Just like the school.

As I step inside, the librarian greets me with a smile. "Anything I can help with today?"

"World War I? Preferably actual letters or local accounts."

"Oh, certainly," she says brightly. "Right this way. We've had some letters donated. This was a staging ground during the First World War. They built a training camp half a mile from town, and well, there's a fantastic source book written by a local author. He's since passed away, but his research was meticulous and included lots of photos. You'll want to start with this . . . oh, and this one too." She's talking as she moves through the stacks.

She taps the top volume as she hands me the books. "That's the best one for your purposes. Mr. Mayweather was something of a legendary figure around here. Not only was he an esteemed historian, he was also instrumental in founding the lab. Half the town works there in one capacity or another."

"Wow," I say, because no other word comes to mind.

"Exactly." She seems pleased that I'm impressed by this deceased local legend and hurries off to answer a question for a fidgety girl in pigtails.

I take my pile of books to an empty table near the back and

open the one she recommended first, *Our World at War* by E. G. Mayweather. The author starts out moralizing, and I detect an unmistakable note of sympathy for the Germans.

I stop reading and focus on the pictures, flipping through the pages.

My mouth drops open as I stare, unable to believe my eyes. I'm looking at the scene I dreamed. Obviously, the only difference is I'm not in the photo, but this train platform with the arriving soldiers? I saw this. And not just the vague idea of it. I recognize these faces because they were in my dream, down to the sad-eyed boy in ragged pants and suspenders. In this shot, he's scared and wistful, and I am freaking out.

How is this possible? I've never seen this book before. Maybe I saw the picture somewhere else? That's wildly improbable. I've studied world history, but the schools I attended didn't place any weight on America's role in various conflicts.

Maybe I shouldn't be shocked, given the other shit that's going down in my life, but the idea that I somehow dreamed this before I saw it . . . this underscores the rest. Somehow, I've become connected to the past, and I don't know how or why.

Shaken, I skim through the rest of the books, but they're all dry and factual, listing dates, names of battles, troop movements, and casualty numbers, like those weren't real people who fought and died. They're not abstract to me anymore.

As I pick up the Mayweather book because it has the most local photos, my phone vibrates, finally a message from Logan.

It simply reads: No. At fort. Bring food. Please.

15

The "no" is a direct response to my question, You okay? Clearly Logan is not fine, and he's hungry too. The "please" is painful to read because it comes across as desperation in such a terse message.

Hell. I don't know if I can find the tree fort on my own. Given my aunt's warning and Tamsyn's missing little brother, I don't want to go out into the woods by myself. I'd be lying if I said I wasn't scared—and why is he asking me anyway? Doesn't he have closer friends who could help?

Even as I'm mentally bitching, I pack up and head for the front desk. I show my ID and get a library card, no need for a guardian since I'm eighteen. Once I check out the Mayweather book, I drop it in my bag. Before I come to a conscious decision, I'm heading for Joe's Deli. I pick up a ham and cheese sandwich, a bag of chips, a fruit cup, and a bottle of water. If he's upset, he might want something sweet, right? I add a brownie to my stash and check out.

Now comes the tough part. My skin is crawling over the idea of venturing into the woods alone. The other day, I was nervous, even with Logan leading the way, likely because of the stories. I remember where he left the path, but I can't bring myself to go there. Dammit, it's going to be dark soon. I don't want to do this.

I can't leave Logan hanging though.

He wasn't at school. He's in trouble if he's asking me to bring food. Sighing, I tap out a grumpy message. Send directions if you want dinner.

In a flash, I get a throbbing red heart emoji and a detailed description of how to reach the tree house. Since the shadows are lengthening and it will be scary-shit-happens-in-the-woods-at-night dark soon, I follow his instructions at a brisk jog. He gives strange landmarks that I never would have noticed as a city girl, but the fallen log and dead tree and flowering bush are all present. I pass them one by one, until I spot the shimmer of light that marks the tree house.

It seems imperative to get off the ground with night closing in; it's weird how I feel the gloom like a physical threat out here. Intellectually, I know there's no more danger than during the day, except the risk of tripping on unseen obstacles, but I still feel that same fear as I scramble up the rope ladder as when I was a little kid who thought monsters would grab my ankles if I didn't leap into bed fast enough.

"You came," he says as I pop my head through the opening in the floor. "I wasn't sure you would."

I shove the paper bag at him. "Here. I didn't know what you wanted. Hope you're not allergic to anything."

"I'm not. Thanks for dinner."

Even in the dim light, I can see his lip is busted, and his face is swollen on one side. At a minimum, someone slapped the shit out of him, and it looks more like he took a few hits to the face. When he reaches for the food, I notice how gingerly he moves, so there's probably damage elsewhere, deep bruises at least. Part of me wishes I'd also brought first aid supplies, but he didn't tell me he was injured.

"You need to see a doctor."

"My ribs aren't broken. I'd know if they were." The simplicity of his answer horrifies me because it seems like he's had broken ribs before.

I remember the damage to his knee, which I attributed to him wiping out on his bike. As I sit on a cushion across from him, I see that pillows are laid out as if he's been lying on them, and there's a pile of afghans at his feet. This tree house is cozy enough to be a decent shelter from spring to fall, though I don't know how it would handle a heavy downpour or a violent storm.

"Did you sleep here last night?"

"That falls under the category of 'when we know each other better' questions," he answers with a lopsided smile, twisted by the damage to his lip.

"Then why did you ask me to bring you food? You should entrust this to someone else, along with the rest of your secrets."

"I wanted you to come," he says.

"But why?" Talk about frustrating. He won't tell me anything about himself, but he's weirdly omnipresent, saving me from trouble at school, giving me rides, and sharing his Wi-Fi.

"Because I want to trust you. I guess you could say this is step one. We'll see how it goes from here."

"I don't even know what you're talking about."

"You haven't told anyone about this place yet, so today I'm letting you in a little more. If you keep my secrets, I'll tell you everything. Eventually. Sorry, even I think I'm being weird around you, but I can't help it."

He peels the plastic off his sandwich and devours it like he hasn't eaten in days. I'm speechless as he works through what I brought, even draining the water down to the last drop. Now I wish I'd gotten two bottles.

Finally, I sputter, "Are you testing me right now?"

He dumps half the bag of chips into his mouth, chews and swallows, before answering, "Don't worry, you're getting excellent scores."

"Did I ask to be rated? From the first day I met you, you've been this extra, like when you asked about my accent. That was rude, by the way."

A flicker of surprise and regret. "Sorry. I just thought you sound cool, that's all."

It's hard to stay mad at him when he compliments me, but I'm determined. "For like five seconds, I felt bad for you. Now, I'm pissed off."

Logan sighs, staring at his hands. "I don't want you to feel sorry for me. If I did, I'd dump my story, and I wouldn't care if you told everyone because then I'd get head pats from everyone who heard how shitty my life is."

That's a tacit admission that he has deep, enduring issues, and that's the truth hidden beneath his goofy persona. "I hear that, but it's frustrating when I have my own stuff going on and I don't know what you want from me."

Trusting and confiding in him might move him to do the same, but there's no way I'm telling him about the letters, which may be a prank, but even if they are, it doesn't explain how I'm live-streaming the past through my dreams. The photo in the book I hid in my bag is haunting and inexplicable.

"Everyone has a life," he says. "But there are layers of what we share with other people. Until I met you, there was nobody I wanted to show everything to."

That is ridiculous. How can he feel that way? I've never had anyone take one look at me and conclude I'd make the perfect confidant. Logan may have decided that based on some criteria I'm clueless about, but I can't linger here any longer.

Because night has fallen, and the trees have swallowed even the faintest glimmer of starlight. Their twisted branches feel like a fortress of brambles, tangled and sinister.

I have to go back soon. In the dark.

16

"Spend the night," Logan says then, as if he's reading my mind. "Call your great-aunt and—"

"Tell her that I'm staying in a tree house with some guy I barely know? No, thanks."

He exaggerates a wince, hunching over from pain that might not be fake. "Ouch, that's harsh. I thought we were bonding."

"I have to go."

Please let me find my way back. I don't want to be added to the roster of the lost.

I almost ask Logan to walk me home, but he's hurt, and it's not that far.

It might as well be a thousand miles, as far as my racing heart is concerned.

"Be careful," he says softly. "And don't follow the lights."

I can hardly breathe as I climb down the rope ladder, phone in hand. My flashlight is on out front and I know which way to go, but I can't see the landmarks as easily in the dark. Every noise sounds ominous, though it's probably a bunny rustling the bushes nearby.

I break into a run because this fear is irrational and immutable. If don't watch my step—

Before I can complete the thought, I trip on an exposed root and pitch forward into a tangle of fallen branches and dry grass, sparsely grown along with moss and clover on the forest floor. My palms sting, and I'm not sure exactly where I am anymore. Running in the dark is a terrible idea, and it's not like I can get walking directions out here: Tía will be worried if I don't get home soon.

Maybe the librarian will be the last one to report seeing me? Since I don't know Logan well, I can't be sure he'd admit to our meeting in the woods. That's the kind of scenario that gets you ranked as a suspect.

Dammit, his ribs aren't broken. I should have asked him to take me home. As I wonder if I can find my way back to the tree house, lights appear in the distance, swirling in the trees.

Oh shit.

At first, I'm simply frozen, but as I watch a little longer, I realize this isn't the same as what I saw before—in the tree house with Logan. These lights are more purposeful, like multiple people shining flashlights around, and they're all the same color, none of the swirling beauty of that first sighting.

It seems like people are searching the woods . . . but for what? It's too soon for my great-aunt to have reported me missing. Did someone else get lost out here? If that's the case, I should ask the search party to help me get out of the woods before I make their lives worse and get added to the list of those they need to find.

Cautiously, I make my way toward those swinging lights, aware that my speculation might be wrong. There could be other, terrible reasons for them to be creeping around the woods at night. Unless I see uniforms and clipboards, I won't show myself. In this town, I'm braced for white hoods and hate crimes I wouldn't survive witnessing.

When I get close enough to see better, I find . . . neither.

Four figures are moving in hazmat suits, carrying high-tech scanning equipment. Their devices whir and beep, according to what they detect, and if this area is irradiated, I am so screwed.

"Give me something, Howard," a woman says, her voice distorted by the suit.

"There are spikes all over the zone," an annoyed man snaps. "We've definitely got bleed, though. I think Edward is right, damn him."

"So you're ready to confirm his half-baked theory?"

"You're seeing the numbers, same as I am. There's no other logical conclusion except that containment has failed. It would also explain the whole cross section of complications. We need to report this and let the higher-ups figure out a solution."

The figure I guess is the woman grabs the other one and shakes him. "Don't be naïve. If you don't realize how they'll clean this up, you shouldn't have clearance for this project."

"Shit. My research!"

"You should care more about your life."

Okay, whatever's going on here, I have officially seen too much. This is where I get scooped up and detained; they'll send me to some private ICE camp and pretend I'm not an American citizen.

I have to get the hell out of here.

Oh my God, my legs won't move. My knees are locked in a crouch, and I'm too scared to shift even a muscle. If I step on a branch and they hear me, I'm done for. Maybe I can wait them out.

How long can they possibly wander around scanning trees and rocks and dirt?

Ever since I heard the words "containment failure" my skin has felt itchy. That's probably psychosomatic, right? It's not like my hair is falling out in clumps as I cower in the bushes.

Though I'm not sure what's going on, this must be related to the lab the Mayweather dude founded. Eunsoo said her parents work there; they're physicists or something. Silently, I run through everything I've learned since I got here, but it still doesn't quell the raw terror keeping me in statue mode.

They're finally moving off, maybe back to the lab. This is not the way to my house.

Once they've gone, I can breathe again, and five minutes later, I straighten with heroic effort, biting my hand to keep from crying out at moving my cramped legs. Sound carries in the forest; even I know that, so better not to risk it.

Using my ears instead of my eyes, I listen for the sound of cars and follow that faint sound trail until I stumble onto a road. It's not the place where I went into the woods, but that doesn't matter.

Now I can get some GPS help. According to the navigation app, I'm four streets away from Tía's house. There's no hiding how scared and shaky I am, so it's a good thing she's in the kitchen when I rush inside, down the hall and into the bathroom. Yeah, I do need to pee, but I'm showering too, washing away every trace of this night's danger. I can't have my elderly aunt worrying about me every time I leave the house. As I catch my frazzled reflection in the mirror above the sink, I note both the dirt smudged on my left cheek and the wild expression in my eyes.

It does not escape me that this town is probably way more dangerous than Venezuela. So much for sending me here to let me experience life as a typical American teen, huh, Ma?

I can already hear Papi saying, "Let's face it, peque, you were never going to be normal. You've always been exceptional."

Which is the kind of cheesy, morale-boosting stuff your parents are supposed to say for your self-esteem, but my father always says it with a straight face.

Tía knocks on the door. "Dinner is waiting. Will you be done soon?"

"Be right out!"

This is my second shower of the day, so she may suspect I have a glandular condition. I rinse off in two minutes and put my rumpled clothes back on with a grimace. She's got another pot of soup, ham and potato this time. Seems like she prefers one-dish dinners. To my surprise, she's no longer hiding the extra bowl. It sits on the table with us, steaming away, like Great-Uncle Archibald will be right with us, as soon as he completes his ghostly business.

"You already know," she says with a shrug. "I won't complain about your taste in music if you can put up with my little idiosyncrasies."

That's one word for it, I guess.

17

There's still no letter from Oliver, which makes me think whoever is behind the joke knows about my laptop security cam. I'm the only one who activates the camera coming in and out of the room; nobody else has triggered it yet.

Eunsoo messages me before bed that night. Anything yet?

Nope. My great-aunt doesn't even come in my room while I'm gone. I'm the only one on camera so far.

This is so weird. You set for tryouts tomorrow?

Pretty much.

I sort of want to tell her what's going on with Logan, but breaking faith with him would mean failing his elaborate trustworthiness test, and I think he needs me. I'm just not sure if I can be who he wants me to be. I'd like to tell someone what he's going through at home, but knowing he lives with the sheriff intimidates me. I feel like he's a big deal in town, and maybe I'll make it worse for Logan by interfering.

He's at school the next day, acting like nothing happened.

People don't pay attention to his bruises, so maybe he's seen as accident-prone. Now I see the reason for the clown persona. If you trip and drop stuff a lot in public, people won't question your story about falling down steps or walking into doors.

I don't speak to him in first period or after, busy conferencing with Kimala for some last-minute tips. She's even nice enough to watch my routine during lunch and give me a few pointers. I can't overhaul the steps, but I will incorporate the minor changes she suggested.

Finally, I'm standing in the gym with, like, thirty other hopefuls. Too bad there are only five spots left by graduating seniors the year before. A red-haired girl stares at me as I stretch.

"You're kind of . . . thick for the team, aren't you?"

My brows shoot up. With a fake sweet smile, I respond in Spanish. The great part is I can cuss people like her out with equanimity, and she's going to feel ignorant as hell. Plus, she won't be able to repeat any of it to get me in trouble.

Her pale face goes rosy and her mild disdain sharpens. "You're in America. Speak English!"

"People can speak whatever language they want in America. It's a free country, right?" I smirk at her and give my hair a toss as I line up.

Probably I shouldn't have provoked her, but she didn't need to say that.

Kimala is standing at the front of the group with a white girl who looks insanely cheerful. Her eyes are both too big and too bright, an electric blue so intense that I suspect drugs or contacts. She claps her hands together and gives a little bounce, as if her excitement can't be contained by standing still.

"Okay, everyone, I'm so excited to see some fresh faces. It's okay, Candace, this is your fourth year, but I'm so proud of your persistence!"

The called-out Candace hunches her shoulders and tries to hide in the crowd, but everyone is looking at her, thanks to the perky co-captain who hasn't introduced herself yet. Kimala catches my eye and gives a faint head tilt, as if to say, "You see what I'm working with, okay?"

I bite my lip to hide a smile.

Perky chatters on. "Most of you know who I am, but for those who don't, I'm Lana Latimer, and this is my fourth year on the dance squad. I'm super-stoked to have been voted in with Kimala as co-captains, and I just know we can make this the best year yet. Now let me explain the rules . . ."

It's basically what the flyer said, so I listen with half attention, until we get broken into groups of five. With thirty of us, there are six mini squads who will later perform the choreography they teach us in the next hour together. Thankfully, I'm not matched with the bitchy redhead from before.

Lana and Kimala each choose a group to teach, and volunteers from the dance team are assigned to the others. It's not a coincidence that Kimala heads directly for my group.

"Hope you all brought your A game," she says. Someone starts the music, and it's a forgettable pop song that would never be my first choice for basically anything. "I'll do this routine once at full speed and then again slower. It'll be up to you to pick it up from there, remember the steps, and practice it as a group. We want people who move well and learn fast since we never do the same routine at halftime."

"Ready," I say, because the rest of my little squad seems nervous. They all look young too, probably freshmen or sophomores.

Kimala waits for some unheard cue in the song, then she starts, and I'm immediately wowed. She's not only mad graceful, but each motion is infused with such joy and confidence that I almost forget I'm supposed to be memorizing what she does so I can perform the same steps.

Beside me, the girls are into it, mocking out the head tilts, arm dips, the circle steps, and the pivots. Next time, she slows it significantly, breaking the routine into chunks so I can see where the moves meld together.

I think I got it. Maybe.

"That's it," Kimala says. "Who's ready to show me something?"

Silence.

Yeah, I'm gonna have to take the lead here. It's not that I think I'm the best dancer ever, but I have more self-assurance than the young ones.

"Let me try," I say.

My version isn't perfect. I notice three mistakes as I run it through, but I can do better with practice. We have an hour to smooth out the rough edges and learn to dance in synch with each other. Nobody mentioned that as being important, but I know it is. If you can't stay in step with your squad, you won't get picked, no matter how slick you move.

"Not bad," Kimala says. "You take point, teach the rest of your group. Wow me in an hour, okay?"

"It seems like you're already friends with Kimala," one of the freshmen breathes. Her voice is light and airy, and she speaks the name Kimala as if she's the school Beyoncé. From what I've seen so far, this is probably true.

"I heard she got a scholarship to a famous dance school," another volunteers.

Also probably true, but irrelevant for our purposes.

"This is why she put me in charge," I say, getting out my phone. "I'm downloading the song as we speak, so why don't we find a private place to practice?"

Being in the loud gym will only distract them. I get them to agree to head to a deserted stretch of hall between the gym and cafeteria, then I start the music and lead as best I can. Lord help them, three are hopeless and can't dance to save their lives. Two are what I'd call adequate, but they'd never find partners for swing dance in Buenos Aires.

If I'm not careful, they'll make me look bad during tryouts. But that's part of the challenge, making the team work as best you can. I bite my lip and show them the steps again. Again. Again.

Finally, we're all on the same basic page as the practice hour ends. I did my best.

They line us up outside the gym, waiting our turn to perform for the judges. After this, it'll be the second part of the audition, the solo trials. If I lose points in group, I can recoup there.

"Group two," Kimala calls.

That's us.

My baby birds are not fantastic, but nobody falls at least, and we are all reasonably in synch. I don't miss a single step, a fact that's acknowledged by Kimala's silent nod.

While I'm waiting, I get a drink from the water fountain. The other girls are sitting on the floor, lounging against the wall, chewing at their cuticles, or fiddling with their phones. Suddenly, I have the same feeling I get sometimes at Tía's house—the crawling sensation that somebody's watching me.

Staying casual, I glance around, but I don't find anyone taking an interest. My skin is chill and prickled with goose bumps, and I swear I feel a faint touch on my lower back.

I spin around, half expecting to see Logan with a water bottle because that seems like a prank he'd play, but there's nobody.

"Jumpy much?" The redhead from before curls her lip at me as her friend nudges her and gives me an apologetic look.

"We're all nervous, okay?"

That quickly, the feeling is gone, and how is that possible? I get why my house feels haunted, but the school . . .

What the hell is going on here, anyway?

18

"Has anyone ever said this school is haunted?"

The random girl who heard the question cocks her head with an amused look. "Did someone tell you that story to scare you?"

What, so there's a story?

"I didn't get all the details," I say, silently willing her to elaborate.

"It's pretty standard. Supposedly there was a boy who died here, like, twenty years ago. Fell off the roof or something. People whispered that it might have been suicide because he was failing a lot of classes and his girlfriend had just broken up with him. But who knows how much of that is true? You know how stuff gets embellished as the legend is repeated." She shrugs. "I don't even know if someone actually died here."

Another girl chimes in, "I totally think it's true. I've gotten chills when the temperature is fine, and sometimes it feels like someone is watching me."

Check and check.

The first girl laughs. "You are so suggestible, though. Remember at Sara's slumber party, when you totally—"

"Shut *up*, Harley."

I tune out and let them bicker over whether the second girl wet her pants because they dipped her hand in water while she was sleeping.

In a town this size, I bet my great-aunt would remember if a boy died at Central twenty years ago. She might even know his name, so I could check the obituaries around the right time. I have so much stuff to check out, although it doesn't seem likely that I'll find much about a secret government lab in the public library.

It's so improbable that everywhere I go, there's a ghost lurking around, though. I mean, what are the odds? Unless the government experiment has something to do life after death. Maybe they're trying to use dead people as a power source? A spirit engine is kind of a cool idea, but a concept more suited for a grim science fiction story.

While I ponder, they finish up the group tryouts, and soon I'm called for my solo audition. The panel of judges is composed of two dance team members, Kimala and Lana, and the faculty coach, whose name I can't remember.

I hand over the USB with my music on it, and Lana plugs it into the laptop connected to the speakers behind me. She flashes me a too-cheerful smile and a thumbs-up. "Ready when you are, Araceli!"

"Good to go."

When the music starts, I forget all the complications, everything weighing on my mind. I dance like my life depends on it, incorporating all the tips Kimala gave me, especially the bits about eye contact and a confident smile. This may not be the most technically perfect choreography they see today, but I have plenty of flair and it's fun watching me dance. People always said that about our swing performances. I finish with a flourish and offer a brief bow.

Per Kimala's suggestion, I don't wait for the coach to tell me the results will be announced later in the week. "Thanks for your time!" I chirp, then jog from the gym, aware they're watching me leave.

Whew. Once I'm outside the double doors, I lean against the cool concrete block wall. It's a little chilly in the hallway, considering I'm wearing shorts and a T-shirt, and I'm also covered in sweat, from both nerves and exertion.

"How'd it go?" It's one of the girls from my group.

"Pretty well. I did my routine and didn't fall over. We'll see."

"I bet you make it," she says in a wistful tone. "You're really good."

Since she was terrible, I don't have any encouraging words. I settle on, "Good luck! See you later."

In the locker room, I clean up a little and put on my street clothes. It's nearly six, thanks to the practice hour and all the waiting. Hard for me to believe it's only been twenty-four hours since I was squatting in the woods, afraid for my life.

The halls are dark and quiet, but the creepy feeling doesn't return. Right now, this place is only a school. As I push open the front doors, I nearly trip on a lanky figure sprawled on the steps.

Logan looks at me upside down, arms beneath his head. "Took you long enough."

"Were you waiting for me?"

"Yup. I owe you for yesterday. I'll give you a ride home."

I snicker. "You think putting me on the back of your bike for six blocks equals a trip out to the tree house?"

"Not so much, but I'm trying here. Get on."

It's better than walking, and he lives right across the street. Refusing would be petty, and I'd get home even later. I'm barely on before he's pedaling like mad, standing up in front of me so I'm not even sure where to hold on.

On Logan's bike, the blocks fly by, and I must admit, it's kind of nice. The horizon is orange and pink, trailing fire above the trees, and the breeze feels clean and fresh on my skin. That's the seduction of a place like this. It seems so safe and whole-some here, but the fact is, that's only true for the right people. The rest of us need to watch our backs.

"We have arrived," he says, stopping in front of Great-Aunt Ottilie's house.

"Thanks," I say, hopping off the back. "Hey, have you taken the SATs yet?"

"Of course. Twice, actually. I did better the second time. Let me tell you, it ate into the money I earned mowing lawns."

"Do you know where you're going to school, then?"

"I'm joining the army first," he answers. "One tour, then I'll have some money for college."

He has to be shitting me; that's the last thing I'd have imag-ined for his future, but he doesn't crack a smile or say, "just kidding."

"Seriously?"

Logan nods. "Men in my family have always served, going back to my great-grandfather. It's kind of a tradition at this point."

"I had no idea. You don't look like the military type."

He's scowling, shoulders in a defensive posture. "Should I shave my head and wear more camo?"

"Get right on that," I snap, whirling toward the porch.

I've taken a few steps on the cracked sidewalk when his soft voice reaches me. "This isn't what I want. It's what my dad expects, what real men do."

I pause without turning, mostly because I suspect he won't want me to see his face right now. That can't have been easy to say. "Ah, well, I'd tell you to be true to yourself, but it's not that easy in the real world. If your dad says he won't do X un-less you do Y, what are you supposed to do? Give up your dreams for the illusion of freedom?"

"That's it exactly," he says. "I'm telling myself I can handle it because after that, I'll be free to do what I want. I won't be dependent on him anymore. Maybe it won't be that bad."

No worse than being slapped around for disappointing his dad, I think. But that's only my private conjecture. Maybe I've taken tiny pieces of a picture of a goat and put them together as a sheep. I turn to face him.

He's standing in the circle of the streetlight, backpack straps twisting in his thin hands, and I can tell he doesn't want to go home.

Hoping Ottilie won't mind, I ask, "Would you like to come in?"

19

Logan's face brightens like he's won the lottery. "Are you sure it's okay?"

"We'll see," I mutter. Louder, I add, "Are you sure you won't get in trouble?"

"My parents are at a town meeting. They won't be home until late."

Town meeting. Why does that sound so ominous?

"Then come on. Maybe wait by the door while I make sure?"

"No problem." As soon as he steps inside the door, he takes off his shoes.

I take mine off too and hurry for the kitchen. It smells like meatloaf. Ottilie is nothing if not an American cook. There are also mashed potatoes. She has potholder mitts on each hand and is carrying a casserole dish to the table. Sure enough, it's a ketchup-topped meatloaf, brown and resplendent in its own juices.

"There's also a salad in the fridge, if you don't mind getting the bowl," she says, instead of hello.

"Looks like you made plenty. Is it all right if Logan joins us? His parents are out tonight. Some kind of town meeting."

Her expression darkens. "They call it that, but they're just looking for ways to make people's lives more difficult." Before I can ask, she adds hastily, "Of course he's welcome. Call him in."

I pop my head out to see him waiting by the front door. "Come on, dinner's ready."

Tía greets him with a hug, and she's gentle with him, like she knows he might have hidden bruises. Easing back, she keeps her hands on his shoulders as she tsks. "It's been too long, young man. I feel somewhat abandoned. I taught you to knit three summers past, and once you had what you wanted of me, I didn't see you for dust."

Logan grins. "Sorry, Auntie. I guess waving through the window while I'm mowing your yard doesn't count as keeping in touch, huh?"

Ignoring that, she tilts his face to inspect his bruises. "What happened here?"

He pulls away, gently but firmly. "As it turns out, I'm terrible at basketball."

While that may be true, I doubt he took a basketball to the face. "I'm starving," I cut in, trying to help him like he helped me with Mr. Timmons that time.

We sit down together, passing around meatloaf, potatoes, and salad. By tacit agreement, the food offering for Great-Uncle Archibald will be left later. No need for Logan to know how weird we are in this house.

"Are your parents well?" Ottilie asks, just as he shovels a huge bite into his mouth.

I can tell from the sparkle in her pale eyes that she did it on purpose, just like servers pop up to check the quality of your dinner as soon as your mouth is full.

His gaze meets mine, pleading for help as he chews. Finally, he says, "Yeah, I mean, yes. They're good."

"I'm glad to hear it. Classes going well? This is your last year, isn't it?"

"It is. I guess they're going all right."

"Let him eat," I say. "This isn't an interrogation."

"I'm old. I'm allowed to question people however I like. Otherwise what's the point of aging?"

It's a compelling argument, but I like to bicker, and I miss doing that with Papi. Under the right circumstances, he'd quarrel with me if I said the sky was blue.

"Not dying?" I suggest with a straight face.

Logan cuts me a horrified look, like he can't believe I said that to my great-aunt. I just grin at them both. She's shaking her head.

Like that, I remember I meant to ask her about the story I heard at tryouts. "Hey, did you hear about a boy dying at Central at any point? A girl told me some ghost story today, and I was wondering if there was any truth to it."

"You're so gullible," Logan murmurs.

Tía taps the table, visibly pensive. "That would have been big news. I'm sure I'd recall if there had been a fatal accident on school property. People would've talked of nothing else, and there would have been a memorial service at Crowe and Son's Funeral Home . . ." Finally, she shakes her head. "There was a bad car wreck, oh, about fifteen years ago, and a teenage girl died. I think the driver was paralyzed, but that didn't happen at school."

"I didn't get a name or anything, but the girl said it could have been suicide. Does that ring any bells?"

"You're really digging into this," Logan says, spooning out another serving of potatoes.

"I'm just curious. Some legends have a basis in fact."

"Not this one, I think." Ottilie serves Logan more meatloaf

as he finishes his first piece. "This town has always been very quiet. I don't remember any reports of suicide. We had an accidental shooting a few years back. A little boy got ahold of his father's gun and accidentally shot his mother."

"I remember that," Logan says. "Luckily, she didn't die, or he'd have been scarred for life. As it is, people called him Gunner until he graduated and left town."

"Poor Greg," she says with a sigh. "I wonder how he's doing."

He got out of this burg, I think. So wherever he is, he must be better off.

"It seems like there's surprisingly little crime here," I say then.

"Reported crime," Ottilie corrects.

It feels like an important distinction, and I'm instantly alert. "What do you mean?"

She hesitates, glancing at Logan, as if she's not sure she should talk about this in front of him. He doesn't seem to pick up on the pause at first, then he looks up from his plate with a twist of his mouth, a bitter expression for sure.

"I don't mind. As the sheriff's kid, I've heard just about everything. I'm not going to repeat what you say to my dad, that's for sure."

Well, that confirms Logan's dad is the county sheriff. If I'm right about his dad knocking him around, that makes it even worse, but men in positions of power often have a narrow definition of what's acceptable for a "real" man.

That seems to reassure my great-aunt. "Well, there are no murders on the books. No suicides either. They write in the paper that this is the safest town in New York State, but here, people just . . . vanish. Their bodies are never found. To me, that's worse than having somebody break in and steal some jewelry. It's . . ." She can't seem to find the right word.

"Sinister?" It makes me think of secret police who round up dissenters and those who don't fit the mold.

It's impossible not to wonder if the disappearances are tied to the town's past—and present—racism, or if it's related to the scientists roaming the woods with scanning equipment. My mind starts racing with ten different conspiracy theories while my great-aunt chews a bite of meatloaf, her head tilted in consideration of the word I offered.

"You're not wrong," she says finally. "If it wasn't for my dear Archibald who was lost here twenty years ago, I'd have sold my house long ago and moved somewhere more hospitable."

"Do you stay because of your good memories with him?" Logan asks.

She gives a small, sad smile. "Perhaps I haven't given up hope that he'll come home someday. Pitiful, I know."

"I think it's sweet," he says.

I'm stuck on the "twenty years" part. Isn't that what the girl said about the boy who died at school? Twenty years. Maybe that was just a random round number, and she might have said ten or fifteen instead.

On impulse, I ask, "How long has it been going on?"

"What, sweetheart?" Ottilie isn't with me; I need to give context.

"You said my great-uncle disappeared twenty years ago, and that people just vanish around here. When did that start? Has it been going on for thirty years? Forty?"

I've seen the pictures in the post office, the number of flyers posted around town. From what I've seen, there are a disproportionate number of *missing* people in relation to the actual town population. There must be a reason, some connection that I can't figure out yet.

She nods, instantly grasping what I'm driving at. "Archibald was among the first. The list of our lost ones has grown over the years, but I don't remember this happening before 1999."

20

"When was the lab built?" I ask.

Ottilie considers for a moment. "I think it was in the eighties. I seem to recall that Mr. Mayweather sold some land . . . oh, I don't remember all the details. You can probably find out more at the library, if you're curious."

Hmm, the disappearances didn't start as soon as the lab started operation, then. But still, this is a definite lead. Now I have a range of dates to put together a timeline. I can also look for information regarding the people who vanished during that time.

I need to talk to Tamsyn about her brother's disappearance.

Eventually, Tía says, "I'm going to my room. You can watch TV in the parlor if you want. I do trust both of you, but it would be disrespectful for you to go upstairs. Understood?"

Oh my God, if I wanted to hook up with Logan, I'd go across the street. He already said his parents aren't home. Sighing, I mumble, "I got it, Tía. I won't drag him to my lair while I'm under your roof."

"Wow," he says, once she's gone. "You have a lair? Villain or dragon?"

I smirk, because I *do* enjoy his sense of humor. "Little from column A, little from column B."

"You're a villainous dragon, then. I thought so. There were

tells." Logan gets up as I do, following me as I start cleaning the kitchen.

"Such as?" I ask, stacking dishes in the sink to be washed.

He gestures broadly, indicating the darkness beyond the kitchen window. "Your massive hoard, the bones of your victims scattered in the backyard."

"What were you doing in our yard?" I bare my teeth at him, scrubbing a plate.

He plucks it from my hands to dry. "Sneaking, obviously. Hiding in shadows. Listening for noise, but I usually fail that roll."

"Are you a gamer?" I met a few over the course of my travels, so I get this is probably a roleplaying joke outside my frame of reference. Rinsing what I've washed, I turn the dishes over to Logan, who is piling them on the counter.

"Points for figuring that out from context. I guess you aren't?"

Shaking my head, I start on the meatloaf pan. Wow, gross. "Not so much, though I did drunkenly LARP once."

He laughs. "That's the worst kind of LARPing. Did you remember your adventures in the morning?"

"Half and half. Actually, it was a costume party that went drastically awry in a cemetery, but I'm calling it LARPing because I can."

"I'd pay to hear that story," he says, drying the last plate.

"That falls under the category of 'when we know each other better,'" I say, pressing my lips together in hopes of hiding the smug smile.

"I had that coming."

"Agreed."

Once the kitchen is spotless, he heads for the door and I don't stop him. The question is scratching away at the edges of my mind. Do I have a letter waiting? If it came now, while Logan was with me, then *I'm* his alibi. I wish I didn't have to send him back home, but I'm afraid anything I do will make his situation worse. Troubled, I watch him put on his shoes.

"Thanks for dinner," he says, shouldering his backpack.

"No problem. Night!"

I'm more eager than I should be, hurrying up the stairs like a startled cat. The heartwood box is on my dresser, precisely where I left it. With careful hands, I open it and lift the false bottom.

I blink once, twice, unable to believe what I'm seeing. There's a letter waiting, but before I read it, I rush over to the laptop I left on my bedside table, open and ready to catch the culprit. Except when I check the output, the *only* new file is the one I made a few seconds ago, and it's still recording. Nobody came into my room, yet the letter from Oliver appeared. Eunsoo is the only one who knew I set up a hidden camera, and she's messaging me right now, sending selfies from her bedroom.

I let out a shaky breath and answer Eunsoo.

You won't believe this . . .

What happened?

I got a letter. There's no video file.

OMG! So this is real?

I have no idea what's going on. There's no other logical explanation, but . . . There's no way to finish that sentence. The rational side of me isn't ready to accept that Oliver is a real person, currently writing to me from 1917, but in my heart, I *want* to believe. I can't tell Eunsoo that yet.

Have you read the letter yet?

No, I'll do that now.

Wait, I want to be there. I'm on my way! You live across from Logan, right?

Yeah. Are you sure? It's getting late.

It'll be fine. I'll borrow my mom's car.

That's the last message I get from Eunsoo, but I figure she's driving. I take the paper out of the box, but I don't unfold it. Instead, I head downstairs to wait for her. I take up Ottilie's offer to watch some TV, just without Logan. Ten minutes stretch to twenty, and I finally ask her what's up.

Are you still coming over?

Did you get in trouble?

Just let me know when you can if something happened at home. I'm getting a little worried.

Now I know how she felt when I was traveling. I'm not exactly sure where she lives, so I send a message to the group chat. Does anyone have Eunsoo's home number? She was heading over here, but it's been almost an hour. Are her parents strict?

It doesn't seem impossible that she might've gotten in a fight about going out at eight on a school night. Maybe they took her phone and sent her to her room? But she could email me . . . I have a bad feeling as I wait for the others to answer in chat.

Tamsyn finally replies, I don't have their number. More than mine, about the same as Kimala's, I think. Well, more than mine used to be. My mom doesn't let me go anywhere since Ronell disappeared.

Nobody has anything helpful to say, and it's now close to ten. Jackson eventually sends me the number, tracked down through some email loop his parents belong to, maybe even started for a circumstance like this. I'm scared to call her parents, even more fearful not to. I think about how my mother handles herself when she's making difficult contacts, and I try for that tone once I dial.

A woman answers the phone on the third ring. "Hello?"

"I'm sorry to bother you so late. Is this Mrs. Park?" Ma always confirms who she's speaking with before providing information.

"Yes, who's this?"

"I'm Araceli, one of Eunsoo's friends—"

"Is she trying to spend the night at your place? I already told her no, not until we meet you. Put her on the phone!"

Shit. Then she's not at home.

My heart jolts so fast and hard that my chest hurts. "That's why I called. She said she'd be right over, and it's been two hours. I'm worried about her."

"She's not there?" I hear the stark terror rising in Mrs. Park's voice. "She never got there at all? I have to go. Eunsoo Appa!"

I'm left with a dead phone, trying not to panic. There's probably a reason Eunsoo lost touch with everyone, but I remember the pitiful flutter of MISSING posters at the train station and a knot forms in my stomach. Because I don't know what else to do, I get on group chat again.

OK, so I talked to Eunsoo's mom, but she's not home, they thought she was here. Anybody know where she might be?

Derek: OH SHIT

Jackson: I'm getting in my car. I'll drive the route between Eunsoo's house and yours. Maybe she had car trouble.

Tamsyn: This means she's . . .

Missing. None of us want to type that word, but I'm suddenly so scared I can hardly breathe. What should I do? Should I go out looking for her?

Logan: Stay put. Stay safe. Mrs. Park just called my dad. Do you want me to come over?

Me: It's okay. I'll just wait until I hear something, I guess. Do you think I should wake my great-aunt up?

Kimala: Can she actually DO anything?

I have to admit the answer is no. It feels like this is my fault; Eunsoo got pulled into the weird stuff happening to me—she was intrigued by Oliver's letters, and now . . . I don't let myself complete the thought. Meatloaf and bile gurgle into my throat. If I don't calm down, I'll be in the bathroom. Stress gives me a stomachache.

I pace the floor for a while before grabbing my phone again. Anything? I ask in chat.

Jackson answers, Not yet. I've driven the route twice, and I can't even find her car. Seems like the county's in on the action now.

Logan confirms, My dad went out. They're mounting a search.

Tamsyn sends, Sorry. I . . . can't do this. I'm not leaving chat, but I'm shutting my phone down for the night.

Nobody's judging her. This must feel so much like the night her brother, Ronell, went missing. The group is silent for a while, then Kimala says, I've hit up everyone I know that's in drama club. No word from Eunsoo.

I let out a deep breath, conscious that my hands are shaking. That deep unsteadiness goes all the way down to my knees, and it's hard for me to carry my wobbly self up the stairs to my room. I want to be out there searching, I *do*, but I'm aware that I don't know the area well and I'd probably just cause trouble and maybe get myself lost.

It's past midnight by the time I settle on my bed, and the rustle of paper in my pocket reminds me I have a letter to read. Part of me doesn't even want to now. Yet curiosity nibbles away at me, married to desperation for something better than this drowning guilt.

Yeah, I want to see what Oliver has to say. These secret glimpses into the past fascinate me. Even if he's terrified of what he's about to face, it's an escape from the bleak reality of what's happening here and now.

By the glimmer of lamplight, I yield and try to take comfort in Oliver's words.

Dear Araceli,

I don't understand what's happening, if you're a sprite, an angel, or a ghost, but your words make me feel less alone. It troubles me to confess I don't rightly understand everything you say. I didn't get that much schooling, left in the eighth grade, otherwise Lester and me would've starved. He's the only family I got. Our folks died of influenza when I was about ten. It near took Lester too. I think that scares me most of all, the prospect of being alone.

Came to camp with other fellows from the city, but we're all too tired to get close, and I guess I'm not the only one thinking about how hard it'll be over there when one of my pals gets blown up. That's my reason for keeping to myself, but you don't know how I envy the men who get care packages and cards from home. So far, I haven't got nothing, except what I hear from you. It'll be worse when I'm over there. Already, I'm hearing stories, but I won't soil your eyes with grisly tales.

Anyway, before, you told me about yourself and you sound pretty as a picture. Smart too, to the point that I don't know why you're writing me, as I'm not very interesting and I can't figure out what to say to make a good impression. I'm pretty tall, I guess, skinny as a stick. My hair is dark brown and I have brown eyes. I got a scar on my elbow from rolling into a fireplace when I was little. Burns just don't go away.

It's odd, what you said about your dream, because it does sound like when I first got to town. You think we're connected? I kind of like the sound of you dreaming about me. You'll let me think so, even if it's not true, I hope.

I spent so much money buying this paper to write to you. Don't know when I'll be able to get more, so pardon me if my writing gets crabbed up. That's just me being thrifty. Have to sign off now. Hope to hear from you soon.

Oliver

21

I cry myself to sleep that night, for Oliver and Eunsoo, Tamsyn's brother, and even my great-uncle Archibald.

First thing, I check group chat to see if anyone has heard about—or from—Eunsoo. The last message is from Logan: My dad came home past three, and it seems like they'll be searching again, come daylight. Try not to worry too much. They'll find her.

In this town, it's hard to keep hope alive, but I'm trying. Before I get ready for school, I make a flyer, using the selfies Eunsoo sent me just before she vanished. I'll print these in the IT room and ask if I can hang one on the bulletin board at school. After school, I'll go around downtown and put them up wherever they let me. My chest hurts just thinking about this, and it's hard to breathe.

I leave a note for Ottilie about what happened with Eunsoo and ask her to check in with Logan's dad. He seems more likely to answer an adult.

Breakfast is a banana and yogurt because I don't feel like cooking, not even toast. Way early, I head out in search of the rest of the group.

I find Tamsyn near her locker. Like me, she looks like shit, deep shadows beneath her eyes. This morning, we're both sad, down to the bone. We're not in a place yet where I can hug her automatically, but I'd like to. I settle for asking, "Do you want a hug?"

"Please," she says softly.

We lean into each other, and my eyes burn with the threat of scalding tears. I don't have to ask to know she's scared for Eunsoo, and this must have brought all the terrible grief and uncertainty back. At this moment, she's probably reliving her brother's disappearance. That was heartbreaking to hear about, but now? With Eunsoo MIA, it's something I have to resolve. Ma and Papi would understand why I'll follow this road to the end, no matter where it leads.

"Do you have time to talk?" I ask.

"Sure." Tamsyn doesn't look too enthusiastic, but she follows me.

I draw her out of the gathering hall traffic. The bathroom is the natural place for a private chat, but I check all the stalls first.

She watches me with a wary expression. "You're freaking me out. Are we about to do something clandestine?"

I shake my head. "Just being careful. Before, you mentioned your little brother went missing. Can you tell me more about what happened? It's not idle curiosity. I want to find out what happened, both for Ronell and Eunsoo."

A flicker of loss makes her face drop, and she says, "This has been hell for my family. We rented a house here in good faith, not realizing what this town is like, and now we can't even leave, because . . ." Though she doesn't finish, I know what she isn't saying.

It's the same reason my great-aunt hasn't sold her house and moved on. They're all waiting for their loved ones to come home. Closure would let them accept the loss, but there are no answers coming.

Just fear and silence.

"My great-uncle disappeared years ago, and my auntie still

isn't over it," I tell her. "If I can, I want to help her. And the Park family. And you."

She gives me a "yeah, right" look. "How're you gonna do that when the sheriff doesn't give a shit? They ran search parties for like a day and then closed the case."

With a twist of my mouth, I acknowledge how common that indifference from law enforcement is, especially when cases involve people of color. "I don't know yet, but my parents do this stuff all the time, so maybe I can too."

"That could be dangerous," Tamsyn says.

I know that, but we can't trust the sheriff, and the deputies belong to him, too. "Guess I'm more like my mother and father than I realized. They've lived their whole lives going after people who had bad shit to hide. Dragged down a couple of corrupt regimes with their coverage too. I never wanted to make a job of it myself, but I can't do nothing when I'm slapped with something this dirty."

She's undecided, I can tell from her body language. Understandable since she hardly knows me. I probably wouldn't tell me a lot of personal stuff either. As I'm about to say, *It's cool if you don't want to,* she nods firmly.

"We don't have time for me to go into details right now. Let's meet at Pizza Inn after school. We'll talk more then."

I agree to the meet, and then hustle to the IT room, where I print two copies of the flyer I made. One is going up here, if I'm allowed; the other one, I'll use to make copies at the library. That handled, I bolt to class and barely make it before the bell.

What a long, terrible day this will be.

. . .

Pizza Inn is everything I never wanted in a restaurant. It smells deeply of garlic and stale Parmesan cheese and is decorated to look like a monastic retreat. By which I mean, the walls are half plaster and half faux-brick with recessed niches that hold melted candles. There are four booths on either side with ten smaller tables in the middle and an order counter where you tell an angry-looking middle-aged man what you want to eat or drink.

I get a Coke and a personal pepperoni pizza since they don't sell by the slice. "Number ten," he says, handing me a flag. "I'll call you when it's ready."

I guess they stay in business by being the only game in town. The place is half-full right now, though it's an odd hour, partly high schoolers like me and the rest are older men nursing pitchers of beer. Maybe it's cheaper than the tavern up the road?

Tamsyn joins me five minutes later, right after my food is done. She's out of breath, dumping her stuff on the torn vinyl booth. "Sorry, a teacher caught me and wanted to talk about an essay I wrote."

"Mr. Timmons?" I guess.

"How'd you know?"

"He seems like the type."

"You're not wrong." She takes off her jacket and drapes it over her backpack. "Okay, so what do you want to know?"

"First, you want some of this?" I nudge the pizza toward her.

"Sure, thanks. I didn't get lunch today. I was working on something."

I did notice she wasn't at the table. No great loss, everyone was silent and morose, unable to look away from the seat Eunsoo normally occupies. "No problem. Anyway, I'm not even sure what to ask. I'm trying to remember what you told me before . . ."

"We honestly don't know much," she says. "But I'll go over it again. Ronell was last seen leaving his friend's house around four p.m. on a Wednesday, six months ago. I had told him repeatedly not to use the shortcut through the woods, but it takes a lot longer if you stick to the streets. That day, an old lady said she saw Ronell head through Elliot's backyard and into the forest. That was the last time anybody ever saw him. We scoured that shortcut path, the area around it. Never even found a trace, not a shoe or a scrap of the shirt he had on. He was carrying his backpack, and we didn't find that either. It's like those trees swallowed him whole."

She bites her lower lip and takes off her glasses to press a napkin to her eyes. I feel bad doing this to her in a place like Pizza Inn, but I doubt my great-aunt would approve of the questions I'm about to ask.

"This may sound weird, but I promise I'm not playing around or making light. Bear with me through some strange questions, okay?"

"Go for it," she says. "I'm braced."

"Do you ever feel like he's close by, but you just can't see him? Has anything odd ever happened at your house?"

Her eyes widen. "Are you seriously asking me if he's a ghost? What the hell is *wrong* with you?"

"Don't get mad. I'm only asking because I swear there's something going on at my great-aunt's house." To earn her trust, I need to put my cards on the table. Before she can leave—and I can see she wants to—I tell her about the disappearing food, the light cord being tugged, and the sensation of being watched.

Her initial anger seems to settle as she listens. "You're for real with all this?"

"Would I tell you otherwise? If you repeat this story, everyone will dish about how my poor tía needs mental help."

"That's true."

The pizza is gone, and my drink is watered down with melted

ice. I stir the light brown liquid with a straw, then say, "If you haven't noticed anything at home, then never mind. But I swear I'm not making any of this up."

Tamsyn hesitates for a long time before saying, "To be honest, my mom has said stuff. She's home the most. After Ronell disappeared, she quit work to focus on the search. We all thought it was grief . . . and stress. But now, you got me wondering."

"So she's noticed something?"

"I think so. She says she feels him at times, like he's right there in the room. And she also claims that food goes missing when nobody admits to eating it."

"Wow," I breathe.

I wonder if other families are experiencing this too. They say two isn't enough to compile data from, but if I find another case like this, it becomes a pattern, right? It's too soon to ask the Parks about this, but there may be other families I could contact, people who have been missing longer. Plus, I'm not ready to give up on the possibility that we'll find Eunsoo.

"Does this help in some way?"

"I'm not sure yet, but it might. I'm still gathering info."

Tamsyn pushes her red glasses up on her nose and shoulders her backpack in a smooth motion. "Let me know if you find anything out. I need to go now. Have to check on my mom. Thanks for the pizza."

We leave together since I paid at the counter when I ordered. This has given me a lot to think about as I run my finding-Eunsoo related errands. I did get the flyer on the bulletin board at school, and about half the businesses let me post one somewhere on the premises. I try to keep hope alive—that any minute somebody will call me and say they've seen her.

But Monday rolls into Tuesday to Wednesday, and our group chat is dead quiet. Until Logan says, I have news. We all chorus, What?! pretty much at the same time, but my stomach is churning hard.

Logan: They found the car Eunsoo was driving, abandoned on the other side of the forest.

Derek: Shit, out by the race track?

Kimala: What else??

Jackson: That is NOWHERE near your house, A.

Tamsyn tapped out of this chat when Eunsoo first went missing, so I don't expect her to reply. Since I'm new to the area, I don't know if what Jackson said is true until I pull up a map. Damn, that's practically in the opposite direction. I have so many questions right now. Did Eunsoo really head that way or did someone move her car after they took her to throw suspicion off someone who lives close by?

So far, nobody has called about the flyers I put up. Her family must be terrified. I can see the future, based on what's happened to Tamsyn's family, and I feel like crying. Somehow I get through Thursday, but a pall still hangs over our table. Nobody can smile, and we all pick at our food without appetite.

On Friday when I get to school, I find a crowd clustered around the notice board. Kimala is there along with co-captain Lana, congratulating people who made the team. Right, results were being posted today. Though I've lost some enthusiasm because of my worry over Eunsoo, I wriggle past the crowd and find my name as the last on the list, just above the two alternates. Guess I didn't blow anyone away, but I did well enough to make the cut.

"Congrats!" Lana calls, grabbing me. Great, she's a hugger. She does some jumping too, pulling me along with her, and with my eyes, I plead to Kimala for help. No mercy. I suffer the full onslaught of Lana's jubilation.

"You were so great," she gushes. "I'm so excited you're bringing some Latin heat to the team."

Uh, what? No.

"I heard that your dad's Mexican," she chatters on.

I need to stop this girl before she says something dim-witted and terrible. "When is practice?" I cut in.

I'm defensive of my family in Monterrey—and constantly on guard—but that's because other people have been offensive. I heard stuff I didn't entirely understand when I was little and visiting my mom's family in Kentucky. Now I get the subtext, and it sucks that I need to deflect, but I'm choosing not to call her out before I start on the squad. She might be the fragile, vindictive type who will make my life untenable if I confront her.

Hell, sometimes people even get mad when I subtly quell their bullshit, but Lana doesn't seem to mind, or maybe she didn't realize I shut her down on purpose. Either way, points for not insisting on saying whatever, against my objections.

"Monday, Wednesday, and Thursday. We perform on Friday nights, so you'll need to wear your uniform to school on all game days. We'll talk more about everything on Monday, okay?"

Kimala links her arm with mine, leading me away. Once we're out of range, she says, "I find it's best not to listen when she talks."

"I'm getting that impression."

"Congratulations, and thanks for coming on board. I could use a break from all the Brittany bullshit. You know there are four of them on the team?"

"How does that work? Do you call them by their middle names too?"

"Nah, it's Brittany B., Britney D., Brittney L., and Brittni Y."

"I think I'll be asking myself that a lot," I say, grinning.

She busts out laughing, the first belly laugh I've ever heard from Kimala. Then she immediately looks guilty that we could've forgotten about Eunsoo, even for a second. That's how those left behind live, tentatively and with tiny increments of joy, stolen like small trinkets.

22

Friday night and the neighbors are having a cookout. They're also blasting an old song about it being Saturday night and how the singer ain't got nobody.

To be honest, I can relate.

I send messages to my parents, who have been good about dropping emojis in chat every now and then to let me know they're alive. Ma doesn't know how they work, though, so I get weird random stuff like a shooting star or a bunch of cherries. Sometimes I put them together to form bizarre sentences, like "cactus poops on dinosaur."

It's my turn to write to Oliver. I'd rather do that than read the messages waiting for me in group chat. Tamsyn is having a breakdown, and she thinks we'll never see Eunsoo again. My stomach aches just thinking about it, and I can't find the right words.

I wonder if small objects transfer or only paper? That limitation would make no sense, but none of this adds up logically. My jewelry box is small; I don't have a lot of necklaces, but I pull out one of my favorites, a green agate pendant strung on a leather cord. My dad said it was a protective amulet when he gave it to me, and I don't think a guy would be embarrassed to wear it. Before I can overthink it, I drop the necklace at the bottom of the treasure box.

We'll see if it's still there tomorrow. In the meantime, I write something to go with it.

Dear Oliver,

I shouldn't burden you with my problems, but I can't think of anything else right now. One of my friends is missing, and she was on her way to see me when she disappeared. That makes it my fault, right? It was so late, I should have told her not to come. Now her family is heartbroken, and I'm so scared.

It's so awful for me to complain to you when you're all alone and frightened too, but everyone else knew Eunsoo better than I did. Or maybe that's not true. She and I knew each other long distance, kind of like you and me. We'd been talking that way for years, even if we only just met in person. I'm not sure what I want to accomplish by writing this down, maybe just a hopeful response. Nobody else can give me that.

Let me get myself together and think about what you said in your last letter. I'm not a sprite or a ghost, definitely no angel. I'm so sorry to hear about your parents. Mine are safe for the moment, even if they're in another country doing dangerous work without me. You must have been terrified on your own, looking out for Lester. When you say you left school in eighth grade, I guess you mean that you got a job? What did you do? Where did you sleep? Sorry for asking so many questions. I'm just trying to put myself in your situation. I'm also sorry to hear about the burn scar. Those are so painful. I once steamed all the skin off my fingers. I won't bore you with the details of how, but I can sympathize on how much it hurts.

You sound handsome, actually, and if you look anything

like the boy I dreamed about, you must have a beautiful smile too. If you ever run out of paper and you can't get more, I can send you some, though it won't be like what you're used to. If you need anything small that I can send, I'll enclose it along with my letter. I'm sending something my father gave me for protection. I hope it keeps you safe as well.

It helps me a lot knowing I can write to you when things get unbearable here. So I hope I can give you that same comfort. I'll be waiting for your next word.

Yours,
Araceli

Around three a.m., I wake with a strange feeling. Out of habit, I check the heartwood box, and I'm astonished to find the necklace and note gone with a reply already waiting, the fastest the magical mail has ever come. I unfold the note, my heart skipping a bit. It feels so much better to focus on Oliver than to deal with what's happening at present in the real world. Eunsoo wouldn't want me to leave him hanging, right?

Dear Araceli,

Please forgive my poor penmanship, as I'm writing this from belowdecks on the USS Mallory. We shipped out early this morning. I hear it will take weeks for us to get there.

I'm not looking forward to that. I could complain more, but I'll just take it as you can well imagine it's bad. I thought things were tough when me and Lester were camped out in the basement of a condemned building and I couldn't find work. Let me tell you, this is worse. You asked what I did after leaving school. Mostly just labor, loading and unloading carts, sometimes I'd haul stuff on the docks or carry messages. Won't lie to you, I thieved some when times were bad. In good times, Lester and me would rent a room in a boardinghouse, but most times, we'd camp out in abandoned buildings and run the streets looking for any opportunities to earn a penny. I was scared, but when you're cold and hungry, that's the most pressing thing. I can't even describe how it feels to starve, and I'm back in the belly of the beast again.

I got your present. The guys all gave me guff and asked where I got such a fancy thing. To be honest, I had no idea what to say, so some stupid joe said I stole it, and I didn't even argue, just put it under my shirt, and right now, I'm holding onto that green stone and thinking about you.

Everything feels like a dream now, like my real life never happened. I'm surrounded by strangers and writing to you in the middle of a dark sea. I can't believe you'll find a way to answer me here. None of this makes any sense, so this seems pointless, but I think maybe if I don't set these words down, then I'll end up like my bunkmate, who's crying in his sleep.

They're about to whip him for being a pansy and a mama's boy, and I don't want none of that. It's all I can do not to attract bad attention. I told Lester I'll be fine, and I'm trying my best to keep that promise, but the closer I get to the front, the more I can't breathe. I hear we'll be some days in Liverpool, take some training in the countryside, and then they're sending us straight to France, probably somewhere I couldn't find without help on a map.

Why is somebody like me going to war? I don't even understand what it's all about, really, except that the Germans are our enemy now. They're marching for the Fatherland and to make everybody eat sausage and kraut? I got no idea, I never had a spare nickel to get the paper and find out more.

Oh, I almost forgot to say this. Your missing friend, that's not your fault, dear Araceli. She wanted to see you, and if some bad person stopped her from getting there, it's on them, not you. I know well enough that it's hard not blame yourself when something bad happens. Since I'm all Lester's got, I sure did take on the fault every time he stepped off a curb wrong. If he'd vanished on my watch, I think I'd have lost my mind.

That's why I'm worried about him. Lucy said she'd look after him some, but he's a lot to take on. Maybe you could see how they're doing for me? I'm waiting to hear from you. Even if it's impossible, even if it makes no damn sense. Don't let me down.

Yours,
Oliver

Oh my God. He signed off as "yours," just like I did. I'm ecstatic he likes my present, baffled as to how any of this is possible. But I *want* to believe in magic now. With Eunsoo missing, I have to believe that beautiful, inexplicable things are possible, because that leaves the door open to the idea that she can come home again. I refuse to consign her to the realm of the permanently lost, souls whose flyers will fade in the seasons and their frozen smiles will never change.

I'm too sleepy to write back this instant, so I snuggle beneath the covers still clutching his letter and close my eyes. This time, a dream catches me like a dark river, and I feel the rocking of the waves—

Wait, that's not right.

I open my eyes in the crowded hold of a boat. The bunks are narrow and there's little room between them. It reeks down here, piss and feet, salt and sweat. A range of noises assails me, as men crammed into tight quarters like this could never be quiet. Someone is snoring, somebody else is snuffling in his sleep, and from a distant bunk comes a slick skin-on-skin sound that I identify as a soldier jerking off, trying to be stealthy about it.

I guess that's one way to get your mind off your misery.

This is the strangest dream I've ever had, doubtless influenced by Oliver's letter, but it's just so damn real—from the rocking of ship down to the sights, sounds, and smells. I drift between the bunks silently; it doesn't matter because I'm not really here, but I'm absolutely looking for the boy I saw at the train station.

Unexpectedly, I find him, sitting up in his bunk. He's exhausted and unshaven, wearing only military-issue boxers and a despondent look. I move closer and sit next to him, wishing I could speak some words of comfort. I like everything about his face, especially the thick, unruly brows and the dark stubble, the sharp curve of his jaw and the strong nose that gives him an interesting look.

I'm the invisible dreamer, doomed to watch but not interact, so I'm dead shocked when he reacts when I touch his shoulder. He twists, knocking his head on the wall, and then he stills. Just like on the platform, it's as if he sees me.

He swallows hard, so scared he can barely get the words out. "Are you a ghost?"

"I'm asleep right now," I answer, so soft that nobody outside our little space could hear, even if the other recruits weren't being noisy pigs. "Asleep and dreaming you."

"That's downright strange, miss. Why would you dream of this? Or me?"

Since none of it is real, I might as well indulge myself. Smiling, I touch his cheek gently and his breath catches. "You know why, Oliver. Isn't it obvious?"

That's who he is, after all. I've dreamed him just as I want him to be, the perfect product of an overactive imagination.

"You're her," he breathes. "Araceli."

Of course he recognizes me. How could he not? This is my fantasy, and I'm starting to enjoy the incredibly vivid nature of it. He's even got the burn scar above his left elbow, puckered and purple. I skate my fingers across the damaged skin, and he gasps, probably at my boldness. He's a product of the early twentieth century and I'm definitely a twenty-first-century girl.

"This is impossible. Unless you're a witch." He says that with complete seriousness, like he's been hexed before.

"Is that what I am? I'd be a bruja, actually."

"What does that mean?"

"It's Spanish for witch. A good witch is a curandera, kind of a healer."

"Then you must be a curandera. Nobody as pretty as you could be wicked." Ever so slowly, he reaches toward me, but before he makes contact, the dream shakes apart and I'm staring up into my great-aunt's worried face.

I don't understand why she's crying or why she's hugging me so tight. "Thank God," she finally says.

My head feels weird and thick. It must be the middle of the night, so what's the deal? It doesn't feel like I've slept more than an hour, if that. Slowly I notice the sunlight streaming in the window, and register it's not night.

"What's wrong?" My voice is rough and raspy.

"You have the nerve to ask me that? You've been asleep since Friday night, and I couldn't wake you."

"Friday . . . night?" Something about that seems wrong, or—"You mean last night?"

"No, I do not. It's Sunday afternoon, sweetheart. I had a retired doctor look you over yesterday, but he said you were just exhausted. Even so, if I couldn't rouse you today, I was about to call nine-one-one and your parents."

"I'm okay," I say. "Don't call them. I was just tired. I'm not sick or anything."

Yeah, I say that calmly, but my head is a mess. I lost an entire day. Somehow. While I was sleeping.

Before, I thought I was dreaming. Now, I'm not so sure. As ridiculous as I feel for even thinking it, I entertain the possibility that I might really be going somewhere in my sleep, and judging by how bad my body feels, there's an energy cost for the trip.

I'm scared to find out what price I'd pay to see Oliver again.

23

"You look tired," Logan says as I sit down in first period.

Since I don't feel much better than I did yesterday, it's a valid observation. I manage a smile, opening the book we're reading on my phone. I need to skim the last chapter Mr. Timmons assigned or he'll call on me first thing. He seems like a teacher who has that deadly sixth sense—let's see, who came to class unprepared . . . Araceli!

Fortunately, I've read *Dracula* before; I just need a refresher. I'm nearly done when I realize Logan is still staring at me, waiting for a response.

"What can I say? It was a wild weekend."

Logan nods and takes his seat while the rest of the class trickles in. Mr. Timmons strides in right before the bell, brisk and ready to discuss literary themes with gusto. As I expected, he does demand my input toward the end of class, and I'm able to give a sensible answer, thanks to my quick review.

I can't face the usual lunch table without Eunsoo. Waiting for the phone to ring sucks, but I don't know what to do for her, other than the flyers. I've taken to calling her cell and listening to it ring. I also send messages she's not reading, wherever she is.

Oliver asked me to find out about Lucy and Lester. I have no idea how I'm supposed to do that without a last name. Regardless, I head for the school library. This is the first time

I've set foot in there since my enrollment, and it's smaller than I hoped. I probably won't find much here—and I'm not even sure what I'm looking for—but I can't ignore what happened this weekend. Part of me is already sure that Oliver is/was real, and the dreams aren't amazingly vivid facsimiles of what his life must have been like.

But I need some proof. Well, more proof. I'm assembling it, step by step, with the lack of video from someone sneaking into my room and the photo I dreamed before I saw it in the Mayweather book. There has to be more.

What details has he given me? I should have brought the letters, but I left the house in a mad scramble this morning. Yesterday, I was only awake long enough to eat and reassure my great-aunt that I don't have some strange sleeping sickness, then I passed out again, as if I hadn't already slept long enough to last me a week.

The librarian already has two students at her desk, so I wander the stacks myself until I find a small section devoted to World War I. I still have the Mayweather book at home for perusal, but I didn't bring it with me. Though I don't find anything so locally focused, I do come across a book about the troopships that carried the soldiers to Europe, starting in April of 1917. I page through it without much hope, but one name on a list jumps out at me, and I stare in wonder:

USS *Henry R. Mallory*, April 1917–18.

I'm 90 percent sure that's what Oliver wrote; it's the ship he was on. It might also be the ship I visited in my dream. The book doesn't have any photos that will help me, so I search on my phone, looking for confirmation. I find a picture of the ship circa 1919, but since I was only in the berths belowdecks, that doesn't help me at all, and I can't find any pictures online to show me what the inside of the ship looks like. That makes sense since taking a photo was a big deal back then, and it required a lot of equipment that took a long time to set up.

With a sigh, I close the book. This counts as corroborating evidence, and it proves I'm not losing my mind. I get up to put the book on the cart to be shelved—the sign firmly states that students shouldn't do it themselves—when I nearly bump into Mr. Timmons. His brows shoot up at encountering me in the library during lunch, which probably doesn't bode well for my social status if other kids learn about it.

"Are you taking history this term?" he asks.

I shake my head. "This is personal research."

He brightens visibly, the first real smile I've seen from his dour personality, and then he plucks the book about army transport ships from my hands. "This is pretty dry fare. Are you interested in World War I?"

"More than you might imagine," I say.

"That's uncommon. Usually, students are more intrigued by the Second World War."

I try to invent a normal reason for my fascination. "I can understand, I guess, but don't they say World War I was the first modern war? The weapons that were new at the time, they changed everything, right?" That's a stretch, dug out of the deepest recesses of my memory.

But he's a fish chewing on my bait. "Definitely. The armored tanks, air strikes, submarine warfare, mustard gas . . . there had never been such potential for devastation before. Are you thinking of studying history in college?"

"Maybe," I lie. "Right now, I'm just trying to learn more on my own."

"That's so commendable. I'm glad you haven't succumbed to . . . what do the kids call it—senioritis? So many students are afflicted with ennui their last year, and they don't do more than the bare minimum to graduate."

"I'll keep working hard," I say, because Mr. Timmons doesn't seem to realize the conversation is over.

As it turns out, I'm right, and he talks my ear off about World War I until the lunch bell rings, indicating our break is over. At least this wasn't a total waste of my time. I confirmed the name of the ship Oliver traveled to Europe on, and I earned points with Mr. Timmons.

I doze through my afternoon classes and recall as I leave the last one that I have dance team practice tonight. There's no way Kimala will forgive me if I dodge on the first day, no matter how tired I am, so I shuffle to the gym, wishing I'd remembered to pack my practice clothes. Since I'm wearing yoga pants and a T-shirt already, this will have to do. Today my outfit screams *I woke up late and I don't care.*

The rest of the squad is already there, warming up. I slip into their ranks at the back and do stretches I'll appreciate later. Lana is cheerful and excited while she briefs us on the first routine we'll be learning. I want to be excited about this, but the miasma from that spirit-sapping dream still has me in its clutches, and I ache whenever I think of Eunsoo. Even if Oliver absolved me, I carry the blame for her absence in my bones.

The song Lana favors has half of us rolling our eyes, one of those painful pop songs that becomes an immediate earworm the minute you hear it. I'll have to cleanse my musical palate with something better when I get home. My entire body feels heavy and sluggish, so it takes a bit to get into the swing of things. I'm out of step, learning the moves with a lack of aptitude I'd find embarrassing if my ass wasn't dragging. By the end of practice, though, I feel more alert than I have since before I fell asleep on Friday.

Hmm, seems like exercise helps. Good to know.

"Good job, everyone!" Now that Lana is finally done talking, Kimala offers concise positive reinforcement. She jogs over to me as I grab my bag. "You okay? I noticed you seem kind of out of it today."

That's a polite way of saying my dancing was for shit. I'm aware. "I'll be fine. Thanks for worrying though."

"I voted you in. Don't make me look bad."

"Wow, really? Did you cast the deciding ballot?"

"Maybe," she says, smiling.

I sling my backpack over my shoulder. "Well, I appreciate it. I'll be sharp next time, I promise." Provided my soul doesn't go sailing off to the Western Front.

24

This is a grisly task, and I can't believe I'm doing it, but I have no choice.

With grim resolve, I note the names and dates of those who have gone missing. Most of the flyers posted also include a phone number. If I'm lucky, that will let me get in touch with the families, so I can ask about their experiences.

Ten people in the last ten months. That's a lot. Eleven when you add Eunsoo. And she's the whole reason I have the courage to channel my mom's methods and tackle this task. Otherwise, I could never work up the nerve to contact people who are already suffering. If there's any chance of unearthing a common link that will lead me to Eunsoo, I have to try.

Whatever's happening here, it seems to be escalating and I can't give up on her.

It's hard not to let my mind run away with me. The scientists in their hazmat suits, talking about containment failure. Maybe the lab bred some kind of monster that got loose and is living in the swamp, eating people?

Yeah, I sound like I should be posting on a special interest forum, raving about crop circles and exsanguinated livestock.

I've just finished taking pictures of all the MISSING posters, and I turn to find the sheriff, Logan's dad, propped against his squad car, silently watching me. He's wearing mirror shades that hide his eyes, and he has the severe haircut of a man who has no tolerance, not even for his own hair.

"What do you think you're doing, miss?" His tone gives me the chills, and I haven't even done anything wrong.

It takes all my nerve to stroll toward him, like he's not radiating intimidation. "Taking pictures of the missing posters." That must have been obvious, so there's no point lying about it.

He escalates from disapproval to open hostility, jerking his sunglasses off to reveal icy, bloodshot eyes. "That's a sick hobby. You should be ashamed."

Excuse me?

"I don't understand," I say. "I just wanted to have the pictures on my phone in case I see someone who looks similar. I can verify right away, rather than rely on my memory, then call the family if there's a match. Isn't that the best way to help?" Honestly, I'm proud of this explanation; it sounds plausible and civic-minded. "My friend, Eunsoo, disappeared recently, and I want to do my part."

His mouth tightens. "I know law officers who do that with wanted posters. Aren't you new in town?"

"I've been here a few weeks," I answer, wondering if this will turn into an interrogation.

Did my picture-taking put me at the forefront of the "investigation" as a person of interest? From what Tamsyn said, Sheriff Reed isn't really looking for the people who've gone missing. Maybe that means he knows something about the secret lab.

Poor Logan. Now I understand the tree house and why he built it alone. This also explains why he hasn't told anyone about his bruises. Are you supposed to call the cops when it's a cop inflicting the damage? I've also seen on the news how clannish law enforcement can be, how they close ranks to hide any implication of wrongdoing.

He eyes my phone as if he wants to confiscate it. "You're staying with Ottilie Groening, aren't you?"

"She's my great-aunt." I feel like I need to extricate myself from this interchange before the questions get intrusive. "Speaking of which, I should get home. She'll wonder where I am. It was nice meeting you."

Manners, manners, manners—Ma would be proud I didn't kick him in the shins. Seriously, I don't like *anything* about that man. Feeling his gaze burn into my back as I rush away gives me the creeps.

Every step I take, I half expect him to snatch me back. It wouldn't surprise me if he's the one yanking people off the streets. Unable to help myself as I turn the corner, I break into a run and don't stop until the door closes behind me.

"Are you home?" Tía calls from the kitchen.

Today's snack is orange wedges and graham crackers. I swear to God, I'm starting to like pretending I'm five, because when I was five, I didn't realize my parents had dangerous jobs or that there was major injustice in the world.

I also didn't have any problems that couldn't be cured with a nap.

"Yep, back from dance team practice."

"Any word about Eunsoo?" she asks.

I shake my head. There's nothing I can add, and she must read my sadness because she changes the subject briskly. "Kimala sounds nice. You should invite her over for dinner. I'm glad you're making friends."

I'm not sure if Kimala would want to come over, but . . . "I might ask her."

"And what about that nice Reed boy? I think he likes you."

Oh Lord.

"I'm not interested in dating right now. I need to focus on school and plan for my future." Surely she'll approve of that.

"Understood, dear. But you know what they say about all work and no play. There's no harm in eating pizza or going to a school dance."

"Fair," I say.

I can't believe my great-aunt just politely told me to lighten up. She has no idea of the pressure I'm under, though. Eunsoo is lost, waiting for someone to find her—to figure out this town's terrible secret and bring her home. I don't know if I'm that person, but I'll do my best. Oliver is also waiting to hear from me, adrift on a dark ocean alone. This is a lot of damn pressure for someone who also needs to prep for college and take the SAT.

"I'm just saying, if he asks you out, don't be afraid to accept. I can personally attest to the fact that he's a good boy. How many boys would learn knitting to keep an old lady company? Or mow the lawn for free?"

"What about his dad?"

I've learned her expressions well enough to register the flicker of disapproval. "He's a strict man. No nonsense about him."

"You don't like him," I guess.

"Let's not gossip about the neighbors. Go do something productive," she huffs.

"Fine, I'm going."

Good to know my aunt isn't on board with Sheriff Reed's bullshit. He reeks of offenses like abuse of power and venal corruption. I'm sure he knows something, that asshole.

Focus, I tell myself.

Homework first. SAT stuff. Driving manual PDF. It seems dumb to memorize rules of the road when I've never even sat behind the wheel of a car. For a couple of hours, I play the good student while fighting the urge to write to Oliver. My mom would be glad I'm no longer attached to my phone, I guess, but now I'm addicted to a wooden box. That . . . is probably not better. I don't mean to open it—I'm not even expecting a letter since I still need to reply—but to my delight, there's another note waiting.

The hand is even shakier than before, not solely because of the ship's movement, I think. He doesn't even use a salutation this time; that's how rattled he was when he wrote this.

> *This can't be. I'm losing it. You were here. I saw you. Almost touched you. Are you an angel or am I a lunatic?*
> > *Yours in madness,*
> > *Oliver*

Yeah, this reply can't wait. Like Oliver, I omit the greeting and get right to the point.

> *Neither. The truth is neither. I don't understand how this is happening, and I'm afraid to tell you the truth. For one thing, I'm afraid you won't believe me. I'm also scared of causing major damage on an unimaginable scale.*

I pause, weighing whether I should elaborate. No, if he finds out I'm writing to him from the future, who knows what impact it will have? I don't want to be the reason the Germans win the First World War. Maybe I'm exaggerating the impact my interference could have on the timeline, but I know about the butterfly effect. I need to be careful.

I continue with:

> *That's all I can tell you right now. When I'm more positive about what's going on, I'll say more.*

I'm not a spy. I'm not an angel.

But I do believe we are deeply connected, even if I can't explain how or why. I'm still here for you, still waiting eagerly to hear how you're doing. Is the crossing rough?

I shouldn't write this. I have no right to. But I miss you.

I'm glad I got to see you. And maybe you can't believe this either, but I'm with you. Not just in the amulet, but through our treasure box too.

Yours at heart,
Araceli

25

I've left a lot of people behind.

You'd think we'd keep in touch online, right? It starts off that way; we mean to. But contact dwindles. People pay attention to what's right in front of them, and even if I mesh well with somebody, they don't do much more than like my pics on social media or click the heart button on something I posted. In time, they stop doing that.

Usually, though, I don't lose touch until I leave. But it feels like I've already started separating from the people I met here because we've all been avoiding each other since news hit about Eunsoo. Part of me fears they blame me too, even if nobody's saying that. Jackson looks so damn sad and thin that I'm starting to suspect he has a thing for Eunsoo. She didn't mention it; maybe she didn't know.

"Did Eunsoo ever mention what her parents do at the lab?" I say into the silence.

Derek shakes his head. Kimala offers a shrug, then answers, "I think she said they signed an NDA. She rarely talked about her folks, but I do know they're physicists."

Tamsyn is silent, like she always is, and I suspect she doesn't have any hope or suggestions to offer. Not after waiting six months for Ronell.

"I was thinking . . ." I start, but I'm not sure how plausible my idea will sound to people who haven't been at the center of the strange vortex with me.

"The lab might have something to do with the disappearances," Logan says into the silence.

How does he know that? I think back to the conversation he overheard between Tía and me. Did he make a guess based on the questions I asked and/or something he's seen in the woods? He's out there a lot, so it's not improbable he's seen scientists, just like I did.

Tamsyn stares between Logan and me, eyes wide. "Is that true?"

"It's only a theory right now," I hedge. "I haven't been able to get any of the family members to agree to talk with me."

"How'd you track them down?" Derek asks.

"I'm calling the numbers on the missing posters," I answer.

Jackson shakes his head with a sigh. "No wonder they don't want to talk to you, dumbass. You get their hopes up with a call, but it's not somebody who can find their missing son or whatever. It's just some girl who wants to poke at their problems."

When you put it that way, yeah, I won't be able to get answers this way.

"Shit," I say. "What should I do, then?"

It's a general inquiry because I'm lost here. My parents might be able to give me some insights because this is what they do, but they'd also vastly disapprove of me doing the same thing, especially under these circumstances. Asking the wrong questions in our weekly video chat might prompt them to get on a plane and drag me off to Venezuela.

And I'd never find out how this story ends.

Ottilie would probably let me take the treasure box with me, but I can imagine how heartbroken I'd be, living to hear from Oliver, aging as he does, only we're living in a strange, connected parallel, unable to meet except briefly in dreams.

I'll end up as a legendary cat lady with twenty-seven felines who eat me after I die.

Kimala has finished her lunch in silence, ignoring my bullshit. Finally, she glances up from her salad and says, "Are you set on causing this kind of trouble?"

"Yeah, I'm afraid so. It's in my blood or something. I can't let it be."

"Then . . . I know one of the families. They go to our church. If you come to service with us, I'll introduce you, but if you hurt Mrs. Wallace—"

"I'll be careful," I promise. "I really appreciate this. I'll make it up to you somehow."

"Just stay focused during dance practice. And don't start any talk. You're new here, so you have *no* idea how hard it is to survive in this town."

Since she's one of two Black families living here, she's speaking truth, I'm sure. I nod soberly, aware of my passing privilege. I'm biracial, but racists wouldn't hassle me at first glance. That comes later, once they find out my dad is Mexican. People say the most heinous shit without a blink. I remember being seven or so, visiting my dad's family in Monterrey. His abuela was of African descent, so some of the family is darker than others. One of our cousins, a sweet man named Marco, went to hug me, then he stopped and said, "Don't be scared, okay?"

At seven, I had no idea why he said that, and later, my dad had the shitty task of explaining colorism to a little kid. When I envision the reactions that make Marco feel like he needs to reassure small children, I want to go nuclear on the world.

"Understood. Can I go to church with you this Sunday?"

Kimala nods. "We drive half an hour, so be ready early. You need to be at my house by 8:30 or you're getting left."

My parents aren't religious. My mom's agnostic and my dad is lapsed Catholic, so I was baptized and that's about it. I've never taken CCD classes or been confirmed. We go to midnight mass once a year at Christmas, and it's a somber occasion in most of the countries I've lived in, so I'm not sure what to expect.

"Dress code?" I ask.

"My mother goes all out, so you'll want to wear something nice or she'll tell me about it later."

"Let's all go to church with Kimala!" Jackson says.

"Nope." She gets up before this can become a topic of conversation and exits after she banks her lunch bag off the wall, landing it neatly in the trash can.

"Is it me or is she . . . effortlessly cool?" I ask the rest of the table.

"It's not you. We've all been trying to soak up her aura for the last three years," Tamsyn says.

"With varying degrees of success," Derek adds.

I leave shortly after Kimala, mentally making a to-do list. Logan catches up to me at a jog and throws an arm around my shoulders. "Look, I know you're worried. I'll do anything I can to help with the search for Eunsoo."

"Anything?" That's a tempting offer. And maybe there's no substitute for recon. Logan knows the woods well, right? It only makes sense to ask him for help, but that would mean telling him what I saw the day I got lost.

Nothing ventured, nothing gained. I pull his arm off my shoulders and take one of his hands in both of mine, hoping that conveys the urgency of the request. His eyes widen, and he doesn't seem to notice we're getting shitty looks from kids rushing around us, like we're rocks in a river made of people.

I tow him to the side and give him my best, most charming smile.

God, I feel awful. He smiles back, eyes locked on how our hands are touching, like this is a huge step forward, intimacy-wise. He might also be dazzled by a glimpse of my ankles, should I show them.

I shouldn't do this. I shouldn't get him involved, given what I know about his relationship with his terrible father.

"Serious question: how do you feel about doing something deeply ill-advised after school today?"

26

"You had me at ill-advised," Logan says. "I'll meet you out front when classes end."

"Sounds good." I let go of his hands, conscious that this might qualify as playing him.

I get the vibe that he's into me, and I'm emotionally involved with someone unattainable. To be honest, I have a history of this, maybe because it's safer than falling for people who might like me back. This is why I joined the 7TOG forum when I was twelve, endlessly dreaming of seven boys who would never be interested in me, even if I did meet them in person.

It's Tuesday, so I'm clear to scramble once school is over. No dance practice tonight. As promised, Logan is waiting for me on the steps. When he spots me, he unchains his bike.

"Where are we going?" he asks.

"Let's start at the fort. We'll talk, and if you're still on board, we can move from there."

"I'm intrigued already."

We can only ride his bike so far, then he wraps the chain around a slender tree near the edge of the road. From there we go on foot, and I don't say much. This isn't a conversation I want to have on the move.

Finally, we're sitting on the floor face-to-face, and I have to start somewhere. "You guessed that I think the missing persons problem is related to the lab. How did you know?"

"It wasn't that far of a stretch, based on the questions you asked Ottilie the other night."

Only if you've seen something yourself, I think.

There's no help for it; I'll just lay my cards on the table. "Okay, so here's the thing. When I brought you dinner that night, I got turned around and headed for the lab compound instead of the road. I didn't realize I'd done that until . . ." I tell him everything about the scientists I saw and repeat their words to the best of my recollection.

"You were lucky," he says softly. "If they had found you, maybe you'd be on the missing list right now."

"See, that possibility occurred to me too." Along with a lot of less plausible theories.

"Whatever they're researching, if they've spent enough money on it, I'm sure they wouldn't hesitate to eliminate people who get in the way of finishing the project."

I agree with that too.

"Have you seen anything out here?" I ask.

Logan sits quietly for a moment, head turned to stare at the greenery outside the window. It seems like he doesn't want to answer.

"Would it make a difference if I said yes?" Bitterness laces his tone. "We can't do anything about it, Araceli. If those people were abducted, they're not safe and sound in some government hotel."

I clench my jaw, anger sparking at the back of my head. "We might uncover answers. One time, my parents broke a story about student protestors who were secretly executed by the government, their bodies dumped in a mass grave. When those kids were exhumed, the people in power had to pay and the families finally found out what happened. It doesn't make up for anything, but closure is better than sitting at the window wondering if someone will come home.

"I have to do this for Eunsoo. It doesn't matter if it's dangerous. I won't be able to live without knowing I did everything possible to find her. We've been friends since I was twelve, do you get that?"

"We can't break into the facility," he says finally. "What do you think you'll learn creeping around the perimeter?"

While I don't want to argue, his attitude is pissing me off. "You said you were up for something risky!"

"Suggest something that makes sense, like shoplifting burritos from the QuikMart or shitposting with a Sharpie on the bathroom wall at Pizza Inn."

I can't stifle the smile. "Toilet humor? Really?"

"It's never a bad time for that."

"Fine. If you won't show me where the lab is, point me in the right direction. I want to scope the place out. I feel like I might get some inspiration from seeing how tight the security is."

"Sure you will," he scoffs.

"If you're not helping, get out of my way." I'm full-on angry as I get out my phone. Shit signal out here, barely enough for me to pull up a map.

This is pure bravado, as there's no way I can find Fairhaven Lab without his help. I couldn't compass myself to the nearest tree. Okay, that's an exaggeration. Trees are everywhere; I just couldn't find a specific one.

He closes his eyes, and I start to leave, but he grabs my wrist with a surprisingly firm grip. "Fine. I'll go with you, but if we get detained and executed, I expect you to entertain me for at least a hundred years in the afterlife."

"Deal. Do you like card tricks? I can also pull a coin out of your ear."

"For real?"

"Guilty. I went through a magic phase when I was like ten. Mis abuelos thought it was super-cute to have me perform at family parties. Afterward, they'd pass a bowl around . . . I'd collect a few pesos and all the marzipan I could eat."

"Maybe you won't want to hear this, but your life sounds so amazing. You're my age, but you've lived in so many countries and you've seen stuff I can only look up on the internet." His wistful tone makes me glance up at him, as I'm already climbing down the ladder in preparation for our stealth recon mission.

"Some of that is cool, but saying goodbye constantly gets old, and it's exhausting to make connections repeatedly. After a while, I started feeling like there was no point because nobody ever tried to hold onto me when I was leaving."

"I'll hold onto you," he says, grabbing my arm in a dramatic gesture.

That's so cheesy, I laugh. "Get off me, we have a job to do."

"Sadly, the pay is terrible."

"I'll buy you that burrito you mentioned."

"Those are terrible too, so why do I love them so much?"

Probably I should act superior because I've had some legitimately delicious burritos in my day, and the frozen, microwavable ones barely qualify as food, but I really like the beef and bean ones. Why am I like this?

I drop down onto the forest floor and wait for Logan to join me. He sets off quickly, so surefooted that I'm certain he won't get us lost or end up face-first on the ground.

"This way," he says.

"I'm with you."

Fortunately, I wore sneakers today. If I had on my cute, wedge-heeled boots, I might break an ankle. Logan, on the other hand, is surprisingly quiet. Before, I couldn't imagine him in the army, but based on how he moves out here, maybe he's slick enough for special forces. That reminds me of Oliver, still waiting for me to write. And I haven't learned anything about Lucy and Lester either.

"If I say stop, you freeze. If I say drop, you hide, okay? No questions, no arguments."

In principle, I don't enjoy being bossed around, but I'd like being snatched by lab security even less. Silently I nod, sticking close to Logan as we move through the woods. It seems like he knows better where to step, though, because he's much quieter. Even if I think I'm avoiding dry leaves and twigs, I still rustle like a toddler making off with a bag of chips.

Logan cuts a clear path, though not one I can see etched on the ground from frequent travel. A swampy smell drifts from the east, but he's avoiding that area, and we walk steadily as the sun sinks lower in the sky.

How far is the lab anyway?

As I wonder that—but I don't want to irk him by asking since this was my idea and he went along with it against his better judgment—the trees thin out. Instead, there are scrubby bushes and tall grass bordering a chain-link fence topped with razor wire. From this distance, I can't read the warning sign, but I'd guess it says KEEP OUT or HIGH VOLTAGE, maybe both.

Beyond the fence, there's an industrial complex that looks like it was built in the eighties, all blocky efficiency, no charm at all. Exactly what you'd expect from a secret facility. Headlights flash on the other side and Logan orders, "Drop."

That fast, I'm on my face, waiting for the shit to hit the fan.

27

The patrol vehicle passes while I'm barely breathing.

I start to get up, but Logan puts a hand on my back, stilling me. At first, I don't hear it, but then I catch the sound of booted feet. They have guards on watch, walking the fence in case of a security breach. Logan laughed at the idea that I could learn anything helpful from their exterior setup, and now I'm positive he's right about the danger. The managers and scientists here would kill to keep their secrets.

A distant radio crackles. "We may have a potential incursion in sector Alpha. I'll check the perimeter and confirm."

Shit. That sounds bad. Logan is already crawling away from the fence, his face pale in the dropping dusk. "Run," he breathes.

No single word has ever infused me with so much terror. He was right; we shouldn't have come here.

Too late for regrets. I bounce to my feet and follow as fast as I can. The boy can bolt. He's like a gazelle bounding through the underbrush toward the cover of the trees. Behind us, I hear men swearing and more crackles of the radio. I put on more speed, desperate not to be caught.

It's bad enough when they're chasing us on foot, but soon enough comes the roar of ATVs. They're damn well hunting us now. My breath rattles in my lungs. Dancing has kept me fit, but I'm not a long-distance runner. Not even a sprinter, really, and I'm getting tired.

Logan pulls out ahead like he could run for ten more miles while roots snake up from the ground to trip me. He slows, reaching for me, but the whine of an engine sounds nearby. I shake my head, frantic, and veer away, waving him off. Now we're running in the same direction, but not together. That should make us harder to catch, right? Branches rip at my clothes and scrape over my skin. Each thud sends echoes of impact through my whole body, the pain of multiple scrapes and scratches overlaid by the fear of those guards finding me.

Dread makes me glance over my shoulder once too often, and I slam into a tree and go down, rolling along an incline that leads to swampier ground. An enormous willow tree spreads across a patch of mossy-green water, and I come to a stop at the edge of the pond. I don't think Logan meant to leave me behind; he's just faster.

Probably better that we split up. Without me slowing him down, he can make it to the tree house, no question. Since I'm the reason we went to the lab in the first place, I should play bait. But where the hell am I?

As I try to get my bearings, a hand snakes out and drags me beneath a camo tarp. I didn't even notice the hunting blind, and I was right on top of it. I fight whoever's got me, at first, but then a deep voice rasps, "Settle down, unless you want to get both of us killed."

It smells ripe in here, sweat and stale corn chips, but I listen to my captor. Whoever this is, he obviously doesn't want to meet up with the assholes from Fairhaven Lab, which makes him a potential ally. I still and curl up into as small a package as possible, necessary considering the cramped conditions.

Neither of us speaks.

My heartbeat nearly drowns out the hum of the ATVs currently scouring the woods for us, but my pulse eventually slows as I calm down. It's dim beneath the tarp and netting; my host has dug a small trench, large enough to hold his prone body, but it's cramped since I've joined him. The amount of refuse suggests he's been using this spot for a while, but I can't ask any questions yet.

Finally, the forest goes quiet, but he signals me to silence until the animals start to chatter around us. Fun fact—the sounds I thought were coming from birds when I first arrived here are made by squirrels. Their reassuring noises let me relax a little.

He whispers angrily, "Now we can talk. Just who the hell are you and what're you doing out here?"

"I could ask you the same question," I snap.

"Since I saved your life, you owe me the courtesy of answering first."

Dammit, he's right. It sucks when there's no reasonable counter to an argument. "My name is Araceli. And I was out here to poke around at Fairhaven, but it's way more locked down than I imagined."

Like, DEFCON 2 levels of alertness.

"Are you stupid or lacking in common sense?"

"I hope it's the second thing. Otherwise, my future looks bleak."

I surprise a laugh out of him, which he quickly quells. Close up, he's an attractive man in his early fifties, rough around the edges, dark skin and close-cropped hair sprinkled with silver, along with an awesome pair of horn-rimmed glasses. He looks a little nerdy, which makes me wonder what he's doing out in the wilderness. Maybe the same as me—he's just smarter about it.

"My turn for explanations, then?"

"I guess. Your point about saving me still stands, so you

don't have to tell me anything. I can disappear without learning what your deal is."

"Don't put it like that," he says somberly.

"What, disappear? Ah, yikes. I mean, I can leave. Not vanish. I'd rather not find out firsthand where all the missing people are. Well, unless I have an escape plan set up. Before I go, I need to know the way back."

"That . . . is not an easily solved equation."

"Are any of them?" I mutter.

"Math must not be your strong suit." The man pauses, waiting out a splash nearby, then comes a weird "jug-o-rum" repeated call. "Bullfrog. They're more active in the summer. Anyway, I'm Dr. Edward Perry. I have no reason to trust you, so I'm not telling you why I'm here. Don't tell anyone you saw me. I'd consider it a personal favor."

"Who am I gonna tell?" It's a small ask, no issues there, but the name pings in my memory. I heard about an Edward recently in these woods—can that be a coincidence? Maybe, because it's a common name. Only John would be more generic.

Still, I take a shot. "You work at Fairhaven, don't you? And you have a theory that the experiment's fatally flawed and . . ." How did they put it? "Experiencing bleed. There were energy spikes all over the zone, which can only mean one thing. Containment has failed."

I'm only parroting what I heard from those scientists, but Perry's reaction is cataclysmic. He grabs me by the upper arms, fingers digging into my flesh hard enough to leave marks. "Who do you work for? Who sent you?"

With my full strength, I manage to knock his hands away. "Nobody. I've been gathering intel, that's all. I know the missing people in town are connected to the lab, and I'm trying to save them. How can we do that?"

Perry stares at me long and hard, but I don't break eye contact. We're eye-dueling to see who gives first. In the end, neither one of us wins that challenge. He sighs.

"I can tell you're digging, and I won't tell you more than what you've already gleaned. It's dangerous. You have no idea what you're doing, and you should stop before you fall down the rabbit hole and break your family's heart."

"What rabbit hole?" I never liked *Alice in Wonderland*, to be honest. The story struck me as weird in a bad way, long before I knew how problematic Charles Dodgson likely was. I mean, his hobby was taking intimate pictures of little girls, and he allegedly fell in love with Alice Liddell when she was seven.

"Don't drink from any strange bottles and stay away from the pretty lights. That's all I'm telling you, so thank me for saving your ass and get out of here."

28

I'm lost.

I couldn't expect Dr. Perry to give me directions or guide me out of the woods, so I feigned confidence when I said bye, and that isn't working out so well. It's getting dark, and while I haven't fallen into the swamp, I can smell it to the east, feel traces of it when the ground becomes marshy beneath my feet. I veer west, according to the compass on my phone, but that isn't helping a lot.

It's cold too. Not enough for me to suffer from exposure, but chilly so that I'm shivering and feeling sorry for myself as I creep through the trees. The very air feels oppressive, heavy in my lungs, and I know that's just my imagination, lingering fear from being hunted before.

Regardless, I'm probably never going to like the forest.

Think. Is town north of here? My head is scrambled, and I can't visualize where it should be. Plus, it's not like I've memorized any local maps.

I am not prepared for any of this. Really, I could crouch, curl up in a ball, and cry, but that would be an open invitation for any guards who might still be patrolling the woods. There may also be scientists scanning after dark, like they did before.

In my panic and because of the gloom, I nearly trip over a person sprawled at the base of a tree. As I kneel, Logan stirs and grabs my hand; his skin is alarmingly cold to the touch, and his eyes won't focus.

"What happened? Did they do something to you?"

For a few seconds, he struggles to speak, but no sound comes out. Then he manages, "Lights."

"The ghost lights?" Shit, this can't be good. "What do you mean?"

With him clutching on to me, I haul him upright, but he's heavier than he looks, and his legs can barely hold him. I step under his arm and take his weight. I'll carry him if I have to.

"It's hard to . . ." He wheezes, like his lungs can't get enough air. "Almost got me."

"The lights did?"

He nods in the direction we need to take, but that gesture is affirmation as well. "Give me a bit."

"It's fine, I've got you."

This the least I can do, considering I talked him into this. With unerring instincts, he leads us back to the tree house, but he doesn't attempt to climb, just collapses at the bottom like he might not stand again. I sit beside him and wait for his breathing to steady.

It's late enough that I need to call my great-aunt, but I'm not sure what to say. Finally, I ring the house, and she picks up on the second beep. "Araceli, where are you? The streetlights have been on for almost an hour. I didn't think you had dance practice tonight."

"Yeah, sorry, I got caught up working on a project with Logan." Not a complete lie. "We're about to eat dinner. I'll be home before bedtime, don't worry."

"If this happens again, I think I need to speak to your parents about basic consideration between housemates," she says, her tone sharp with disapproval.

Awesome, I pissed her off.

"Understood. Sorry again. I just got busy and forgot to call sooner."

Also I was being hunted.

As soon as I hang up, Logan says haltingly, "You . . . can go . . . if you need to."

"Nah, I'm not leaving you here. We'll go back together, once you feel up to it, and after I hear what the hell happened after we split up."

"Funny story . . ." he starts, but he can't finish the attempt at a joke.

"Stop trying to be cool." To distract him, I tell him about my encounter with Dr. Perry and the bit I learned from bluffing before he got wise to my tactics.

"Huh." Since he's having trouble talking, that's an eloquent response. I'm sure he'll say more later.

It takes about fifteen minutes more before his breathing eases and the rigidity leaves his body. Logan leans hard against my side. "Better?" I ask.

He nods. "When the lights hit me, there was like . . . this enormous energy pull. I can't explain it, except it was like being tased while getting sucked into vacuum. I couldn't breathe. And the ghost light only grazed me as I was running. If I'd passed through it completely, I think it would've killed me."

"Damn. Do you think they're working on a weapon at the lab? Molecular dispersion field?" I'm taking a wild guess, based on his report of the symptoms he felt when he made contact with the ghost lights. Really, I have no idea what's going on, but Dr. Perry does. Seems like he's no longer on board with the work either, if he's watching them in secret. But did he quit or did he take time off to do surveillance? I can't imagine a place like this calmly accepts resignations, then lets you go to work for another company, though.

"All I know is, the ghost lights aren't natural. They aren't swamp gas. I feel like shit, and my left arm is still tingling."

"I'm sorry."

"Eh, it didn't happen right outside the lab, so I can't blame you. It might have happened at some point during my normal wanderings out here."

He's being nice. Under usual circumstances, he wouldn't be running for his life, distracted enough to get buzzed by the ghost light. I've seen how careful he is in these woods; he just doesn't want me to feel guilty. Too late, there's no cure for my remorse.

"Okay." I pretend to accept that, but inwardly, I'll be poking myself hard with the self-blame stick for quite a while.

"If you're really sorry, pet my hair and tell me I did well."

It's such a small request, but I'm thinking about Oliver too, wondering if he would mind. That's pointless and I know it is. We'll never have the kind of relationship where we have a right to be jealous.

But I still wonder if he would be. It's too soon to think that way, even with the strangely lucid dreams. Yet as I wrap my arms around Logan, I picture Oliver's face.

"You did great," I whisper to Logan. "Nobody could have done better."

He sucks in a little breath and hides his face against my shoulder. "I've never heard that before."

"Seriously?" My parents are all about positive reinforcement, so I grew up hearing that they're proud of me, no matter what my grades look like or how many friends I make.

"I'm a constant disappointment to my father," he says softly. "And my mom . . . if I bring home four As, two Bs, and a C, she lectures me about the C and tells me I'll never get anywhere as an underachiever."

"Does she know he hits you?" That's a risky question; it could make him retreat since he's already denied it once.

Long silence. Finally, he answers, "She pretends not to know, and that's kind of . . . worse? She'd rather preserve the illusion of peace than try to protect me. Part of me doesn't blame her, because if she stepped in, he'd hurt her too, and I don't want that, so . . ."

So you take it and stay quiet. Because your dad's the sheriff and you're afraid people won't believe you. I wonder if child protective services could help Logan or if Sheriff Reed has contacts there, too. This is such a small, insular place that I'm scared to take the risk.

"Yeah." Right now, I want to call my parents and thank them—for loving me, for dragging me around the world with them for most of my life.

"I've never talked about this with anyone before," he says.

"Listening without judgment is just one of the many services I provide."

"Thanks. I'm good to go, if you'll hold onto me." The light is enough for me to see the brilliant warmth in his eyes, the shy hint of a smile so different from his usual goofy grin.

He's thirsty for me. I've seen the look enough to recognize it, but I pretend not to know as I lever him upright and give him a friendly pat.

I can't worry about a crush right now. His real concern should be his exposure to the ghost light and whether he's got radiation sickness. If I wasn't concerned about freaking him out, I'd search for the symptoms right now; I hope they don't include numbness, trouble breathing, or tingling extremities.

"Come on," I say. "Let's get out of here."

29

The next day, Logan isn't at school.

I hope he's not sick. Before first period, I hastily send a message. You okay?

There was no note from Oliver waiting, and I'm scared what might be happening to him, based on my scant knowledge of World War I. It seems like more time is passing for him than for me between our letters, but I can't ask without revealing my future origins.

No response from Logan either. This Wednesday is shaping up more like a Monday. It took a bunch of fast talking last night to keep Ottilie from grounding me. She wanted to call my parents even after I got home, so I sweet-talked her and watched an old movie with her on DVD.

Now I'm tired, concerned about both Logan and Oliver, and I have dance team practice this afternoon, like my life has the space for such normal stuff. Though I'd have an icon blinking if anyone had called about Eunsoo's flyer, I check my voicemail anyway. Nothing. I want to ring Mrs. Park to ask how she's doing, but I know the answer. She's wrecked, just like I am, and no matter what I do, it's not enough.

Tears start in my eyes as I study the last selfies she sent me. I've looked at them a hundred times, so I've even memorized what photos she had up on her bedroom wall.

My head hurts from pondering the stray bits of info I've collected, and it feels like I should be able to assemble the pieces by now, but there's one crucial bit missing. I don't know what that is. I start to make a list in my notebook, but Mr. Timmons comes in and I don't want to get caught. He might read what I've written to the class and I can't afford for people to realize how much headspace I devote to conspiracy theories. I've already got a rep for being quirky after the ghost thing.

To my dismay, Mr. Timmons ambles down the aisle after setting his briefcase on the desk and gives me a warm smile. "Are you still researching World War I?" he asks, loud enough for everyone to hear.

Inwardly I sigh. "When I have time."

"Sometimes I wish I'd taken my specialization in history instead," he says. "There's so much we can learn from the past."

Someone near the front pipes up, "Those who don't learn from the past are doomed to repeat it."

"Yes, Jeff." From the exaggerated patience of Mr. Timmons's tone, Jeff is not his favorite student.

I can see why, judging from the shirt he's wearing. It reads GET IN LINE B*TCHES, which I can read because he's sprawled across his desk, facing the wrong way. Probably teachers haven't noticed the slogan yet or he'd be wearing it inside out. Though I hope that's my last interaction with Jeff, life has other plans.

After class, he tries to talk to me. "Hey, so, I hear you made the dance team. I wasn't sure whether to rank you as hot or not, but since you can work that body, I'm putting you on the doable list. Wanna hang out sometime?"

"No," I say.

There's no room for debate, and thankfully Tamsyn happens to be passing so I run after her, glad to have an excuse to get away from Jeff. At first, she won't even look at me, but I follow her with a desperation that's only half-driven by Jeff-dodging.

"Will you stop avoiding me? Please?" I haven't imagined her silence at the table, and she doesn't make eye contact with me anymore. I wonder if she blames me for Eunsoo's disappearance and is prickly over me asking personal questions about her brother.

She finally stops, books clutched to her chest. "I'm not. I'm just in a hurry right now. Class starts in three minutes."

Eh, true, but she's definitely hurting, and I'd be a terrible friend if I didn't reach out to her. We haven't known each other long, but it feels like trauma is a bonding agent, and these short weeks have been a crucible. "Then can we talk during lunch?"

"Yeah, that's fine." Tamsyn sighs and pushes her red glasses up on her nose. "I know everyone's worried, and I'm sorry about that. I had to hermit for a while after Eunsoo . . . well, it brought everything back. My mom's on depression meds, and it's a struggle to get her to eat. Some days, I don't even want to get out of bed myself."

"If there's anything I can do—"

"We'll talk more at lunch," Tamsyn says. "Promise."

I rush off after we go our separate ways. Whew. I barely make it to my next class on time, and I keep checking to see what's up with Logan. No reply as of lunchtime, dammit.

I head off to the cafeteria, where most of the group is already at the table, Tamsyn among them. Only Kimala and Logan are missing. First things first. I open a container of cookies Tía baked while I was lost in the woods yesterday.

"It's a shit day, who wants a cookie? These do have peanuts in them, by the way."

Jackson scrambles back. "Why didn't you say so sooner?"

"Oh my God." I pull the plastic tub back toward me, eyes wide. "I'm so sorry!"

Tamsyn elbows him. "You shouldn't joke about allergies. My cousin is allergic to nuts and he almost died because someone thought it would be funny to see what would happen if he accidentally ate some."

"That's not a joke," Derek says darkly. "That's attempted murder."

Now that I'm clear that Jackson was messing with me, I pass the peanut butter chocolate chunk cookies around. When the bin comes back, it has one broken cookie left in it. Jackson isn't eating otherwise, and he's already so skinny that I'm worried about him. Tamsyn pokes at her salad, eyes lowered, and I wonder if I should bring up the stuff she confided in the hallway. Maybe she doesn't want everyone else to know? She makes eye contact with me a few seconds later, and I raise my brows silently asking.

"It's fine," she says. "Derek and Jackson already know about my family situation."

Derek immediately wraps a muscular arm around her shoulders and shifts his body so the rest of the cafeteria can't see her crying. I don't know if I did the right thing by making her talk, but at least she knows she's not alone.

Jackson reaches across the table and pets her head, then he takes the last broken cookie. "I hate that there's nothing we can do," he mutters.

Good, it seems like we've cleared the air. I start eating my lunch and vaguely wonder where Kimala is. Before I can ask, someone plops into the empty seat next to me where Logan would usually be. Oh God, it's Jeff of the B*TCHES tee, which has been replaced by his gym shirt. It seems like I'm on his radar now. This is not excellent.

"What's up, party people?" He beams at everyone at the table like he can't imagine he wouldn't be welcome.

I immediately stand. "See ya later. I have to do a thing."

Pulling away from Derek, Tamsyn grabs her stuff and is moving with me. "Yeah, me too. We have a thing."

Derek and Jackson give us the side-eye, but they can't leave with us or it will seem like Jeff is being shunned, Mennonite-style. I keep a straight face until we get into the hall, and then I can't stop laughing.

"I know why I'm fleeing the scene. What did he do to you?"

Tamsyn answers, "He's so dense. Just turn him down eight or ten times. He'll get the message. Eventually."

"My life did not need this embellishment," I mutter.

"Nobody's life needs more Jeff," Tamsyn says.

I feel a bit bad for laughing because it's kind of mean, but it's also true, and I'm glad Tamsyn is talking to me again. Full-time hermitting is not the best way to deal with emotions, and in a town like this, I need all the friends I can get.

After school, I get through dance practice somehow. Lana isn't there, which makes everything better. I love how efficient Kimala is; she wastes no time on pep talks or squad gossip. We warm up, drill the routine, and that's it. I'm curious why she wasn't at lunch, but she looks okay, and I have two boys to check on.

I rush home without showering. Though my first instinct is to run upstairs and look in the treasure box, I force myself to greet my great-aunt and chat a bit over snacks. Today, it's grapes and goldfish crackers.

Only after I finish do I ask, "Is it okay if I go over to see how Logan's doing? He wasn't at school today."

Her expression softens, maybe even enough for her to forgive me about yesterday. "Is he . . . sick?"

Something in her tone communicates that she's aware his father isn't a kind and gentle parent. I mean, she saw his bruises recently. If she hasn't reported it by now, there must be a reason. If I had to guess, I'd say she fears making life worse for Logan at home, too.

"I'm not sure," I say quietly. "I'd like to find out."

"By all means, visit him. I won't worry if I know you're right across the street." That's a pointed jab if ever I heard one.

"Yes, Tía."

"Hold on, let me get some soup ready for him. I'm not sure if he'll have healthy food at home, and if he's sick, he'll need something light on the stomach." She bustles around the kitchen making a care package, forgetting I'm a whisper away from being punished.

"Here you are."

"Thanks. I'll be back soon."

30

I knock three times, loudly, and Logan still doesn't answer the door.

As I contemplate going in the window—probably not a great idea at the sheriff's house—I hear shuffling footsteps within. Eventually the door swings open, revealing Logan, who looks terrible. His hair is standing up, and he's swaying on his feet, clinging to the doorframe for support. No new bruises, so this must be the aftermath of ghost light exposure. He's so pale that he looks green, and the circles beneath his eyes make it seem like he hasn't slept in weeks.

Holy shit.

"You rang?" he jokes.

"Have you eaten today?"

"I don't know. Don't think so. I'm so freaking tired."

"My aunt sent over some soup. I'll heat it up for you." Same dated house and nicotine-stained walls. Hiding my instinctive revulsion to the smell, I cross into the kitchen. The microwave sits on a little cart by the wall, so I pop the soup container in and let him hobble toward me. There must be a way to make him feel better, right?

I did check on the symptoms of radiation poisoning, but he wasn't displaying them last night. "Uh, so, you haven't noticed any hair loss, bloody stool, sloughing of skin, nausea, or vomiting, have you?" There could also be spontaneous bleeding, mouth ulcers, and excess fatigue.

Crap, he has that last symptom. I need to take him to the hospital, but I don't know how to drive. Ottilie was right, dammit.

He props himself against the doorframe, trying to make that desperate lean look casual. "You think I'm irradiated."

Damn, he's quick.

"Maybe a little. Is there a doctor in town? You should get checked out."

"My mom will be back from my grandma's tomorrow. If I'm not better by then, I'll ask her to take me in."

"I don't think you should delay," I protest.

The microwave beeps. I serve his soup and watch him eat it, mostly to make sure he can keep food down. If he's lying about the nausea and vomiting, I'll carry him to the ER on my back if I have to. From what I read, those are the first symptoms of radiation poisoning, and since I don't know what energy spikes they're scanning for in the woods, the ghost lights might be super-dangerous.

Soon, he's scraping the spoon against the side of the bowl. "Your auntie makes delicious potato soup. Thank her for me."

"She worries about you," I tell him.

"Is she the only one?" That's a flirty line, but I don't respond in kind, and when I don't, he adds with a crestfallen expression, "You should go before my dad gets home."

"Okay. Call me if you start feeling worse." I say that because I don't think he'd tell his father, and his mom is gone.

I hurry back across the street, feeling like I've committed a crime. Can't let the scary sheriff catch me in his house. I've only been back for maybe five minutes when I spot the squad car roll up, and as I predicted before, he parks in the garage and goes in through the side door. Logan's life really sucks, and I'm making it worse.

I should stop involving him in my business. Since I'm the one who wants to dig up the answers, I shouldn't ask him to help me anymore. Using someone when you know they have feelings for you is all kinds of wrong, and I'm not that person. I won't be.

But my patience is now at an end. I can't wait any longer to check the heartwood box. A hot flush washes my cheeks as I open it and remove the velvet bottom to find—

Dearest Araceli,

(Oh my God, I'm "dearest" now. That's progress, right? Right back at you, Oliver.)

Hope I've not offended you with that familiar greeting. That's how I'm thinking of you since the night on the ship. Now that I've seen your face, I'll never forget it.

I've passed through England on my way to the front. We didn't stay long, just enough for the others to get puking drunk. I tried some dark lager, but didn't like it much. The countryside there was so different to anything I've seen at home. Farmland is the same, I guess, but there are hedges all along the roads, and all of the buildings are so old, hundreds and hundreds of years. We passed a church that a local joe said was built in 1107. I had to ask him if I heard that right.

He said, "sodding yanks" and spat like I was the enemy. I stopped asking questions after that. We were there less than a week while our COs were getting orders. Now I'm in France. Those are not words I ever thought I'd write, but I haven't seen much of the country. We landed on the coast and have been marching since. I want to describe some of the horrors I've already seen, remainders of battles fought, but part of me thinks I oughtn't do that to you, my sweet girl. What I seen should not be for your eyes, yet I recollect you did say that you'll hear me out, no matter what.

So I'm writing it down so if anybody's left after this terrible war, somebody will know what I thought and felt in my time on earth. France has become hell on earth, no way around it. Great runnels in the dirt, piled high with bodies, and you can't tell a Jerry from a Brit from a Sammy. (That's what they call us over here, on account of Uncle Sam, I guess.) Death makes every soldier the same. Nobody is coming for those men, not to give them services or say a few words or even bury them. The birds pluck out their eyes, so I guess at least the crows and ravens are doing well enough in the war. Entire villages are shelled to rubble, some so bad there's just signs standing to tell you what used to be roads.

We were on the move and a whole airplane came crashing down, maybe two miles off. We heard the explosion clear as anything, then they shelled the area to be sure. I can't sleep for the noise, and I haven't been dry since I left England. We made camp tonight, and the officers are on edge. I'm told not to ask questions, but I can hear the distant sounds of the battle we're being ordered to join.

I don't want any of this to be real. I wish I could vanish like you do. I wish I could go where you are. There probably aren't any guns roaring through the night, are there? Thinking of you keeps me from fretting on what's to come.

These days it's hard for me to think of anything else. I sleepwalk through playing soldier boy, and at night I try to dream you up, if that's what I did before, but it doesn't work.

The stars are pretty here. They're not making us hunker down because we're moving soon, but I hear there are Jerries close by. We'll see action soon. I pray I last long enough to get another letter from you.

I don't question how anymore. I just wear your necklace as I wait, hope, and believe.

Yours at heart,
Oliver

I ache so much that it's hard to breathe. His fear, his suffering seems as real to me as my own life. From the pictures I've seen online, I imagine what his camp in the French countryside looks like. Is Oliver patrolling, or is he off duty, shooting the shit with other recruits?

Stop wondering and answer him. That's what he wants, just as bad as I want it when I'm waiting to hear back.

My Dearest Oliver,

No, I'm not offended. Not by the greeting or what you told me about the war. I'll take anything you give me and hold it dear. I wish I could send you more than words. Come to think of it, I can send you small things, anything that fits in the treasure box, so if you want sweets or any little comfort to remind you of home, let me know and I'll get it to you.

If I could ship myself the way our letters travel, I'd go. And I don't say that lightly, even knowing there are people who would be so sad if I went, knowing I can never come back again. It would be worth it, I think. I want to be with you too, more than you know. I see your face when I close my eyes to sleep. I find myself thinking of you when I should be focused on other things.

I hate that I can't think of anything wise or profound to say right now. What unit do you belong to? If I know that, *maybe I can tell you something useful next time. It would also help me if you dated your letters going forward. Maybe, well, I won't make promises. We shouldn't do that. All I can offer is my unconditional support. I hope that's enough.*

I'll just add this—it's fine to be scared. It would be strange if you weren't, and if you have to choose between being a hero and staying alive, I hope you choose the second option. What I want more than anything is for you be safe and happy.

Right now, you're neither, but the war won't last forever. You have to come home to make sure Lester is all right, remember? So don't talk about lasting long enough for one more letter ever again. You just about made my heart stop.

I miss you. I'm longing to hear from you again. I do wish you could dream me up, or I could dream you, but . . . that's tough. Before, you asked if I'm a bruja, and if that were so, I'd say we must remember the price for such dangerous sweetness. Don't tempt me to make promises I can't— or shouldn't—keep. Don't make me want more than I can have, please.

I might risk everything for you.

> *Yours at heart,*
> *Araceli*

At first I looked on Oliver as a pen pal, and then it was like a visual novel where I play the role of the fiancée left behind during the war, except it doesn't feel like history or fiction anymore. The way I feel connected to him, despite the impossibility and the strangeness. I'm fighting with everything I have not to fall head over heels. His honesty—and the way he needs me—those qualities are damn near irresistible. This is a fantasy, I know it is, distracting me from a difficult situation in my current life, but this relationship feels truer all the time. I'm frightened for Oliver, as much as I'm fretting about Logan and scared to death for Eunsoo.

I only hope I can help everyone who needs me . . . and I'm not forced to make a terrible choice somewhere down the line.

31

I've bitten my cuticles down to the quick, but Sunday's finally rolled around. Tía is surprised I'm going to church with Kimala's family, but it's not the sort of thing she'd object to. "Have a good time, sweetheart! Or should I say 'peque' to remind you of your father?"

It's sweet she's noticed he calls me that, let alone remembers it.

"Either is fine. How do I look?" I smooth the white sundress and adjust the blue cardigan I put on with it because I'm not sure it's appropriate to show so much skin on the Lord's day.

"Very pretty. I'll see you this afternoon."

Normally she wouldn't be up this early, but she made an exception when she learned I had morning social plans. This is the first breakfast she ever cooked me, and I must admit, her biscuits are freaking delicious. And I'm not even a huge pastry person, unless we're talking about crema pastelera, my absolute favorite.

"See you later," I call as I snag my purse and head for the door.

I checked the map last night, and it should take me about twenty minutes to walk to Kimala's house, leaving me ten minutes before departure. There's a nice breeze, a hint of autumn sun peeking through wispy clouds, so I enjoy the walk, but I take it slow so I don't get sweaty. Kimala's house is a well-kept blue ranch built on the newer side of town.

There are still five minutes to spare as I rap on the front door, red for good luck. Pretty sure that's from China, but the custom has spread all over the west too.

Kimala answers, and wow, she looks beautiful. She's got on a gold sheath dress, her hair is twisted into the most sophisticated style I've ever seen on a girl my age, and her makeup is photo-app flawless. Like, she could be heading to a runway, not to church.

"You look amazing," I say, because not acknowledging it is unthinkable.

Her smile says she knows, but she offers a gracious, "Thank you," while waving me in. "I'm still helping the youngers get ready. Give me a minute. She's here, Mama!" she calls, heading down the hall.

I hear Kimala snap, "Pants are not optional!" from one of the bedrooms, and I stifle a snicker.

A gorgeous, dark-skinned woman comes out of the kitchen; she might be Kimala's mother, but she looks young. I decide to play that card for points.

"You must be Kimala's sister," I say.

"Stop. You won't win me over by sucking up." But the twinkle in her eyes says she didn't hate hearing that. "I'm her mom, as I'm sure you know. It's a real pleasure to meet you, but I was a little surprised. Kimala's never invited anyone to church before."

"I'm excited. I've only ever attended Catholic services."

Her perfectly shaped brows shoot up. "Are you looking to convert?"

"No, I just wanted to learn more about Protestant beliefs. I'm not a devout Catholic or anything. I've never been confirmed or taken communion."

That's the right thing to say because she's smiling. "Well, everyone is welcome in God's house. Let me go help Kimala, or we'll never get there on time."

There are two younger siblings, one boy, one girl, who trot out in their Sunday best. I'm guessing it was the younger brother who didn't want to put on his pants, but he looks cute as a button in his white dress shirt and red bow tie. The little girl has puffs on either side of her head and is wearing a lemon-yellow dress with ruffles all the way down and a pair of the shiniest white shoes I've ever seen.

I get in the back with the kids before they can offer to let me ride up front. As her mother takes off, Kimala asks, "When's Pop coming home, anyway?"

"Tuesday, I think. He has meetings after the conference on Monday."

The little boy, whose name I still don't know, pokes me in the side. "My dad is a big deal. He's in Washington DC right now. That's where the president lives."

"Cool," I say.

But I've already lost his attention because there's a bug on the windshield. Kids are funny.

I listen to the conversation and don't say much on the ride to church, trying to figure out how to question the woman Kimala will introduce me to without it seeming obvious that I came to do exactly that.

Be cool. Keep it casual.

We pull into the church parking lot just before nine. Looks like they attend First Baptist Church of Silver Lake, half an hour closer to NYC and way friendlier to people of color. Inside, I feel immediately more at home, tension I didn't even know I was holding draining from my shoulders.

I'd say 70 percent of the congregation is Black, with a few

Latinx people, and some East Asian. No more than a handful are white, a complete flip from the creepy town I live in.

Kimala takes the kids to children's church, whatever that means, and then rejoins us as we're taking our seats in the main hall. I do my best to follow along with all the cues, but it's quite different than Catholic mass. The singing is fun, exuberant and active, but there's no standing or kneeling in response to the minister's requests, after the music ends. As the preacher speaks on, I notice the audience is way more engaged and animated.

There's fellowship after the service ends, and Kimala takes me by the arm. "See the woman in the blue dress with the black hat? That's Mrs. Wallace. I offered an introduction, and that's where my part ends. Do not cause trouble."

"I won't," I promise.

She leads me through the crowd, periodically stopping to chat or answer a question about who I am. Finally, we get to Mrs. Wallace, who turns with a tired smile. I can see she hasn't been sleeping well, maybe since her brother went missing.

"Kimala! You brought a friend today. What's your name, baby?" She pats me warmly on the shoulder.

"Araceli, ma'am. It's nice to meet you." I make casual conversation for a few minutes, struggling with how to open the topic, before I find the perfect segue. I sigh a little, staring up at the stained glass above the baptistery, and I let my expression fall.

Since Mrs. Wallace is a nice lady, she asks, "What's the matter?"

"My auntie loves stained glass." I have no idea if this is true, but it could be. "I wish she could see this. Your church is beautiful."

"Is there some reason she can't? Is she sick, or . . ." Delicate question, not quite asked—*is there something wrong with her?*

I'm so glad you asked. Let me tell you.

"She doesn't go out much these days. Since my uncle disappeared, she hasn't been the same. She says she can feel him in the house sometimes. Once, I saw her leaving food on the table for him."

Mrs. Wallace staggers, catching herself on the pew in front. "Is that true? Your poor auntie."

From the flicker of her eyes, I can tell I've said something familiar. Time for my finishing move.

"I thought it was strange, and I was going to talk to the school psychologist about it, but then I spoke to my friend at school and she said her mom does the same thing. Isn't that amazing?" I try to keep my expression earnest and open. "The Lord really does work in mysterious ways."

Mrs. Wallace grabs my hand with a fervor I'd find startling, if I didn't already have an inkling why tears are in her eyes. "He sure does. I think He must have sent you here today to let me know I'm not alone. It's funny how grief moves some of us in the same way."

Elation rockets through me, brilliant and electric. That's an admission—that she feels her lost brother close by and she leaves food for him. Maybe he even eats it?

That's not the commonality of grief. It's a pattern.

32

"I'm telling you, I'm not sick. At least not with anything they can identify," Logan insists. It's Tuesday afternoon, and he's sitting on my front porch, waving a clinic receipt.

"You're not reassuring me. At all."

"My leukocyte counts are a little weird, nothing alarming. The doc said it reads like I've been fighting an infection for a while, but that's not the case."

"Did you mention—"

"The ghost light? No. There would be questions about what I was doing in the woods, word would get back to my dad, and he'd burn down my tree house."

I wish that sounded like an exaggeration, but that outcome wouldn't surprise me. "Are you really feeling better?"

"I'm fine."

I decide to accept that as the truth because I can't prove otherwise. "Then do me a favor, if at all possible."

"Again? You almost got me killed last time."

"It's nothing to do with the lab. Do you know how to drive?"

"Yeah. My dad insisted on teaching me when I turned fifteen, something about a rite of passage. I tried to tell him that ride-sharing apps mean it doesn't matter as much these days, but a real man knows how to drive, so y'know. But I don't have a car, if that's what you're hinting at."

"Ottilie does, and she wants me to learn. Would you teach me?"

"Seriously?"

"Unless you have plans." After the scare in the woods, I want to be able to take someone to the hospital if they get hurt. Feeling helpless sucks.

"Your aunt will be okay with that?"

Eh, probably not. She wants me to find a qualified teacher, which sounds complicated, an extra step I don't have time for. My life is messy enough already.

"We can ask if you can borrow her car, so we can . . . go to the mall?" There must be one within driving distance. "Then instead, you'll find a road with very little traffic and teach me how to drive."

Logan doesn't seem enthused about lying to my aunt, but if we're careful, it'll be fine, right? Finally, he agrees, and I head inside to do the talking. Ten minutes later, I exit triumphant, dangling her keys in one hand.

"The car's in the garage. Wonder what she used to drive."

I jog along the gravel path to the single-car detached garage at the back of the house, built at least fifty years after the original construction. Logan levers up the door, groaning almost as much as the rusty chains. I glance into the shadowy space and realize that Tía's idea of a "perfectly good car" is different than mine.

I'm positive she bought this thing before my great-uncle disappeared. It's a bright orange Plymouth Horizon hatchback, circa 1985. She said it still runs, and it's not rusty or anything, but this is a clown car. It might take a literal emergency to get me behind the wheel.

Logan nudges me. "Are we sure about this? Like, completely sure? I'm not good enough at driving stick to teach you."

"Well, let's look inside."

Black cloth interior, musty smell, oh my God, spider! I jump out, screaming, and won't come back in for ten minutes. Why is this my life? Logan takes care of the arachnid guests and checks out the interior.

"Good news, it's an automatic. Bad news, that's about the only thing it is."

He's right; the doors have to be unlocked by hand, and for the windows, there's a handle you have to turn. I feel like I've traveled back in time, which is sort of fitting, I suppose, given that Oliver has never been on a plane and couldn't imagine an invention like my cell phone.

"Pull the car forward," I say, sighing. "I'll shut the garage door."

For good or ill, the Great Pumpkin starts with a little coaxing from Logan and settles into a steady idle. At least this isn't a land boat like they had in the seventies. I have no confidence in my ability to steer something that huge. After checking the garage door closure, I hop in the passenger side.

Oh hell, there's an actual cassette player in here. Is there a tape?

There is.

"Let's find out what your greats jammed to back in the day." Logan pushes the button, and some guy comes on singing about how we can call him Maurice.

"Wow," I say and switch it over to the radio, which surprisingly still works. "Any idea about where we can go for our next secret mission?"

"You make everything sound so dramatic," Logan says.

"Guilty as charged. And that's no answer."

"They built a racetrack around here, but it closed down, like, five years ago. The parking lot is huge, and there won't be anyone out there. Plus, there's nothing for you to hit. That should be pretty good for driving practice."

"Genius. Thank you for doing this, seriously."

Logan glances over at me with a smile. "Any chance to spend more time with you is a good thing. Never thought I'd be grateful to my dad."

Since I don't want to talk about Sheriff Reed—or Logan's crush—I decide to share some personal info. "My dad taught me how to dance. I was small. I remember standing on his feet. I've loved dancing ever since."

"You must've been so cute." Logan gets a dreamy-eyed look, staring like he's imagining my childhood face.

"Not really. I got lice when I was six, and my mom tried to shave my head. I threw a fit, and she compromised with a pixie cut. Let me say, it did not suit me. I spent two weeks with her grooming me with a special comb and a smelly hair treatment."

This is not a story you tell a guy you're trying to impress. To his credit, Logan doesn't seem repelled, which means he's not shallow. He's also . . . not Oliver.

"At least you didn't end up bald. I did one summer as punishment, and I found out my head is slightly lopsided. Here's our turn."

I read a faded sign as he makes the right—CRESTWOOD DOWNS—and we drive maybe five more miles in comfortable silence. Another turn's coming on the left—and a rusty barricade should prevent us from progressing down this private road, but Logan swerves around it, half going off-road. The Pumpkin bounces but doesn't buckle under the rough treatment, and then we're back on the weathered pavement leading to the defunct racetrack.

It's as he described it, with nothing but space. Rain and snow have scoured away the lines that told people where to park, but that's no deterrent to driving all over the place. I only have to manage not to hit the external walls of the stadium seating on the other side, and if I can't do that, there's no way I'll pass a driving test later.

"Let's swap seats," Logan says.

This is the first time I've ever sat on the driver's side, and it's kind of cool. He runs through a list of things I need to check, like seat belt, multiple mirrors, and seat adjustment, then I learn where my lights and wipers are.

"This will be different in another car, so be ready for that."

"Si, maestro," I tease him a little, but he's having none of it.

"Stay focused, Flores Harper."

Ooh, last names, this is serious. I listen to his short lecture, though of course, I know the difference between gas and brake.

"It's best to use your right foot for both. Otherwise you might panic and stomp on the wrong one at the worst possible time." I hear ten-and-two hand positioning, signaling—honestly, he might be able to do this for a living. We've been sitting here for half an hour, and the car hasn't moved.

Finally, he wraps up the talk. "Are you ready to try it out?"

Belatedly I realize his overly detailed explanation gave me a chance to settle down behind the wheel. I'm not even remotely nervous anymore. He's sweet.

"Absolutely," I say. "Let's get this party started."

33

Nobody is more surprised than me when I turn out to have an aptitude for driving. I've been looping around the parking lot for half an hour, and my stops are good too. Now I'm practicing my turns, and it all feels perfectly natural.

Finally, Logan says, "Are you sure you haven't done this before?"

"Positive, unless you count racing games. In that case, I've logged many hours with my cousins in Monterrey." Probably best if I don't mention I got points for maiming pedestrians in that game.

"Not the same. I wasn't going to move this fast, but since you already seem comfortable, should we try this on the road? There won't be many cars out here, and you can practice staying in your own lane."

Okay, that's slightly scary. Even if only one car passes me, I still have to keep from hitting it, and I don't have a driver's permit. Tía agreed to let Logan drive her car, not for him to teach me.

"Sure, why not?" I project a confidence I don't feel as I turn down the rutted path that leads back to the public road.

When we get to the barrier, I stop and make Logan drive around it because I'm not confident I can make such quick, intricate turns without putting us in the ditch. He gets us around it easily, then we swap seats, and I take a bracing breath before turning onto the county road. Like he said, there aren't many cars.

The first time one passes me going the opposite way, I tense up, but I don't jerk the wheel and it's fine. Logan leans over to check my speed.

"You're going really slow. If you're not careful, you'll get pulled over. Only people who are slightly high drive this much below the limit."

"Don't even joke!" I do press down on the gas, but it's like his words have the power to predict the future because a couple of minutes later, I see flashing lights in the rearview mirror.

"Shit," Logan says. "It's my dad. Pull over and swap seats with me. Hurry!"

At first, I think he's kidding, but another glance in the mirror and I identify the sheriff's car. This is not a drill. As his old man gets out of his vehicle, we scramble in the Pumpkin, knock heads, and get his shirt button caught on my hair. By the time his dad gets to the window, Logan is in the driver's seat, and thank God I didn't get caught. I don't know why I'm so scared, but this man radiates ice.

"What are you doing all the way out here, son?" That last word might sound like an endearment coming from anyone else, but it's more of a warning in this scenario.

"Coming back from the mall," Logan answers.

It's such a strange coincidence that we ran into his father out here, a place we chose specifically because it was deserted.

"The highway would've been a lot faster. Guess you're taking the long way home." His dad sets a hand on the car as if to prevent us from driving off and leans down to make eye contact with me. "We meet again, miss. Isn't this your aunt's car?"

"She gave us permission to borrow it. You can call her to ask if you want." I'm sweating, despite the fall nip in the air.

"No need. This isn't a vehicle kids would steal for a joyride."
Pleasant tone, which makes the look in his eyes feel worse,
dead and humorless. "While we're talking, I had a report of
some trespassers out near the lab recently. Do you know anything about that?"

He knows.

I don't know how, but he does. Or suspects anyway, if
he doesn't have direct evidence. The fact that he gets reports
from the lab isn't just sinister; it suggests he's part of whatever
is happening there, playing a role in keeping the community
quiet and compliant.

I shiver. My mouth is too dry to answer. Logan must be
more used to this because he shrugs. "Why would I?"

"Anyway, tell your aunt to get the rear taillight checked.
It's fritzing, probably a short. That's why I stopped you. I'll let
you off with a warning this time, but there will be consequences if I catch you like this again." He slaps the roof
with his palm. "Take the lady home now, Logan. I'll see you
soon."

That sounds like a threat, but Logan maneuvers back on
the road, his brows drawn in a scowl. "I'm sorry."

"For what?"

"Partly because he's my dad, but also because I forgot to
turn off my phone. That's how he tracked us."

My mind races. If the sheriff has a GPS tracking app that
pings him with Logan's movements—

"Did you turn it off when we were in the woods the other
day?"

"I always do before I head to the tree house. Otherwise, he
would have razed the place years ago."

That's why his dad was fishing. He got a report from the
lab, but he doesn't have any suspects. It could be anyone in
town from a bereaved family member to a bored high school

student. Good thing we didn't give him any ammunition to use against us.

I calm down over the drive back. It helps to know where the sheriff's allegiances lie. Now I understand that we can't ask him for help under any circumstances. In this town, Tía is the only adult I trust, and her ability to assist is limited.

We're only a few streets away from home when my phone buzzes. Message from Tamsyn. I open the app to find: URGENT. Come over as soon as you get this.

She includes her address, which I read off to Logan. "Do you know how to get there?"

"Are you kidding? Nobody lives more than five miles away if they go to Central."

"Then take me there. Please. I think something's going on."

I've learned my lesson, though, and I call Ottilie as he wheels away from our neighborhood. "Hi, Tía. Logan and I are back, but my friend just messaged me and asked if we could stop by her house tonight. Is that okay?"

"It's fine, as long as I know where you are. Which friend is it?" She sounds pleased, I think, that I have Logan to drive me around and a friend to ask me over.

"Her name is Tamsyn Leon Salazar. She lives on Aspen Drive."

"I know where that is, and the detour is fine, but do call if you're going be out past ten."

Since it's only 7:30 right now, I doubt that's the case, but I agree and hang up as Logan pulls into the gravel driveway, behind two cars already parked in front. We rush up to the white house and ring the bell. Tamsyn answers right away and pulls us inside.

"Everyone else is already here. Hurry."

I have no idea what's going on, but she dashes up carpeted stairs and leads us to a good-sized room with a peaked ceiling that's lower on each side. Though she said everyone, I'm still surprised to see the whole table assembled: Derek, Kimala, Jackson, and someone I never could have expected—Mrs. Park, Eunsoo's mother. I have no idea what's going on.

Jackson glances between us. "Normally I'd have a lot to say about you two rolling in together, but consider yourself mocked and let's move on."

"What happened?" I ask, kneeling next to Kimala, who's trying to comfort Mrs. Park.

Logan takes a seat as Tamsyn shuts the door, as if she doesn't want her family to hear what's being said. Her grim expression worries me, though.

"What is it?" Logan asks.

Derek isn't wearing his headphones, so it must be serious. You'd think Tamsyn's mom would be a part of whatever this is, but I'm guessing she's in bed, still struggling to cope. Finally, Mrs. Park raises her head to reveal red and swollen eyes. She's obviously been crying nonstop for a long time. It takes her a couple of tries to calm down long enough to reply.

"It's my husband. He said he had a little bit left to do at work, so I got a ride home with a colleague. He never reached our house, and I can't get any answers from my supervisor. He's missing, just like Eunsoo."

34

Tamsyn pulls me aside in the guise of making tea, the beverage of choice for offering comfort. "I stopped by to check on Eunsoo's parents," Tamsyn explains, as we wait for the kettle to heat, "and Mrs. Park was just . . . hysterical. I didn't know what else to do, so I brought her over here and sent out the message to the group chat. I didn't think she should be alone."

"Good thinking. Did she file a report?" Even as I ask, I know it won't do a damn bit of good. I saw firsthand how useless Logan's dad will be. We have to do something, but hell if I can figure out what.

Tamsyn nods, getting out the tea bags. "The sheriff left shortly before I arrived, I guess. But I've seen that play out too often to have any hope they'll do their jobs."

"True." I help her with the mugs, and by the time we get back to the den upstairs, Mrs. Park is more or less composed. Kimala has done a great job calming her down, and the woman looks resolved now. Whatever we plan from this point, I think we can count her in.

We pass out the drinks, then Kimala says, "Araceli, you were right when you said we should take action. We can't keep losing people like this."

Mrs. Park reaches out to Tamsyn, taking one of her hands. "I've had misgivings for a while about our research at the lab. I'm so sorry that I didn't take action sooner." She sweeps our faces with a haunted, weary gaze. "If they think they can keep me quiet by doing this, they're dead wrong. This is personal for a lot of us, and I'll help you however I can. I'm taking a leave of absence, but my badge will still work and I can help you from the inside, if necessary."

Imagine how desperate Mrs. Park must feel to offer to join up with a bunch of her daughter's friends to investigate her former employer. With her entire family missing, Mrs. Park has become the most dangerous of enemies, one with nothing to lose.

Kimala asks, "Do you have any of Mr. Park's work stuff at home? His laptop, maybe?"

Mrs. Park nods. "We're not allowed to take much home, however. And we were working on different aspects of the same project. They keep the research quite compartmentalized, so our department doesn't know what other teams are focused on."

"That's not shady at all," Derek mutters.

"Maybe there's another way," I say, remembering my encounter with Dr. Perry.

"What are you thinking?" Logan asks.

I lean forward to get Mrs. Park's attention. "See if you can find contact information for a Dr. Edward Perry. Do you have any idea who that is?"

Eunsoo's mother stares at me, visibly startled. "How do you know that name?"

"I met him. Why?"

"He's the second-in-command at Fairhaven, answers only to the big boss. I've seen him around often. Her, not so much. How did you run into him exactly?" Mrs. Park asks.

Everyone else looks like they want to know too, so I loop them in about the recon mission I went on with Logan, then I explain how Dr. Perry saved me and said some stuff that makes me think he's no longer fully on board with Team Secret Project.

"If we get in touch with him," I finish, "we might be able to recruit him to help us."

Jackson is nodding. "That's way better than letting Mrs. Park poke around covertly. They will so be watching her. And he definitely knows what's going on in there, and he's positioned to help us stop it."

"Assuming that's possible," Derek mutters.

Kimala says, "Well, I agree that we have to try. This is where we draw the line." She digs her fingers into the pale carpet and dishevels the pile to emphasize her point. "Nobody else goes missing. Not without us getting answers."

"I hate that I have to say this," Logan cuts in, "but you can't trust my dad. Probably best to avoid his deputies too."

"Talk about redundant," Derek says. "We'd be wary of the cops in a regular town. But here?" He shakes his head as if he can't believe Logan thought he needed to say that.

"Never mind, then," Logan mumbles.

"Do you want an invite to our group chat?" That's a weird thing to ask, but Mrs. Park is one of us now. It's reassuring not to be a bunch of kids united against the forces of evil, even if her hands are tied by surveillance. She still has insights about Fairhaven that we desperately need.

"Please," she says.

Kimala's already tapping at her phone. "On it. And done."

"Awesome. Message us when you find a number or an email for Dr. Perry. I need to get him on board with whatever we plan next."

"I'll go over my husband's laptop, see if there any clues in his research, and I'll post Dr. Perry's info when I find it." Mrs. Park stands then. "I appreciate the way you're looking for

Eunsoo." Such a heartfelt tone that I can't handle all of the sincerity.

"We'll find her," Jackson promises, his eyes overly bright.

Derek nudges me. "Look at you, it's like you have experience leading covert missions or something."

Though I know he's joking, I answer, "Not so much, but I've seen how my parents work. Before they can take down a corrupt regime, they start with one irreplaceable asset—a credible source. Dr. Perry can fill that role, and based on what he said before, I don't think it'll take much persuasion."

"Too bad you didn't get his number in the woods," Tamsyn says.

I cut her a look. "Even if I'd asked, he would've refused. Because back then, it was just me poking around, dragging Logan reluctantly with me. That's not a movement. Now, there are enough of us prepared to act that he has to take us seriously." I'm including Mrs. Park in our ranks, and she nods emphatically.

Jackson seems to have signed on for permanent pessimism, as if his ability to hope vanished with Eunsoo. "That seems unlikely. Who listens to teenagers?"

"So many protests have started in high schools. If people don't realize we have power, they're just not paying attention. Look at Emma Rodriguez." I could name a lot more influential young people as well, but the others aren't in the mood.

"Yeah, we get the point," Derek says. "Nobody ever thinks, hey, today's the day I become a hero. It just happens. Or it doesn't. But we won't know the outcome until we take our best shot."

"Exactly," Kimala says.

Logan finally speaks up. "Then the plan is to get in touch with Dr. Perry, and if he agrees to help us, what then?"

"That depends on what's going on at the lab. Maybe we get

the media involved, get the place shut down if the experiments are dangerous and/or illegal." I still think they might be building a weapon, but I don't want to derail this productive meeting with my wild theories about radioactive death rays.

The minute I start talking like that, I suspect Derek and Jackson will tap out. They won't listen to someone who might as well be ranting about crop circles. But they didn't see how those damn ghost lights affected Logan either.

I notice he hasn't mentioned that. For good reason, I suspect.

"I should go home," Mrs. Park says wearily. "I have some digging to do, and it will look more natural to any observers if I stick to my usual routine."

"I'll give you a ride," Jackson offers.

Mrs. Park favors him with a gentle smile, and in that moment, she resembles Eunsoo so much that I almost start crying. I breathe through it and follow everyone else down the stairs, trying not to make it worse for my friends. Logan touches my arm by the front door, silently asking if I'm okay. I shrug. The answer is "not really," but it's nothing anyone can fix. Before we go, I hug Tamsyn, wave at Derek and Kimala, and follow Logan out to the car.

"Well, everyone is fired up now," he says, starting the Pumpkin.

"I'm sorry this happened to Mrs. Park, but her husband is the tipping point."

Backing out, he gives me a shaded look. "Don't say that in front of her."

"I wouldn't! But you know I'm right. She didn't want to take action against a company she knew was messed up until she lost people close to her. That's how everyone is, but since she works at the lab, this is a unique opportunity."

"Mrs. Park is a person, not an asset. You're not a CIA

operative, and her pain is not an opportunity, Araceli. How can you say that when we don't know if she'll ever see Eunsoo or her husband again?"

"What's with you tonight?" I demand.

"I should be asking you that. To me, it looks like you're treating people's damage as incidental. That you're more interested in getting answers than in making them feel better."

Okay, he's right, and I hate that he is. I got carried away. I was thinking about what connecting with Dr. Perry might let us achieve, not how hurt Mrs. Park is right now, and how much pain Tamsyn has been in for months.

This isn't a game; we're not playing to win. The best we can do might be in offering closure when we crack open the secrets of Fairhaven Lab. I subside into silence as we cross the few miles to my great-aunt's place.

"Fair," I mumble. "I'm sorry."

"Just don't be an asshole in front of other people. Save that especially for me."

I eye him as he pulls into Ottilie's drive. "Why on earth would you want that?"

"Do you really have to ask?"

To be honest, I do. I told him my lice story. I haven't even been that nice to him, so why is Logan like this around me?

Smiling, he puts the car in park. "Because it means you're not putting on a front when you're with me. I prefer you uncut and unfiltered."

I have no idea what to say. Thankfully, Ottilie saves me by flipping the porch light on and peeking out the front door, likely to make sure we're not getting hot and heavy in her Plymouth. I open the door quickly.

"You can put the car away. We trust you. G'night!"

35

Waiting sucks.

The next day, Mrs. Park messages us that she doesn't actually know the password for her husband's laptop, and her guesses resulted in an admin lock, so she's taken the computer to a friend who can probably get into it. In time. She's given me Edward Perry's contact info in group chat. So far, no response.

In movies, people are always like, I must talk to you. We need to meet.

And then the person with the crucial info ends up getting iced.

Ergo, that won't be my first move.

I download an encrypted texting app that promises end-to-end user security with messages that can be set to self-destruct, leaving no trace. While I can't be sure this is foolproof, it's better than a basic service. My parents use this when they need to communicate in countries where data might be compromised, and it's held up for them so far. If Dr. Perry won't download the app and doesn't respond, I'll have to risk less secure channels. For now, though . . .

We met in the woods. It's vital I talk to you ASAP. Use only Telegram. Don't risk regular Wi-Fi, cell towers, or regular email. I'm waiting for you to get in touch. THERE ISN'T MUCH TIME.

I set the message to self-destruct in twenty-four hours.

If he hasn't replied by then, I'll try the direct route, even if it's risky. The lock the lab has on local law enforcement makes me suspect they could easily be spying on people in town.

With all of that going on, you'd think I wouldn't have the mental energy to worry about Oliver, but he sits at the forefront of my mind. The fact that I still haven't heard back from him is terrifying. Oliver might have already seen combat. He might be—

No, I won't think about that. Yeah, Oliver is gone in my time, but he didn't die in the war. I won't let that happen. He has to make it through and go home to look after his little brother, Lester.

Dammit, I keep forgetting to ask for more info about Lester and Lucy. That's the one thing he asked me to do, but I don't know enough to do an internet search for their descendants.

And I need to find these missing people in my time; I only wish I knew more about what's happening, how the lab is turning people into ghosts.

The house is quiet when I get home, which means Great-Aunt Ottilie has gone out for one of her rare afternoon meetings. She's part of a book club, and they get together once a month to discuss what they read. It seems like it's all elderly ladies, half of whom are widowed. I hope they read cheerful books at least. Since she's not home to insist, I skip the afterschool snack. I still have the Mayweather book, and on a whim, I open it to the page where I found the picture of the scene I dreamed at the train station. So wild that I can see Oliver like this, anytime I want—

Holy shit.

It's different than I remember. This time, Oliver is facing the camera instead of looking away, and he's smiling. Like he did in my dream. A chill runs through me as I stare at this old photo. What the hell is happening? Shivering, I check the heartwood box. No matter how many letters Oliver writes, the thrill at finding a new one is always the same. With trembling hands, I pluck it out and unfold the page.

My Dearest Araceli,

You have no idea how it feels to write that and know you're happy to see it. I'm alone here as I never have been in my life, though I'm surrounded by men sharing a common state of misery. We're all alone, waiting for the next explosion, the next engagement. I scan constantly for your face, as if you might be hiding in the bushes along the road.

I have only bad and worse news to report. I killed my first Jerry and threw up afterwards. They called me names and said it would get easier. I'm heartsick that it did.

I don't throw up anymore. Don't feel much of anything except hungry and cold.

It's bad here, worse than anything I could have imagined. There's no glory, and I still don't know why we're fighting. If anyone on our side got a hold of this letter, they'd probably hang me, but since I know I can trust you, I can leave these words in your care. The trenches are filthy, and sometimes our wounded die quietly alongside living men. You don't know they're gone until you shake them, and they drop their guns.

My friend John took one in the gut, bad way to go. Took him hours to go west, and we were all freezing next to his body in the trench during that first long hour of hate. Daisy cutters all over, until our archies took out their bomber.

I can't live like this. You probably think you've heard the bad and the worse, but . . . I took one in the shoulder. Not bad enough for them to ship me home, but it hurts like hell. I'm scared of losing my arm. Medic says no chance of that unless it gets infected, but I'm wallowing in mud, up to my knees, and it's been raining for two days now. I nearly forgot what the sun looks like.

We're dug in here until they send reinforcements. Don't have any idea when that will be, but you asked for the date. It's September 12, 1918. My unit info is written below.

I'll close now because I can't think of anything else to say and the light's going. I'm running out of paper too. You offered to send me little things. I don't know if you have money, sweet girl, but I'd take some chocolate, a few peppermints, a tin of sardines, cigarettes, and a little something that smells like you, unless that's too expensive, too forward, or both.

Think of me as you can.

Yours at heart,
Oliver

Dammit, he's hurt. I should have asked for more information sooner. The cautious part of me that was worried about the butterfly effect is being violently choked by the rest. How much impact can it possibly have on world events if I send a few judiciously timed messages to Oliver?

While I ponder, I pop out to the QuikMart. The stuff Oliver wants isn't too much money, though I'm not sending cigarettes; I might even warn him that they're dangerous and will give him lung cancer. I wonder what he'll make of these modern products. Though he didn't ask for it, I add a tube of antibacterial cream to his stash. Maybe this won't help a bullet wound, but it can't hurt, right?

Pensive, I spray a bit of perfume on a handkerchief, simple floral cotton, but it doesn't look anachronistic. Then I test whether everything fits in the box; it does.

Before I make a conscious decision, I'm cross-referencing

the date Oliver sent, and I find out fast there's a big fight incoming. From the comfort of my bedroom, I can report German troop movements, even tell him what time the attack begins. I don't let myself overthink it. I just scrawl a quick message of support on the top of this intel and then stuff it into the box along with his goodies.

What if they don't believe him? He might just attract attention and end up being interrogated over this. A random grunt having this kind of information will likely raise all kinds of red flags. I hope he's smart about this, but when I open the box five minutes later, already worried about what I've done, the letter and the small bits are gone.

Well, shit. In addition to trying to lead a resistance movement in present day, I'm also meddling in the past. So be it.

Before I can truly start obsessing, though, my phone rings. It's strange for anyone to call me, and I find Logan's number on the ID screen.

"What's up? Something too important for a text?"

"Araceli . . ." His voice sounds strange, wispy and distant.

"Hey, are you okay? I'm coming over."

"I don't know what's happening."

That's sufficiently alarming that I bolt from my room, down the stairs, and out the front door without even putting my shoes on. I don't knock; I just come blazing into his house. Nobody's home but Logan, or his parents would be yelling at me by now.

"Where are you?" I call.

"Bedroom." He doesn't sound any better.

If anything, the reality is worse when I hurry into his room. He's crouched on the floor, and I can see an echo of the ghost light burning beneath his skin. Sick sweat trickles down his temples, and he's shivering from head to toe.

He needs treatment, but what doctor would know how to

fix this? Only the assholes at the lab could help, and they're more likely to let him die and dissect the body for science.

I drop to my knees next to him. "What should I do?"

He shakes his head, trembling too hard to talk. Desperate, I grab his comforter, drag it off the bed, and wrap it around him. This is so wrong. I might as well pat his head and make him tea if I'm trying useless shit.

Logan grabs my hand, and a strange shock passes through me. Not like static, but deeper and more unpleasant. There's an empty feel to it too, as if Logan could vanish entirely if this strange energy devours him from within.

Dammit, we need to talk to Dr. Perry. I've already looked, but the lab doesn't have much of an online presence, certainly no staff listed, and I can't find any records of Dr. Edward Perry. It's like his existence has been scrubbed from the internet, and with this black ops bullshit, I'm not remotely surprised. The contact info Mrs. Park provided leads to a voicemail box, and she only has a work email for Perry. I'm not foolish enough to send a "hey, want to join the resistance" email to the server manned by the evil overlord he works for.

Logan holds onto my hand so tight that my fingers go numb, but I don't let go, even when I feel the nasty burn travel up my arm toward my shoulder. His breathing is so loud and ragged that it reminds me of an asthma attack. Finally, the light shimmers out, leaving normal skin, and Logan curls up on his side, panting hard.

"Bath . . . room," he manages.

I basically drag him there, and he crawls inside, shutting the door in my face. Outside, I pace until he comes out a few minutes later, damp hair, towel around his waist. He's better built than I would've guessed. Focus, not the time.

"Better?" I ask.

"Somewhat. Let me get dressed." He's trying to be positive,

but he still hugs the wall to stay upright to make it back to his room.

Fear wraps icy claws around my throat as I realize this might be how people fade from healthy human to unseen ghost.

Dammit.

We're running out of time.

36

"You should go," Logan says.

I don't want to leave him, but he looks exhausted, and his parents will be home soon. His dad can't be trusted to look after him, but hopefully his mom has an iota of maternal instinct.

I hesitate. I don't feel good about going home with him in this state. "Are you sure?"

He can't manage a smile. "Not really, but there will be drama if you stay. I'm too tired to deal with it. My dad will leave me alone if I don't provoke him."

That statement breaks my heart. With a last, reluctant glance, I limp back across the street to Ottilie's place. There are a bunch of scrapes on the bottoms of my feet, some deep enough to bleed. That's what I get for running off without my shoes. I go into the bathroom to wash up and put Band-Aids on the worst of it. They won't stick if I keep walking around, though, so I put on a pair of socks.

At this point, I'm too tired to want dinner, so I leave Ottilie a note:

Went to bed early. Hope you had fun.

It's almost too much trouble to brush my teeth, but I persist then drag myself up the stairs. As I'm about to climb into bed, the group chat pings with a message from Mrs. Park.

I have access to my husband's laptop and I'm looking through his online accounts. Didn't find anything pertinent saved on local drives.

Thanks for letting us know, I send. Still waiting on word from Dr. Perry.

Damn, I'm aching all over. Dance practice was brutal earlier—and the scare with Logan didn't brighten my day. Hopefully my feet feel better in a day or two, or I won't be able to perform Friday night. Maybe I'm a bad person for caring about that when I have so many problems, but I don't want to let Kimala down. Her vote put me on the squad, and I plan to show up for her like she has for me.

Last thing, I plug my phone in and pull the covers up. I'm out as soon as my head touches the pillow, and . . . Oh shit. There's no rest for the wicked.

Here I stand in the middle of nowhere, nothing but a dirt road and trees and bushes. But in the distance, I hear gunfire. I'm pretty sure I'm standing in what historians call the Western Front. Oliver said he's been trying to wish me up, and here I am.

Last time this happened, I went semi-comatose because I lingered.

Despite realizing this, I still follow the sounds because I can't leave without at least glimpsing Oliver. At this hour, he might be on patrol. I close my eyes because it's no use searching that way. Before, there was a tug, and that's how I found him on the boat. I feel that same pull now, delicate and tenuous, so I move that way and find him standing at the edge of camp in a rumpled uniform.

He looks older now, face filthy and drawn. Killing other humans has left his eyes deep and haunted beneath those thick brows.

This time, I don't have to speak or touch him for him to

register my presence. He whirls when I approach, raising a gun I didn't even realize he was holding. Then he lets out a soft breath.

"You found me again," he whispers. "Let's go, before someone catches you."

I'm not sure if he realizes that nobody would notice, even if I got right up in their faces. Probably best not to test that. Sometimes I wonder if we're both asleep when this happens, so we're meeting across time in our dreams. If that's the case, then he doesn't need to worry about consequences either. I'd rather not risk it.

"Did the information I sent help you?"

He takes my hand in a gentle grip, leading me to a small stand of saplings that will hide us. "Boy, did it ever. They're talking about giving me a commendation."

"How did you explain it?"

"Said I found some papers on a dead Jerry. Luckily, the attack was imminent, and we were scrambling to get ahead of it."

"I'll do my best to keep you safe," I promise.

I can touch him in this dream, so I do. There's no reason to hold back. When he drops his weapon and opens his arms, I slide into them like I belong there. God, he stinks, but even that makes this feel more real.

"Don't worry about me," he whispers. "Just take care of yourself, doll."

If a dude from my time called me that, I'd probably kick him until he fell over, so why does it feel so delicious to hear it from Oliver? I have no rational explanation.

"Did you get my care package?" I ask softly.

He nods, his bristly chin rubbing against the top of my head. "We had ourselves a little party with everything you sent. I'm keeping the peppermints for a special occasion. Oh, I put the ointment on when I can. I think it's helping." His arms tighten on me, and he's using both, so his shoulder can't be too messed up.

"I didn't send the cigarettes because smoking is bad for you. The chemicals could give you lung cancer."

He draws back to stare at me incredulously. "Come again? We're in the middle of a war, but you're worried that smoking is bad for my health?"

"I know it sounds odd. Promise me you'll quit?"

Oliver strokes my hair, half-closing his eyes as if this is the best he's ever felt. Such a small gesture, but it must feel like more to him because attitudes toward physical contact were different then. Holding someone's hand was a major deal, so he's probably not going to kiss me unless I show him a little modern style.

"Fine, sweetheart. I'll give up the gaspers for you. Happy now?"

From context, I can figure out that "gaspers" are cigarettes, but I've never heard that slang before. "It will make kissing better too," I say.

He raises a brow, shock and amusement warring in his expression. The moonlight shows me everything he feels, all the doubt and longing. "Are you trying to get me stirred up?"

In answer, I stretch up on tiptoe and cup his face in my hands; I feel the heat of his skin, the scruff on his chin and jaw. Then I press my mouth to his, light and soft. He drags me closer and kisses me like our lives depend on it, all heat and desperation. I can tell he hasn't done this a lot because he's fierce and clumsy and utterly dear. In soft little movements, I teach him, not something I can say has happened before. We kiss and cling until I can barely breathe.

At last he breaks away, panting, and rests his brow against mine. "I'm not sure I can handle it if anything gets better than that," he whispers.

My heart pounds like a runaway train—no, more like the shells I can hear dropping. That's new. Will I be in danger if I stay? The ground rumbles.

"I don't want to leave you." What happens if I choose not to wake up? I wonder if I'd become real in 1918, or if I'd be a ghost that only Oliver could see. My heart hurts because it feels like I'll be forced to choose—save Logan and Eunsoo in my time, or keep Oliver safe in his. Maybe that's irrational, but it's how I feel. The air smells of pitch and burning, with a tang of decay in the bitter wind.

He kisses my forehead then, such a tender gesture. "Even if you're Resistance, it's not safe for you here. I couldn't go on if anything happened to you, but my God, sweet girl, I'd forgotten anybody could smell this clean and good."

I hold him harder, feeling how thin he is, the jut of his bones against my softness. He was a boy at the train station, but in the time we've been writing, he's become a man far too soon, one whose eyes will never have that same innocence and clarity. He's not alone in that, but Oliver is special. Oh God, I've fallen for him. Such a dumbass thing to do. I need to go back, now, before I'm tempted to stay.

"Did you have the chocolate?" I ask.

"It was incredible. You're like our own Sofia Bruner," he says.

"Who?"

"Legendary German lady spy. She's stolen from two different allied camps now. Without you, I think we might really be suffering." From his tone, he still thinks I'm some Houdini type, capable of amazing sleights of hand and magical beyond reckoning.

Maybe it's easier to cling to that unlikely prospect than to wrestle with more improbable explanations. If he doesn't believe I'm an angel, he must imagine I stowed away on his ship and have been covertly tracking his company across half of France. Shit, I wish I were that girl.

Because then I wouldn't feel the burn of exhaustion. My head wouldn't ache, and I wouldn't be hearing this immense roar in my ears.

"I have to go." Hugging him hard, I reach up to kiss his cheek, and then I take two steps into the darker shadows of the trees.

From behind I hear a man shout, "Where the hell are you, Private? You better not be AWOL, you dumb son of a—"

"Here, Sergeant!" My last glimpse of Oliver is him grabbing his gun and running back the way we came.

I'm in my bed, and my phone is blaring. My alarm is set to get louder if I don't touch it, and now it's screeching at max volume. My arms feel like rubber when I reach to turn it off, and it's impossible for me to get out of bed.

I'm trying, but I just don't have the strength. When I study my fingers, they're trembling. Like this, I can't even let Tía know I'm sick.

Eh, she'll figure it out eventually.

Though I'm no judge of such things, my cheeks feel fever hot while my hands are so cold they hurt, and the chills just keep coming in endless waves. Looks like I'm missing school for the first time here.

I can't bring myself to worry about what might happen in my absence. With a groan, I close my eyes and fall back into the dark.

37

It's late afternoon when I wake. No idea what day.

Ottilie is sitting on the side of the bed, and there's a cool, damp cloth across my forehead, along with various over-the-counter medicines. She lets out a relieved sigh when she sees my eyes are open.

"You're pushing yourself too hard," she chides. "If you're not ready for the SAT next Saturday, you can take it next month."

She thinks I got sick studying too hard? Best to let that misconception stand.

"What day is it?"

Great-Aunt Ottilie laughs like this is a joke. "Very funny. I called the school around noon. It's past five now."

So I didn't lose a full day, at least. That much is good, but the fact that I got physically ill might mean these dream travels are stressing my body too much.

"Thanks for looking after me," I say.

"No need to thank me for that. I'm happy to be needed. It's . . . been a long time." A shadow falls across her face.

Maybe she's remembering the last time her husband was sick and she sat by his bedside. Ottilie gets up with a soft groan.

"When you feel up to it, come down for some chicken soup. A bath probably wouldn't hurt either."

Now that she mentions it, I can smell the sourness of my own skin. Nasty.

She'd probably yell at me if she knew where my priorities lie, though, because once she shuffles out of the room, I snag my phone. Telegram is still silent, much to my dismay, but there are sixty-seven messages in group chat for me to catch up on.

I skim the back log and don't find anything that requires an immediate response, so I make my shaky way downstairs and collapse in a kitchen chair.

"Mission accomplished."

Tía smiles as she serves my soup. "Times like this, I really regret not being able to have children. I wouldn't have been alone after Archibald vanished, and I might even have grandchildren by now."

"It wasn't a choice?"

I'd never really thought about it. There are lots of reasons a married couple might decide not to reproduce, though I guess that choice is probably rarer among the older generation.

She sits across from me, glancing at the empty chair. My skin prickles, a sensation I recognize from the attic and the school. Archibald is here. I'd swear to it.

Wistfully she replies, "Not at all. We tried for years, and I went to various doctors. Never got any good answers. Nowadays they could test us both and pinpoint the problem."

"I'm sorry."

She waves that away, seeming to take pleasure in watching me eat. My stomach feels cavernous. I might be the lone survivor of some dreadful famine, the way it's rumbling as I gulp the food down.

"None of that. I was just thinking out loud, not trying to make you feel bad. Why don't you have a bath? I'll tidy up the kitchen."

"That's my job."

"Not when you're sick. Listen to me or I'll call your mother."

She totally knows how to motivate me. I don't want my parents worrying about me while they're working on the Venezuela story. They might make a deadly mistake because they're concerned about me . . . yeah, no thanks.

I take her advice literally and climb in the bathtub because I think I might pass out if I try to scrub up on my feet. The water fills the tub around me, and I lean back, still exhausted, but at least I'm not ill. I can't skip tomorrow. The group is counting on me to bring Dr. Perry on board.

We can't progress unless that happens.

I stare hard at my phone, and as if I have the power to warp reality, Telegram finally buzzes to life. I accept the request and find myself in a private chat with someone called Imperator.

That must be Dr. Perry. I haven't contacted anyone else using this app. My handle is Cassandra, chosen for the prophetess who warned everyone of impending doom but had been cursed so nobody would ever believe her.

A little on the nose, maybe.

Imperator is typing, then the words appear: This could be a trap.

You know it's not. There's already unrest in the project. They wouldn't go to these lengths to trick you. From what I overheard, you've already established yourself as a dissenter.

Imperator is typing: That's true.

Okay, making progress, I tell myself. Keep it up.

So if they decide you're a liability, they won't bother with an app. You'll most likely be liquidated. Probable, yes or no?

Imperator is typing: Yes. You know WAY too much for someone your age. Are you ready to tell me who you're working for yet?

I stifle a laugh while turning off the tap. This man would die if he knew I'm only a high school girl with an unconventional life in the rearview.

I swear, he really thinks I'm undercover with the NSA or something.

Conversely, here I sit in my great-auntie's bathtub, trying to work out my master plan. I send back: That's confidential. I do have a contact inside but the situation is volatile.

Imperator is typing: Fine, don't tell me.

That's beside the point anyway. You need allies to help you clean up this mess. From my observations, you CANNOT be happy with how this experiment is proceeding.

Imperator is typing: Then convince me it's in my best interests to align with you. I know what I bring to the table. Dazzle me with what you're offering in return.

Dammit, he holds all the cards. I desperately need to learn what he knows, and I barely have what could be considered a glimmer of a plan, let alone a brilliant strategy to entice a scientist of his caliber. I'm assuming he's a genius anyway, if he's the second in command at a top-secret lab.

Let me say, I do not want to get on this man's bad side. Which makes what I'm about to do even riskier.

When you're a holding a shit hand and you can't afford to lose, what's your best option? Time to bluff.

I send back: I don't have clearance to tell you who I'm working for, but did you hear about the protests in Sudan? Let's just say, I have ties to the people who made that happen.

(Sorry, Ma and Papi. I'm taking credit for your work.)

If that's not enough, I've also got people in town, willing to do anything to correct this course.

Hopefully I'm selling this well, selling it hard, because Dr. Perry needs to believe we have the power to back him up. He won't spill his secrets unless I'm convincing as hell.

Imperator is typing: Anyone can talk big on the internet. Let's hear something about Sudan that only someone who was inside would know.

This is easy; I just need to tell him the worst thing that's ever happened to me, something that gave me nightmares for years after.

I was young at the time, and for my parents' sake, I pretend I don't remember, but the truth is, it's all in my head like it was burned there.

Dust, desert wind blowing across the square. I'm on my mother's hip. The kids are protesting, shouting, waving signs.

A shot rings out. The student leader goes down, bleeding from his head, and it's all mayhem, all running and screaming. The buildings burn bright in the relentless sun. We're hiding behind a car, and Papi is pleading with me not to cry.

With grim resolve, I send him that account. There's no doubt I was on the ground in the plaza that day. Then I play my final card, going all in.

What you'll never find on the news is, the sniper wasn't an insurgent. He was American, planted to foment unrest.

At least, that's what Papi said, and I've never known him to get his facts wrong. Something about oil rights and destabilizing the region. I wait, hardly daring to breathe.

Imperator is typing . . .

38

Dr. Perry sends, Give me twenty-four hours to think about it. If I commit to working with you, things will escalate fast. There will be no going back.

Understood, I reply. I'll talk to you here, this time tomorrow.

Then I exit the app and finish my bath. If I don't hurry, Great-Aunt Ottilie will think I fell asleep and drowned. Sure enough, after I finish scrubbing up and rinsing my hair, a knock sounds.

"Are you all right in there?"

"Fine." I pull the plug and let the water start draining.

Bathrobes are towels for lazy people, and I shrug into mine with dwindling reserves. With the last of my energy, I say good night and haul myself up the stairs. Ottilie changed my sheets while I was downstairs, and they feel crisp and cool when I slide into bed.

This time when I sleep, there are no dreams, and I wake feeling nearly human. There's a residual throb in my temples, so I pop a headache pill along with my quick breakfast. Hopefully all my neurons will be firing by lunchtime. I haven't updated the group on my progress with Dr. Perry yet, and it'll be safer to do that in person.

To my surprise, Tía gets up as I check my backpack. "Are you feeling better?" she asks.

"Mostly. Thanks again for taking care of me."

"My pleasure. Do you have dance practice today?"

"I . . . think so." My answer is none too confident because I've lost track of what day it is. Maybe my connection to the past means my link to the present is slipping.

"Well, take it easy. I'm sure the leader of your dance troupe will understand."

I stifle a smile at her verbiage, but I don't correct her. "See you after school."

The walk wakes me up a little, though I'm watching for Logan's bike as the blocks go by. No sign of him yet as I get to school—the first bell rings as I climb the steps. His bike isn't at the rack either.

Now I'm worried, remembering the burning beneath his skin. Maybe he walked to school or his mom dropped him off. I rush to first period, and my knees nearly give way when I spot him slumped at his desk.

He doesn't look great, no better than I feel, but he's here at least.

I take my seat right before Mr. Timmons gets to class, so there's no chance to talk to Logan before the lesson begins. Idly, I notice that Jeff's desk is empty. He seems like the type to skip early and often.

Because I'm in a hurry for lunch to arrive, the morning drags on forever.

Finally, I can head to the cafeteria to brief everyone, but in my haste, I'm first to arrive at the table, so I get to wait more. People show up slowly, and when we're all seated, I say, "I got in touch with Dr. Perry."

"What's our next move?" Tamsyn asks.

"He asked for twenty-four hours to consider his options. I'll find out what he plans to do tonight."

Jackson sighs. "So he didn't tell you anything useful?"

"Not yet. He's being cagey."

"It was a long shot anyway," Derek says. "Why would he team up with us?"

"At least he knows we're not corrupt," Kimala suggests.

"I played a hidden card," I say. "I'll explain more later, if it actually works."

They all nod, then Tamsyn speaks. "We're trusting you."

No pressure.

Jackson stabs at his salad with a fork, carefully not looking at Eunsoo's empty chair. "This is pointless. Even if he tells us everything, what the hell can we do?" More pessimism, excellent. If this were a horror movie, Jackson would die first.

Logan has been quiet this whole time, his face wan and weary. "Whatever we can. Right now, we don't know what we're dealing with, but it would be a mistake to quit before we start."

"Easy for you to say," Derek mutters. "If shit gets real, you're the sheriff's son. You think you get shot along with the rest of us?"

I see Derek's point. While things are shitty between Logan and his dad, I have a tough time imagining Sheriff Reed would let his son be taken out by Fairhaven goons. Bribery can only go so far, and that does give Logan a safety net the rest of us don't possess.

Tamsyn says, "Let's not argue. We don't even have our inside man on board yet."

"Soon." At least I hope so.

Group chat shows a message from Mrs. Park: They're watching my house. Two men, black Ford SUV. Be careful, all of you. If I disappear, please don't give up on finding Eunsoo. I can't breathe for a second. That's a mother's love right there. This woman has lost so much, and she's scared to death, but she's still focused on her daughter. My mom loves me that way too, and I wish I could call her.

"Damn," Kimala whispers. "What do we even say?"

Jackson sends, We won't give up. Stay inside. Stay safe.

The rest of the day drags. I feel like putting a doom clock on my phone. At 6:16 p.m. I will find out whether my ploy worked.

Turns out, I was right about dance team practice, so I show up for that and try to bring my A game, but my heart's not in it. Lana even yells at me, which almost never happens. Normally, she's robot-girlfriend levels of fake cheerful.

"Do you want to sit out tomorrow night?" she demands. "Do you?"

Tomorrow night . . . is our first performance. Right.

Silently I shake my head. A few girls smirk, and I feel bad because this reflects on Kimala. When she comes up to me after squad practice, I brace for an outpouring of wrath, but she hugs me instead.

"I know there's a lot going on, I'm scared for Eunsoo too— and hell, all of us, really—but you need to learn to focus. Otherwise, one part of your life will bring the rest down."

I hug her back. "I'll work on it."

"Try to keep it together."

It's not easy, especially when Kimala only knows a portion of what I'm dealing with, but I can't talk about Oliver with anyone now that Eunsoo is gone. Maybe that is illogical, but it feels like the universe punished my friend for what I did. I can't take the risk with Kimala. Plus, she might not even believe me. If I lose credibility, the group won't listen when it comes to working with Dr. Perry and exposing the lab's dire practices—whatever they are.

"I'll be fine by tomorrow," I say.

A bold claim, one I hope I can uphold. With a wave, I hurry off to the locker room for a quick shower. I still don't feel great. My stomach is a little queasy, and I'm more tired than I should be from exertion. Other dance team members are chatting around me, but their words blur together into a noise cocktail.

At this rate, I'll get a reputation for being stuck-up, but I can't force myself to socialize today. I step out into the empty hallway, my hair still damp, and a familiar chill sweeps over me.

I'm not alone.

No phantom touch brushes my skin this time, but I know someone—something?—is watching me. I spin slowly in the corridor. Relief breaks over me like a wave when I spot Logan's figure, silhouetted by the sunlight behind him.

"You waited for me? What's up?" I walk toward him, but as I get closer, I can see something is distinctly *not right*.

What I took for a halo of sunlight is more of that eerie internal glow, but it's not just beneath his skin. The phosphorescent flicker burns all around him, brighter and brighter, until it hurts my eyes.

His mouth moves, but I can't hear him speak. This brightness hurts, forcing me to angle my head, but I keep moving toward him. Last time I saved him. I can do it again, right? I just need to get there.

But it feels like I'm walking through water; the air is heavy and thick, and I can barely focus. I try to run, but my legs are leaden. The world goes white for an instant, whirling with ghost lights, and when I can see again, the hallway is empty.

Logan is gone.

39

I have to tell someone.

Kimala—she's calm in a crisis. My heart is racing so hard that it hurts, and I'm so scared I can't think. Sprinting back the way I came, I check the locker room first. She's not there. Maybe still in the gym?

Yeah, there she is, wrapping up a conversation with the squad coach. I pace and try not to pass out from hyperventilation until the woman leaves. Finally, I rush over to Kimala and start babbling.

"I saw it, oh my God, Kimala. I saw it. I know how people disappear. I saw him vanish."

She grabs my shoulders, giving me a little shake. "Slow down, breathe. You saw who vanish? Wait, Eunsoo's dad? You should have said something sooner!"

"No, Logan, just now. He's gone. Just . . . gone." I drop to a squat because I'm light-headed with reaction.

Kimala crouches next to me to peer into my face with dark, worried eyes. "Did you hit your head? You're freaking me out. Who's Logan?"

What. The. Hell.

"Logan Reed. He sits at our table at lunch, lives across the street from me."

Nobody could fake the blank look she's giving me. "I have no idea who you're talking about."

Before, people vanished, but their loved ones remembered them. This time, it's like Logan has been . . . erased. I tip over and hit the gym floor, fighting the urge to curl up in the fetal position. I wasn't fast enough. I saw what happened to Logan before, and when Dr. Perry asked for more time, I should have persuaded him then. Maybe if I'd gotten the answers yester-day . . .

I could have saved him.

"Come on, get up. If you keep acting like this, Ms. Lovett might catch you and demand a drug test."

Numbly, I let Kimala pull me to my feet. She herds me out of the school and puts me in her car. I guess she doesn't trust me to get home on my own.

"Could you take me somewhere else?" I ask.

She frowns at me, but she's worried, not annoyed. "Where do you think you're going, acting like this?"

"Please. It's important. I promise I'll text you when I take care of this, and then once I get home too."

The meeting with Dr. Perry will go down in less than two hours, but I don't need to be at home for that. As long as I have a cell signal, it will be fine. I give Kimala a pleading look, and she reluctantly drops me off a few streets away. At the turnoff to the path that leads to Logan's tree house.

This time, I don't have any trouble making the turns. There's plenty of daylight, and I recall all the landmarks he specified. The walk takes me fifteen minutes, but when I locate the thick-trunked tree where his fort should be, there's absolutely no sign of it. No wood construction, no strands of solar lights.

I sit at the base of the tree and rest my head against the bark. Before, shock had me too startled to cry, but I'm bawl-ing now, hot tears that scald my cheeks sliding down. My throat hurts and my nose is running, and it seems like nobody in the world remembers him but me.

Why is this happening?

I wish I could just curl up on my side and go to sleep, but these woods aren't safe. With a groan, I drag myself to my feet and trudge to my great-aunt's house, futility dogging my steps like a mocking child. Not only did I fail to save Logan, it might be argued that this is my fault. I insisted on doing recon, and when the ghost lights got him in the woods, it was because of me.

I pass a few people working in their yards, but this isn't the kind of town where people call out greetings. Strangers are met with wary stares, and I'm conscious of hard eyes watching me as I go. Outside Tía's house, I stand on the sidewalk, staring at the Reed place.

Ottilie steps out onto the porch, wrapping a cardigan around her thin frame. "Brr, I can feel autumn in the air. I should make cider this winter. Do you like it?"

I am in no mood for small talk. "How well do you know your neighbors, Tía?"

"Which ones?"

"The sheriff across the street."

"The Reeds keep to themselves," she says. "I don't know how he got elected. I never voted for him, but he must have powerful backers."

"Do they have a big family?" I've learned my lesson about asking directly about Logan, but I need to verify. I feel like if I ask the right question, I'll get the answer I want.

"It's just the two of them. Why?"

"So they never had any kids."

"I just said that, Araceli. You're acting strange. Maybe I shouldn't have let you go to school today. Are you feverish again?" She touches my forehead and eyes me in surprise. "You're so cold. Let's get you inside."

I let her pull me into the house, utterly convinced. That

exchange with Kimala wasn't a fluke. Logan has been freaking wiped from existence.

I eat dinner in a fog and retreat upstairs to nurse my wounds. Get it together. Maybe it's not too late. Dr. Perry is Logan's only hope now.

A bitter laugh escapes me when I realize I don't have Wi-Fi anymore. It's such a small thing, but of course the password Logan gave me for his family network doesn't work, because he doesn't exist anymore.

My cell signal is best in the attic, and that's where I'm least likely to be interrupted while meeting with Dr. Perry. Only ten minutes to go. I can't wait, so I log into the app early.

Imperator is already in the chat. Guess he's impatient too.

Me: Did you make up your mind?

Imperator is typing: I needed to check some things at the lab, confirm if my worst suspicions are correct.

Me: And?

Imperator: There's no hope of salvaging my work. She'll kill me before she lets me take it, and I'm not letting her finish this as she intends.

Me: If you haven't burned your bridges at the lab, why were you hiding in the woods that day?

I have a theory, and I'm curious what he'll say.

Imperator: I took a few vacation days to track the research teams. I suspected Sofia was fudging the numbers she showed me, and I confirmed that through personal observation. You should know, this will get messy before the end.

Yeah, I'm prepared for that. I've already lost people. Seems like everyone in this town has. And his answer squares with what I expected. I mean, I didn't know about the fake statistics, but I guessed he was spying on his own people for some reason. Smart of him not to give evidence of his defection or he'd be dead.

Me: I'm ready. Are you prepared to burn some bridges?

Imperator: I am. Is it strange that I'm both deeply proud of my work and profoundly ashamed of the way it's been twisted? I should have acted sooner, but the last time I tried, they killed my contact. At least I assume so. His family still hasn't found his body. Please be careful.

Shit. Well, this isn't a game. I understood the stakes even before Logan disappeared. I tell myself my parents would be proud of me for staying the course, but in reality, they'd probably pull me out of here so fast my head would spin.

Since I'm bluffing, I might as well go big. I send: Don't worry, my cover is intact. Nobody would suspect me. I even joined the dance team.

Imperator: Good thinking. Do your best to blend in.

I strangle a bubble of hysterical laughter. Yup, doing my best. Typical American teen here. What is up, fellow kids?

It's funny that both Dr. Perry and Oliver think I'm a spy— for varying reasons. Maybe that's my true calling after all.

God, Logan, I'm sorry.

My head is such a mess; I need to wrap up this conversation before I slip up. I don't kid myself that Dr. Perry will stick around if he realizes that my "assets" are regular high school students and a physicist currently on mental health leave from Fairhaven. I throttle the surge of guilt when I consider that I might be endangering Dr. Perry.

I send: Don't worry about that. There's a reason I was chosen for this mission.

Wish I knew what that was.

Imperator: Understood. Uploading files pertaining to the project to this server. Setting a five-minute destruct on the data, so act fast. Once you're up to speed, we'll talk more. This time tomorrow?

Count on it, I answer.

As soon as the files arrive—and they are *big*—I d
them. My data connection may not be secure, but I'm
ing on Telegram to keep us hidden, hopefully long enoug
strike against Fairhaven.

I'm finally getting answers in 3, 2, 1 . . .

40

If you are reading this material, you have been approved for level five clearance on Project Paradox.

Historical overview:

The initial theory for the project was proposed in 1903 by a German scientist, Dr. Hans Weber. He posited that it was possible to send inorganic matter across time. This theory was rejected by Dr. Weber's colleagues and resulted in him leaving the faculty of Heidelberg University to attempt to prove his theory alone.

Dr. Weber retreated to a family farmhouse outside of Stuttgart and devoted himself to his work. Despite many setbacks and struggling in poverty, he perfected the first prototypes in 1909. His assistant, Frau Schmidt, took one box, and Dr. Weber tested his technology by placing a letter in it and setting the time shift for two years later. At first, the test was presumed a failure, as the letter immediately vanished and seemingly went missing for the next two years. It reappeared in his assistant's possession two years later.

He shared this result with former colleagues and potential investors—to no avail. Frustrated by the lack of support in his netherland, he moved to New York in 1912 to find investors. With unrest in Europe, US investors were unwilling to support German ingenuity. This was a heavy blow to his scientific career, and Dr. Weber was further set back when one of his prototypes went missing from his room at the Algonquin Hotel. The First World War disrupted Dr. Weber's research until his death in 1929. He died destitute, completely discredited by his peers.

In 1947, Dr. Fredrick Winslow stumbled upon an old journal containing Dr. Weber's notes and equations. Winslow became obsessed with finding the old prototypes, and he scoured the countryside for Weber's descendants to no avail. In 1950, Winslow founded Project Paradox, determined to start the work from scratch if necessary. He quickly recruited the brightest minds of the time, pulling researchers and scientists from quantum mechanics and theoretical physics.

Unlike Weber, Winslow came from an affluent family. Winslow's family profited from both World Wars, and he poured the funds into a robust think tank to solve the time travel paradox. In 1955, Winslow located one of the prototypes in the possession of Dr. Weber's grandson. Winslow procured the box and studied its inner mechanics to see if he would be able to re-create a bigger one capable of transporting organic matter.

Dr. Winslow died in 1979. His research and experiments reached a dead end, leading to an unfortunate addiction to hallucinogenic drugs, which he took with the mistaken belief they would help him unlock the secrets of time travel. His son, Lawrence, had no interest in his father's research and sold all the equipment along with his documentation to a German company founded by Sofia Bruner.

In conjunction with an international scientific initiative, Dr. Bruner partnered with local magnate E. G. Mayweather to establish what is publicly known as Fairhaven Labs, believed to be researching communicable diseases but, in

...ity, Fairhaven is the home of Project Paradox. She recruited Dr. Edward Perry in 1995. Together, they worked to
refine the ideas first proposed by Dr. Hans Weber in 1903. In
1998, they built the first portal prototype and began testing
on animal subjects.

My eyes widen as I keep reading. They've apparently got
machinery, devices of some kind, installed all over the woods.
The swamp too. There are pages and pages of data readings,
energy spikes like those scientists were talking about, and I
can't begin to make sense out of the equations scrolling on my
phone.

It's not a weapon. It's time travel. So . . . the people who are
vanishing, the question isn't where are they . . . but when?

That means there's a chance we can bring them back,
right? Provided they're still alive in whatever time stream. I'm
guessing the ghost lights have something to do with the experiments too and the field they're trying to generate.

What's the point of that? The endgame must be big. Dr.
Perry said he's not on board with what his boss wants to do . . .
Is he still working for Sofia Bruner?

Where have I heard that name before?

Wait . . . I can't be right, and if I am, it must be a coincidence. Still, I run downstairs to riffle through the letters
Oliver has sent me and don't find anything. Damn, why can't
I—oh. He mentioned her in a dream . . . Sofia Bruner, legendary German spy.

It's a coincidence, right? If she was spying during the First
World War, there's no way she's still alive. It's hard to imagine
she'd be healthy enough to found a company in the nineties.
She couldn't still be working on the project.

I have so much information crashing together in my head
that it takes a minute for it to sink in. This box that I found

in the spare room, it must be the missing prototype. If I smash it, I'm sure I'd find more than wood framework inside.

Smashing it means never talking to Oliver again. He's still relying on me for intel, so I can't do that. This thing took Dr. Weber six years to perfect; it's not just a random memento holder. How the hell did Oliver get this, anyway?

I scrutinize the box, and this time, I notice that the fabric on the top is loose. Gently, I peel it back and find a switch and a dial. Oh my God. The switch just flicks from left to right . . . that's . . .

Oh. I know. I think Oliver and I own the same box—in different times. If the switch is set here, the item goes straight over. If I flip it, I bet I could send something to the other prototype, sort of a pair or dupe transmission. The dial just has numbers from one to ninety-nine, so that probably controls when your item arrives.

That means I could write to Dr. Winslow. Or Dr. Weber, if I change the settings.

I wonder if a warning would work, if it would be enough. I could ask Dr. Winslow not to let his son sell his stuff to Sofia Bruner. For a moment, I wonder why Dr. Perry hasn't tried this, but who knows, maybe he has. Or possibly he doesn't have access to the first prototype. The box might be kept under the tightest security, locked away in some vault.

I have so many questions for Dr. Perry.

This box is way more than a way for me to contact Oliver. It might be the key to saving all those people who've been sucked into the time slippage. That's what I'm calling it anyway since I'm not physics savvy. There's probably a technical term like quantum singularity or something.

Well, I do have one person I can turn to right now. Before, when I was researching World War I, I saw how France is still scarred to this day. There remain miles of trenches and barbwire, tons of undetonated shells. The aftermath laid waste to much of the country, left it uninhabitable. To this day, the soil is still full of arsenic. Only trained personnel can pass into the Zone Rouge, French for the red zone.

Time to write a letter to the heart of that hell.

My Dearest Oliver,

I'm always thinking of you. Pressing problems are keeping me busy, and I don't know what will happen if I can't solve them.

Please, can you tell me how you found our box? I'm sure now; we have the same one. This is more important than you know. I also need to find out everything you know about Sofia Bruner. This isn't a casual question, dig among the other soldiers if you have to.

It was so good to be with you. I wish . . . so many things. I don't know if I should tell you more than I have.

Part of me thinks you need to know, even if it spoils some of the magic between us, so I'll leave the question here. Would you rather learn the answer to a puzzle, even if it meant life lost a little of the wonder? If you say the word, I'll spill all my secrets to you. I trust you.

And I miss you.

I'm closing with more troop movements that I hope will keep you safe. Tell your superiors right away. My intel is indisputable.

Yours at heart,
Araceli

41

My Dearest Araceli,

I can tell you were in a hurry the last time you wrote. If I ever find myself in a town that hasn't been bombed to rubble, I plan on buying you a ring. No matter how complicated things are, I'll wait for you.

I don't care if you're a spy. I don't even care if you're German because you're helping me through this. Our whole unit would've been blown off the map if you hadn't sent me that info.

I'm starting to get a reputation. They invited me to the officer's mess last night, and I hear I'm being promoted. I don't do grunt work anymore. The lieutenant keeps me close, and I run errands for him. It's better than being down in the dirt.

Funny you should ask about the box. My old man bought it as a gift for my mother at a little junk shop around the corner from the Algonquin Hotel. They both took the influenza in '15, it almost got Lester too. I think I might have mentioned that? It's hard for me to remember what I've said. All they left for us was a few clothes and that treasure box. Might've given it to Lucy when we got married if she'd said yes, but that wasn't meant to be.

Now, I could buy that girl a basket of posies because I

owe her one. There's no way I'm meant to be with anyone but you.

You asked about Sofia Bruner, so I looked into it, but it's all fish stories around camp. This one dumb doughboy said she's a witch and can vanish at will. When I heard that, I thought about you. Sorry I can't help. It seems like it might be important.

I thought about your question. Do I want to know the secret even if it spoils the magic? My answer is yes, especially if it's about you. There's nothing you could say that would drive me off.

I don't know how you did it, maybe you're a witch after all, but I'm so wild about you that the world I live in is starting to feel empty, and it doesn't help that death is everywhere, piles of bodies, endless mortars, and the drone of German guns. I haven't had fresh food in a week. I ate one of the peppermints you sent, held it in my mouth for an hour, remembering that your kisses taste twice that sweet. I kissed your lips and your forehead last night, and you left me wanting more. I shouldn't write this down, but I have racier ideas in my head. Sometimes they keep me awake at night, a distraction from the shells.

They're sending us toward the Argonne to meet up with a few more companies. We're all down good men. I've seen so many men I trained with die.

You told me not to think dark thoughts, but it's hard, doll.

I'm fighting for you now . . . and to come home to you one day.

My love always,
Oliver

I don't realize I'm crying until the tear trickles over my lip. It slips onto the page, so I clutch it to my chest. He shouldn't love me. There's no way for him to come home to me, and it will destroy Oliver when I write back with the answer to that question. He wants to know the truth. I don't want to tell him.

Only one of us can get our way.

It would be terrible of me to leave him waiting for me his whole life. For so many reasons, I need to let him go and say goodbye.

Not yet. Not tonight.

I do a quick search online to see what I can find about the next major battle, and when I start reading, fear coils like a snake in the pit of my stomach. Seventy-seventh Battalion, behind enemy lines and cut off from reinforcements. Food was scarce, water only obtainable by crawling through heavy German fire to a nearby stream. It was a grueling battle, but they held their ground against all odds and even faced the additional danger of friendly fire bombardment.

Five hundred fifty-four men went into the Argonne forest, believing they were braced on either side by French and American troops. They pushed forward, not realizing the French forces had been stalled and were surrounded by German soldiers. All runners sent were lost in the woods or fell to enemy patrols. A grueling six-day battle followed. Despite the hardships, the brave men of the 77th, many of whom had been pulled off the streets, caused enough of a distraction the Germans were forced to retreat.

Commander Charles Whittlesey is said to have sent the following message by the pigeon Cher Ami: WE ARE ALONG THE ROAD PARALEL 276.4. OUR ARTILLERY IS DROPPING A BARRAGE DIRECTLY ON US. FOR HEAVENS SAKE STOP IT.

The Germans shot down that poor bird, but he got in the air again, somehow, and delivered the message. Cher Ami had been shot in the chest, lost an eye, his leg hanging by a thread when he arrived at his destination. Talk about unlikely heroes.

One hundred ninety-seven men died. One hundred and fifty were captured. Only one hundred ninety-four made it out alive, rescued by Allied forces.

I must make sure Oliver is among them. Somehow. I don't want to let him go, but he can't be with me. Not really. And digging down for a little selflessness, I do want him to be happy. I wish for him all the beautiful things that are waiting on the other side of war. He's too young to die in a forest thousands of miles from home.

So many soldiers were.

At this point, I'm carrying too much mental weight. Logan is gone. Oliver is in danger.

My remaining friends are counting on me to come up with a workable plan now that Dr. Perry is on board. It's too much, and I freaking want my mom. I curl up on the floor near my bed and cry silently, until my head aches and my eyes are swollen. That choice I dreaded before, it's creeping up on me. I can hear the grim soundtrack in my head.

If Project Paradox has perfected the portal tech, there might be a path I could take that leads to Oliver, but it would mean leaving my family forever and abandoning everyone who trusts me here. Maybe I think too highly of myself, but it feels like if I step out of the picture, all the balls I have in motion will drop.

Dr. Perry can't do this alone or he'd have acted by now.

Tonight, I can't write back to Oliver. The upcoming battle is so major that I can't tell him to advise his superiors to ignore the order to push when it comes. There's a limit even when you've established yourself as a credible source.

How would he find out the French unit won't be able to keep up? That's prognostication, not intel.

Really, I don't want to think about any of this anymore. Logan's loss is fresh, and I'm trying to stay hopeful. I can bring him back, somehow, along with all the others who have gone missing because of Project Paradox.

Need to ask Dr. Perry about that too.

Quitting isn't an option, though. I've come too far. I get on group chat, where they've been buzzing anxiously for over half an hour.

Tamsyn: Did you talk to EP?

Me: I did. Before I brief you, can I show you something, Mrs. Park?

Mrs. Park: I'm not sure if my connection is secure. Is it classified?

Well, crap. She's an actual physicist, but our access to her is limited, and I suspect the lab goons would think it's weird if her daughter's friends come over all the time, even after the girl went missing. On the bright side, as long as they're just watching Mrs. Park, it probably means she's safe.

Me: Okay, new plan. Besides Mrs. P, who's the best at physics?

Derek: My money's on Jackson.

Jackson: B+ last grading period. What's up?

Me: It would be better if you came over.

I'd ask him to use Telegram but talking about an encrypted app on an unsecure channel is a good way to get busted. My parents always have a lo-fi backup when they're working with a source, so it's less suspicious if Jackson drops by.

Nothing to see here, we are average high school students, absolutely no plotting against top secret labs in this house.

Jackson: Give me fifteen minutes. You live at Old Lady Groening's, right?

Tamsyn: Should the rest of us come too?

I think about that, then send: No, an organized meeting will draw more attention, and the sheriff is right across the street, remember?

Derek: Right. Keep us posted.

42

Jackson takes more like half an hour, so he shows up right at dinnertime.

That means Tía won't hear of us going upstairs to "study" until she feeds him a bowl of leftover chicken soup. It's the pot she made when I was sick, but she's frugal and we eat food until it's gone around here.

It's so strange sitting here with Jackson when I remember having Logan over for dinner. My great-aunt doesn't recall or she'd be teasing me, I suspect.

Finally, I wash the dishes while Jackson chats with my aunt. Unlike Logan, he doesn't offer to help me. That's probably because he likes Eunsoo, even if she's MIA, and he's only here to evaluate the equations I got from Dr. Perry.

I drag him up to my room as soon as possible and present my phone. "You can make a copy if you want, but let's use a Bluetooth connection."

"You're seriously paranoid," he mutters, but he follows along.

Once he has the data on his device, all the color drains out of his face. "This . . . is this for real?"

"That's what I'm asking you."

"It's not like I can solve this in a glance, dude. I'm not Stephen Hawking."

"Does it look credible, though?" While I don't think Dr.

Perry would have sent me a dummy file, a second opinion would be nice.

"I'll take the equations home to study them, but this whole story is wild. You read the overview, right?"

I nod, hesitating. Can I trust him with this? No choice. I need to bring someone in, and Jackson is here. Since I don't know him that well, this feels like a risk.

Before I can think better of it, I pick up the treasure box. "See this? It's one of the prototypes." I peel back the red velvet to show him the old-fashioned apparatus. "This is the box that went missing from Dr. Weber's hotel room at the Algonquin."

Jackson stares at me, eyes narrowed. "How do you have this?"

"It was in my great-aunt's junk room. If you're wondering how she got it, I don't know." I'd rather not ask either, because I don't want to draw her attention to it. She might start asking questions around town, thinking it's harmless, and the next thing we know, she's missing like my great-uncle.

Jackson hefts the box, and by the calculating look in his eyes, he's contemplating cracking it open to see the inner workings. I snatch it away and clutch it to my chest, aware I'm being irrational.

"We can't open it up. That might ruin the functionality. I need to ask Dr. Perry about it when we talk tomorrow night."

"Maybe we can use it somehow," Jackson says. "If the more modern experiments are using the same basic equations—"

"Then the box might help us find the devices buried around the facility," I finish.

"Okay, you win. I won't break it if you think it will be useful."

I doubt he'd be swayed if I told him I need the heartwood box so I can keep someone alive during WWI.

"This is all so messed up," I mumble.

"I knew the town had problems, but this . . ." Jackson shakes his head. "We have to shut that shit down, starting with those field generators."

"From what I've seen, it won't be easy. They have guards who patrol even outside the fences, and the scientists take regular readings too. In hazmat suits, which makes me feel not great about touching the equipment unprotected."

"Then we need DIY hazmat suits. It's doable. I'll do some research on it. Anything else you want to discuss while you have my undivided attention?" In anyone else, I'd take this for flirtation, but Jackson is all about Eunsoo.

"Now that you mention it . . . I don't know how techy you are, but I'd like to know where Sheriff Reed goes. I have an old cell phone, could you do anything with that?"

"How old is the phone? Flip or smart?"

"It's a really old smart phone, low-level Android." It's sentimental, but this is the first phone my parents ever bought me. I'll never throw it away, but I could sacrifice it if it means getting the jump on our enemies.

"Then we can install a GPS locator app and link it to your current device. Use your new phone to track your old phone."

"That is . . . surprisingly clever."

I guess I was expecting him to cannibalize my old cell for parts, but this is way simpler. It doesn't take long to charge it up, and he finds an app that will do the job.

"Here we go. There's also an app that can serve as a listening device, for as long as the phone is charged."

I nod. "Let's install that too. We might learn something before the battery dies."

"Does the SIM have any data that can connect it to you if they find it later?"

Good question. "It's a prepaid one from Argentina, so I

don't think so. I'm not sure how much airtime is left, so we may not have a signal for long."

"I think it's worth a try," Jackson says.

I agree. At this point, we need to know as much about the enemy as we can. "Now for the hard part."

"Getting it into his car?"

I nod. "You want to handle infiltration or distraction?"

"Distraction. I'm a good talker, not so much with feats of stealth and speed."

After affixing a piece of double-sided sticky tape to my old cell phone, I say, "Let's do this."

I lead the way. Great-Aunt Ottilie is in the parlor watching a movie, so she doesn't hear us slip through the kitchen and out the back door.

"I'll ring the bell. Wait until someone answers to make your move." Jackson gives me a little shove.

It's not quite full dark, and the neighbors are always watchful. Doesn't matter, I'm doing this. I stay in the shadows as best I can, picking a path across the road. My heart's pounding like mad as I press up against the exterior garage wall.

Jackson comes over then, boldly striding up to the front door. I hear the bell ring, and then he says cheerfully, "Sheriff Reed! I'm Jackson Pruitt. You don't know me, but I'm writing an essay about my personal heroes, and I was hoping I could ask you a few questions. I'm interested in finding out how I could pursue a career in law enforcement too, if you don't mind sparing me some time."

Wow, he's good.

A bass rumble comes in response, and it seems like Jackson is being ushered inside. Now's my chance. I hug the wall, inching toward the back door. Locked. I should have figured. There are windows, though, and one of them isn't shut completely.

I get a stick and wedge it in, levering upward as fast and quiet as I can. Sweat rolls down my back while I work, despite the cool autumn air. Just need a little more . . .

Got it.

I drop the stick and pull the window open, then use all my dance flexibility to wriggle through, narrowly avoiding all the tools and various car-care bottles stacked on the shelf below. I dive forward, tuck and roll smoothly onto the floor. Too bad nobody saw that—even I'm slightly impressed.

Hurriedly I close the window behind me and tiptoe to the squad car. Since the garage was locked tight, the car door isn't. No alarms sound as I open it; I wedge the cell phone beneath the driver's seat and use the sticky tape to keep it in place.

Done.

I can't let Jackson stay in there forever, so I close the door silently and sneak out the back door, which opens from within and locks behind me.

I take two steps toward the yard and a woman's voice freezes me in my tracks. "What are you doing in our yard?" This must be Mrs. Reed. Used to be Logan's mom.

I turn slowly. "Helping my friend look for her lost cat. Have you seen a ginger tabby?"

"No, I have not," she says coldly. "You should get home now. It's getting dark."

"I will. Sorry to bother you."

I take the long way back to my great-aunt's house, trembling so hard I might throw up. Once I hit the porch, I send a message to Jackson: MISSION CLEAR.

43

It's the middle of the night, and I should be sleeping.

Jackson left shortly after we planted the cell phone, and I can't stop thinking about Logan. About Oliver. About Eunsoo, her father, and Tamsyn's brother, Ronell. Insomnia made me check the eavesdropping app, so here I am, listening to the sheriff drive.

Sheriff Reed left his wife sleeping, and now he's on his way to what I can only presume to be a secret meeting. I can hear the roar of the engines through the phone. He's been driving for a while, muttering to himself, so it seems like this is a sudden request, rather than a regular check-in.

Since the phone is under the driver's seat, I can hear the tires on the pavement too, and I register the shift from smooth asphalt to a gravel road. The loose stones ping against the undercarriage, making for strange reverb in my earbuds. I hope it doesn't echo in the old phone speakers, but I'm banking on the ambient noise to drown any strange sounds out.

I hear the engine cut off and Reed sits for a while in the quiet car. Eventually the car door opens, and someone climbs inside. A woman says, "What the hell are you doing, Reed? First, it was trespassers near the facility, and now your man lost Edward. I have no idea what he was doing . . . or with whom. It was a simple surveillance job! I told you to keep eyes on him at *all* times."

Crap. They're already suspicious of Dr. Perry.

"This is absolute bullshit. My manpower is limited, and I don't work for you. The deputies are already asking awkward questions. I can't do more than I already have." The sheriff sounds angry, not a shock, considering that she dragged him out at this hour.

I wonder who this is? Could it be Sofia Bruner?

"Then you should answer them with a cut of the payment I wired to the Caymans. At this point, I'm done dancing around," the woman snaps, her voice cold as ice. "Dr. Perry has become a threat to the experiment and needs to be eliminated. It should look like an accident. You're devious enough to lie to your wife about our meetings, so you should have no trouble arranging an incident that fits the bill."

Holy shit.

This must be Dr. Bruner, and she's apparently concluded that Dr. Perry is a security risk. She's not wrong, but the timing couldn't be worse. We were just talking about making a move. Now we need to step up the timetable. There's no space for doubt or hesitation anymore; we need to strike as soon as possible.

Sheriff Reed takes a long time responding. "You're trying to give me a kill order? I can't believe you think you bought me for fifty thousand."

"I did," she says flatly. "But if you want more, that can be arranged."

"You have the wrong idea, lady. I agreed to look the other way and provide cover for your fun and games in the forest. I never signed on as a hired gun. If you're having . . . personnel problems, resolve it yourself."

She chuckles, the sound devoid of humor. "If you consider your involvement, you'll realize you're already in too deep. If I crash and burn, you're coming with me, Sheriff. You can't afford for this project to fail."

Sheriff Reed says, "I guess we'll see, won't we?"

"Don't disappoint me."

I hear the car door open and shut, movement across the gravel. Seems like Dr. Bruner is leaving. Now there's no sound in the car, except for the sheriff's heavy breathing. Then he slams his hand repeatedly against the dash, a series of wild strikes and angry curses. "What am I supposed to do?"

Nobody answers since he's alone in the car. I am the silent witness to what happened here. There's no way I'm going back to sleep, so I start getting ready for school. At five a.m., I get on chat. It's still early, but this news can't wait.

Me: I don't know if Jackson told you, but we put a bug in Sheriff Reed's car.

Silence in the chat room.

Well, they may not be up yet. I'll explain the situation and they can read the update when they wake. I summarize what I overheard, and then add: I'm afraid the sheriff will be too intimidated to resist for long. She's scary. I'm warning Dr. Perry. I hope he checks his messages before tonight.

I get on Telegram and type up a similar message to Dr. Perry. The other app buzzes me soon after, and I find the first reply.

Derek: Oh shit. That means they'll be watching him even more carefully inside, and it reduces our chances of success. We need to act fast.

Me: Exactly my thoughts.

Jackson: Well, at least we know and maybe we can work around this. We need a plan, like yesterday.

Me: Just got a message, let me check it.

It seems Dr. Perry is an early riser because he's already on Telegram responding to my ping.

Imperator is typing: I wish I could say this comes as a surprise, but I know Sofia too well. I'm sure my lack of faith in the project is apparent to her by now, and she's not one to wait. Thank you for the warning. But I must go about my business and pretend I don't know anything. I'll be wary until we're ready.

Me: When do you think that will be? What do you want us to do? What CAN we do?

Imperator: I do have a plan, don't worry. We'll just need to step it up and move faster than I originally anticipated. The first stage is to destroy the field generators. That should help with the timeslips and the town disappearances. Unfortunately, your team will need to handle that, as Sofia will be watching me like a hawk.

On our own? Sure, no problem.

Me: Any information you have to facilitate that would be helpful.

Imperator: Uploading patrol routes and time pattern data. This will show you when it's safest to strike. I'm also including the collection schedule for the beta team. They're the scientists who take the external readings. This will be dangerous. I can't stress that enough.

Me: We'll do our best to plan the raid, using the information provided.

It's too early for this shit. I'm still so tired, and I can't believe I've signed on to destroy machinery I barely understand.

Imperator: Is there anything else?

Me: Is there anything strange about Sofia Bruner?

I can't believe I'm asking this, but it's better than coming right out with my actual question. Is she immortal? Was she a spy in WWI?

Imperator: In what sense? I find her aims to be exceedingly strange . . . and wrong. Or are you talking about something else?

Me: Never mind. Before, you mentioned the timeslips. Could you elaborate on that? Because I have a theory about the disappear-ances . . .

Imperator: There's no way to confirm without bringing back those we lost, but based on my observations, I think they're currently living between time, a microsecond ahead or behind. Here, but out of phase with our timestream. We can't see them, but we in-teract with the same objects. To them, the town would appear to be completely empty, except for those who get sucked into a timeslip.

Me: That's why certain places feel haunted, why you feel like someone is near, but you can't see them, and food disappears.

Imperator: Your theory matches mine. When we disrupt the equipment, I hope everyone will return. You have no idea how much I hope for that. My wife is among the missing.

Oh, damn.

Me: What about . . . what if someone isn't just lost, but everyone has forgotten them? Would they come back too?

Imperator: That sounds as if the timeline has been changed. Are you hiding something from me? It could be vital.

I don't want to go into details about Logan since I'm already draining data with all the bandwidth this secure app uses.

Me: I'll get with the others, and we'll take out the field genera-tors ASAP.

44

Friday night's performance at halftime goes off without a hitch.

The whole time I'm beaming at the crowd, I have the urge to laugh because it feels like I really am pretending to be a normal high school student. My real life has become a cover for my across-time romance and my secret-agent stuff.

Earlier that day, we made all the plans for our forest raid. We're going before dawn on Saturday morning, and even with the coordinates Dr. Perry provided, this will be a scary game of hide-and-seek.

Not only are we hiding from Fairhaven forces, we also need to avoid the ghost lights. I'm the only one who knows what they did to Logan.

After the game, I tell Ottilie I'm tired and go to bed early. I need the sleep, but I'm afraid I'll dream. Probably a baseless fear since that usually happens after a message from Oliver, but I can't afford to oversleep tonight.

At two a.m. I give up and put on a black hoodie and sweats, the closest I have to proper stealth garb. We had to build travel time into the plan since we'll be creeping around the woods on foot.

There are six devices planted around the facility, three in the woods and three in the swamp. Since they're embedded in the earth, they won't be easy to spot in the dark. That's why

I'm taking the box with me—on the possibility that Jackson is right and the devices will resonate.

I head out early, sneaking through the house with my phone set on silent. When I reach the rendezvous point, Tamsyn and Kimala are already waiting, both dressed in black also. Tamsyn has gone a step further and smeared her face with something dark.

Kimala whispers, "Waiting on Derek and Jackson. Mrs. Park still has watchers."

Within ten minutes, the boys arrive. Derek has tools, including a shovel, while Jackson is carrying a bulging black garbage bag.

"What's in the sack?" Tamsyn asks before I can, and Jackson gives her a look.

"Hazmat suits. If the scientists are wearing them to take readings, we should be as careful as we can. I could only patch together two, though. Who wants to suit up?"

"I will," I say.

Jackson nods, helping me slip into the weird outfit that's made of shower curtains, duct tape, and God knows what else. It's so low-tech that he has to tape me into it, and if the material gets caught on a tree branch, suit integrity will be compromised.

No point in worrying about that now.

"I'll wear the other one," Jackson volunteers. "That means only Araceli and me should approach the site. The rest of you keep watch from a distance."

Derek hands Jackson the shovel. "Then you'll need this."

It feels like we are so woefully unprepared for this, but we'd never be able to match Fairhaven for equipment, so we'll just have to succeed guerilla-style, swift strikes and constant movement.

It'll have to be enough.

"We have a lot of ground to cover before daylight," Kimala says. "Let's get moving."

Tamsyn takes the lead. "I memorized the maps Dr. Perry sent, and I used to be a Girl Scout."

"That makes you uniquely qualified to lead this mission," Derek jokes.

Nobody laughs, and we fall silent. The others hold branches away from Jackson and me, so we can pass undamaged. The first spot is where I saw the scientists before when I got lost leaving Logan's tree house.

The tree house that doesn't exist anymore. I can't think about that or wonder what Dr. Perry meant about a change in the timeline.

"Should be around here somewhere," Tamsyn says.

This seems like the right clearing, but it's dark and the ground is covered with dead sticks and dry leaves, typical of autumn. The device was buried long ago, so the ground shows no signs of that interment.

I pull the box out of my backpack, and at first, I feel silly carrying it around, but as I approach the far side of the clearing, the box vibrates in my hands, subtle but persistent. The low buzz tingles against my skin, similar but not identical to how the ghost lights felt when I was holding onto Logan.

"Here," I call softly.

"That's your cue," Tamsyn says.

Jackson jogs over and starts digging, shallow at first and tapping with the shovel for any sign of buried gear. At six inches, I hear a metallic ping.

"That's it," Kimala says.

She's got her back to us, scanning the woods for any signs of a Fairhaven patrol. No idea what we'll do if we hear ATVs or see flashlights shining in the trees. Run, I guess, and hope for the best.

I squat and use my hands to excavate around the gizmo, revealing what looks like a simple silver canister, but on closer inspection, I see the same tree that's etched on my box stamped on the side. When I bring the two together, light kindles inside the engraving, glowing an eerie blue.

"Whoa, don't let them touch," Tamsyn snaps.

"Why? What do you think will happen?" Kimala sounds interested instead of worried.

Honestly, I'm with Tamsyn, better not to risk it.

"Sledge." Jackson holds out a gloved hand.

I feel like a surgical assistant since I run over to Derek to get it. The other three are giving us plenty of distance, at least twenty feet. Once I deliver the hammer, Jackson motions me back.

"I'm hearing movement," Kimala whispers. "Think maybe we've got company inbound. Hurry up, Jackson!"

He raises the sledge and smashes the shit out of the device. The first hit only dents the casing, but the second cracks it, and the third breaks it wide open. Jackson keeps smashing the hammer down, until the glow dies away and all the internal components are broken into shards.

"I hear it too," Tamsyn says urgently.

"Bury the pieces. Fast." Derek is pacing, spinning in a slow circle.

Now I hear the low hum of the engines too, through the muffling effect of my makeshift hazmat helmet. Jackson rakes the dirt back over the fragments and rushes to join us, hammer in hand.

"Let's go. Tamsyn, which way?"

"I'm going clockwise, so there's one more in the forest before we hit swamp. It'll be slower going there."

Adrenaline rushes through my bloodstream, a powerful combination of fear and elation. The guards are looking for trespassers, not ruined gear. This is a break for us. If the beta team comes out early to take readings, they'll know immediately the equipment is messed up.

"I hope they don't receive remote data," Jackson says, as we hurry after Tamsyn.

Derek blows out a worried breath. "Oh shit. Never thought of that. You figure an alarm went off as that thing went offline?"

"Pointless to worry about that now," Kimala says. "But if it did, we have Dr. Perry inside. He knows we're moving tonight, so I hope he has the foresight to cover our asses."

"There would be more movement if they knew," Jackson points out.

That makes sense to me. "I agree. If the facility was on alert, they'd be sweeping the area with floodlights, chasing us down with hunting dogs. It wouldn't even surprise me if they had helicopters."

"Your basic prison break scenario," Tamsyn adds.

"This is so surreal." Derek has the hammer on his back like he's Thor or something. "I keep asking myself how I got mixed up in all this, and I'm still not sure."

"It's the right thing to do," Kimala says softly. "If this helps Eunsoo or her dad, or your brother . . ." She hugs Tamsyn quickly, one-armed. "It's right, that's all."

We've been walking for a while, and I'm tired from holding my body stiff, keeping my arms and legs away from aggressive branches. Jackson must be feeling it too; he's not exactly the sporty type. Sweat trickles down my spine, pooling at the small of my back, and thanks to my duct tape suit, I can't wipe it off.

Tamsyn holds up a hand. "Less chatter. We're getting close to the next one, but . . ."

"But what?" I ask.

She sighs. "We've got company. Suggestions?"

45

It's not guards.

Beta team is sweeping the area with their scanners, but based on their casual posture, they're taking routine readings. They don't know yet that we broke one of their field generators. If we were really spies, one of us could ninja roll up and take them out, but none of us have that skill set.

"We have to wait them out," I whisper.

If they're moving counterclockwise, they'll check the ruined unit next. And that's when the shit will hit the fan. We might not be able to get to the other four, but failure is not an option.

Kimala nods. "Let's see which way they go."

Seems like she's on the same mental page as me. If they head toward us, we'll have to do—something. Hell if I know what.

"Did you hear?" one of the techs asks.

"What, Howard?" I remember him from last time. He must be the lab gossip. At least the woman's tired tone suggests she's sick of his news updates.

"Dr. Bruner is accelerating the schedule. She hasn't posted the new timetable yet, but I heard from Dr. Milton in quantum. Bruner wants the whole grid active in twenty-four hours."

"That's impossible!" the woman protests.

"I guess Dr. Milton said so too, and Bruner suggested that she make it possible or there would be . . . consequences. Milton was crying when she told me. I don't see how she can finish all the calculations in time. Even a supercomputer couldn't."

"We signed on knowing we were in for death or glory," the woman says finally. "It can't be both."

The five of us sit silent as ghosts while the scientists finish their scans, pocket their equipment . . . and turn toward the swamp. Oh my God, like Tamsyn, they're moving clockwise. Which means we can trail them to each installation, wait for them to finish, and then destroy the device. I wave my mitts in excitement, and Jackson motions for me to settle down. We wait five extra minutes to be sure the beta team isn't coming back, then we rush into the trees where the unit is implanted.

This isn't a clearing, so we have to scramble over a bed of pine needles and low-hanging branches. I'm constantly checking my suit, but the plastic he used is durable.

Derek chucks the shovel at Jackson as I start scanning the area with my box. "Second verse, same as the first."

We're quicker with the disposal this time, and we wrap it up and bury the evidence before the guards can reach this zone. Tamsyn leads us toward the swamp, and the stench is revolting—decaying plant matter, stagnant water, and fetid soil.

"Watch your feet," Tamsyn cautions.

I hear a squelch, and when I glance over my shoulder, Derek looks like he's about to cry. "My new kicks! How'm I supposed to explain this to my mom?"

Since he's a big guy, quiet usually, it tickles me to imagine him cowed by his mother. "We'll chip in to get you a new pair," I say.

"If we survive," Jackson mutters.

"If we don't, nobody's gonna care about anybody's shoes." Kimala is always practical.

The sky is starting to lighten, only a suggestion, but I doubt we have more than a couple hours of night to hide us. We need to step it up, but we can't move faster than the beta team.

What does alpha team do? I wonder.

"I see their lights up ahead," Jackson whispers.

But as we draw closer, I realize those aren't flashlights at all. Ghost lights, drifting through the swamp, and I full-on panic. "Get down!"

I drag them off the path, and Tamsyn nearly topples into the pond, but all I can think about is what happened to Logan. I can't breathe inside this damn makeshift helmet; I pant until my vision goes fuzzy.

"Don't let it touch you. Get *down*."

Derek grabs Tamsyn's hand before she can fall with a splash, hauling her to more stable land. Maybe my fear gets through to them, but everyone drops to a squat, staying low until the ghost lights pass overhead.

I've never been so close to them before, and now that I am, I can see that what I took for hypnotic colors are swirls of other times. This proximity gives me a blurry glimpse of a castle built on a hillside, and that swirl reveals a girl riding hell for leather across a golden field.

"What the hell?" Jackson breathes.

"We might be safe in the suits, I'm not sure. But Kimala, Derek, and Tamsyn aren't." I wish I could tell them about Logan, but they don't remember him.

"Definitely not swamp gas," Derek says.

I shake my head. "According to Dr. Perry, those are timeslips. And I think they have to do with our missing people."

Tamsyn grabs my arm, hard. "Did my brother get pulled in? Are they like portals? Oh my God."

There's no time to discuss theories with her. We have four more machines to break. I'm not sure what they were talking about when they said Bruner wants the grid online in twenty-four hours, but it can't mean anything good.

"Later." I try to play off my extreme reaction as I get to my feet. "Stay away from the timeslips."

Derek keeps sliding me looks when he thinks I'm not paying attention. I don't respond as we close on the third device. My freak-out means the scientists have already moved on, but the guards are probably closer behind us.

They've planted this damn thing on a small hill in the middle of the water. It's not deep, but it's nerve-wracking looking for a solid path in the dark. I'm scared of the sudden drop-off that Logan mentioned, scared of getting sucked in and drowning in this algae-topped water.

"Let's make a chain," Tamsyn suggests.

It would be better if we had rope, but we don't, so we all join hands and pick our way slowly toward the rise. Reptiles and amphibians scatter, bubbling the water around us, and the smell—

My foot slips, and I nearly slide into the water, but Kimala pulls hard, yanking me back toward the rest of them, and they catch me in a messy group grab. I lean for a few seconds, heart racing.

"Okay, let's keep going."

"You okay?" Derek asks.

"Eh." That answer is relative. My legs are trembling, and I almost dropped my backpack. Losing the box means failing this mission and letting Oliver die.

Tamsyn gets us to solid ground at the base of the hill. "We'll wait here. You two got this?"

Jackson has the shovel; I've got the sledge. I glance at him to check, and he nods. "Yeah, we're good."

He helps me scramble up the slope, and as I'm about to take out the heartwood box, I see the orange tip of a glowing cigarette. Oh shit, there's someone here.

Frantic impressions bombard me. Dark clothing, guard, not beta team. What's he doing here?

The man raises his arm—weapon or radio—I don't know, but we can't fail. I rush toward him, and everything else is instinct. With the hammer, I knock whatever he has out of his hand, and then I swing again, as hard as I can, right upside his head. His body goes flying, tumbling down the hill and into the water with an ominous splash.

I . . . killed him?

It all happened so fast. Jackson is frozen, clutching the shovel as I stumble down the other side of the hill. No sign of the man I bashed. If I knocked him out, he must be drowning.

I can't breathe. Drowned, neither can he.

Suddenly Jackson is there, hands on my shoulders. "Calm down. I've got his radio. Now we can listen to their movements."

I killed someone to keep him from reporting in. He wasn't trying to shoot us.

Oh God, now I know how Oliver feels.

46

I can't even throw up.

It would spatter inside my helmet and make my life a living hell. My stomach feels queasy, but I choke down the bile. I can't think as Jackson shoves me back up the hill, his gloved palms flat on my back, crinkling the plastic of my suit. I'm not sure the others know what happened yet.

The radio crackles, and Jackson juggles it, nearly dropping it in his startlement. I can see how wide his eyes are through the clear visor.

"Where are you, Charlie Tango? Come back."

We trade looks as I try to decide if we should risk responding. I gesture at the walkie-talkie. Jackson cocks his head, and I finally shake mine. Better to stay quiet. We don't know what the guard's voice sounded like, so we can't try to match it.

A gusty sigh crackles through the unit. "Keep it up, asshole, and I'm reporting these unauthorized smoke breaks." A pause—he's giving his coworker one last chance. "Well, screw you too. This is going in my official sitrep, right to Doc Bruner. Proceeding to the next checkpoint without you."

Here's what I know about the man I killed—he was a smoker, known for slacking off. He might have a wife and kids, waiting for him to come home. When I let my thoughts wander that way, I could crack, here and now. Regret and revulsion sweep over me, and I hear the dull thud of the sledge smashing into his skull.

No. I clench my jaw. I can't do this. Not now, there's no time. I take a breath, then another. Through sheer will, my nerves settle a little. No matter what, we still have a job to do. Jackson silently turns the radio off, as it will give our location away. He doesn't need to tell me to get busy.

I pluck out the box and walk a circle atop the hill. It reacts toward the far side, close to where the guard was standing. "Here."

He nods. The digging takes on a more ominous note this time, as if we're exhuming the body I sent tumbling into the bog, but Jackson doesn't unearth pale corpse flesh or even dry spindly bones. That's my imagination going into overdrive, as he drags out the third device. I don't hand over the sledge this time. It seems more fitting for me to destroy it myself, considering how grim my actions here have been.

"You sure?" he asks.

I nod. "Back up. I've got this."

True, the shaking has settled. I don't even want to hurl anymore; I'm resolved and numb. I could rationalize what I've done tonight—that guard had to know he was working for terrible people—but the truth is, when my fight-or-flight instinct kicked in, sheer impulse drove me forward, reaction, not rational decision. I might even do the exact same thing if I was given time to consider.

I wind up and slam the sledge into the cylinder. Like Jackson, I bash it repeatedly to destroy functionality, but unlike him, I keep swinging until my arms are sore and the thing is only dented bits of broken mental. Part of me expects him to comment because he doesn't strike me as the patient type, but he only buries the evidence, then heads back down to where the others are waiting.

"The guards are close again," Kimala says. "What took you so long?"

A glance at Jackson, but he says nothing. It's up to me, I guess. Well, I won't lie. "There was a guard slacking off up top. I . . . took care of him."

Tamsyn has already turned, but that stops her in her tracks. Her head whips around, and even in this faint light, I can read her shock. "Does that mean—"

"He won't follow us," Jackson cuts in. "We're halfway there, so let's not stop now."

Kimala nods. "Fair. We'll talk later."

The group is dead silent, though, as we move through the swamp, just the splashing of our feet in shallow water. I can't stop thinking about the noise the body made as it plopped into the pond. Since we didn't weigh him down, he'll surface as the body starts decomposing, releasing buoyant gasses. That means the other guards will find him soon, unless the beta science team stumbles on him first.

Depending on how long he's in the water, it may be hard to tell why he ended up there. It's so macabre, but I hope the fish and frogs eat the skin to hide his head wound. If they have to do an autopsy to inspect his skull, establishing cause of death will take longer. I might even hope they'll be too busy to bother checking into it.

Mechanically, I assist in the search-and-destroy for the one remaining swamp device. We've got this down, now, and we don't run into any more slacking guards. The beta team still seems to have no idea we're moving in their wake. So far, so good.

"Only one more," Tamsyn says, with a tired stretch.

We've come a long way, pure physical distance, at this point, five miles at least. And there's a trek ahead of us too. My thighs are burning, and the sun is coming up, fiery yellow and orange with streaks of crimson. I can't remember the last time I saw a sunrise. Lack of sleep is catching up with me too, as my eyes are blurred and gummy. I can smell myself inside the suit, fear sweat mixed with regular perspiration, and it's almost as bad as the swamp.

Still, it's good to be back on dry ground. My shoes are caked in mud, so each step is heavier than when we started out. Hopefully Dr. Perry hasn't been detained yet. I wonder if they'll interrogate him when they realize their field generators have been smashed. Bruner may have replacements ready to go, but installation will take time. I'm counting on Dr. Perry to prevent that. We're on the other side of Fairhaven now, crossing an open field. My nerves are tight, and I think it's unanimous.

"Are we close?" Derek asks.

The lack of cover is bothering me. I never thought I'd miss the trees, but the shadows may save our lives. I quicken my pace as Tamsyn practically snarls, "You could thank me for getting us this far."

"Listen," Derek starts.

But Kimala gives them both a hard look, shutting that shit down before it can escalate. Thankfully we reach the edge of the woods soon after, and the canopy of fall leaves hides us from watchful eyes. Checking the time will only agitate me more, so I don't get my phone out. This will take however long it takes.

There's no sign of the beta team as we approach installation six. That bothers me, but maybe they don't check all the equipment at the same time? Whatever, as long as we complete the smash and scramble, that's all I need. Jackson rushes us through this removal, and then Tamsyn sets off for the final stop.

So close. Maybe we should check the radio? Nah, safer to leave it off. It might have a tracking device embedded in it.

So I don't say anything as we creep through the woods. Tamsyn silently signals a ghost light, and we all drop to the ground, quiet as death until the timeslip rolls by. The routine feels almost normal now—I scan with the box and Jackson works with shovel and sledge.

We did it.

Maybe it's because we're all so damn tired, but nobody hears the engines until they're almost on top of us. Guards in black uniforms burst into view, bounding over rough terrain on ATVs. They're shouting orders, and we don't have an escape plan. Those are real weapons, live rounds slamming into the ground behind me. I dive behind a tree, tearing at my hazmat suit. This thing has served its purpose and will only slow me down.

"Scatter!" I shout.

Then I run for my life.

47

Bullets pepper the trees behind me, sending up a spray of splinters.

The others don't waste any breath on a response, and besides, anything we say could be used against us. We can rally later, scrub away all traces of the mission, and regroup in chat.

I hope we're all fit enough.

Men are shouting in a mixture of German and English, commands for us to stop and surrender. Yeah, that's not happening. They're using automatic weapons, good for nothing but efficient slaughter. Dark camo fatigues, military berets. Bruner has damn special forces patrolling these woods.

"The one in the black hat is getting away! Break west!"

Black hat, that's Tamsyn. I can't stop to see how everyone else is doing, but I hear someone rushing up behind me and closing fast. Must be one of us, if they're not riding an all-terrain vehicle. Risking a backward glance, I see Jackson sprinting as hard as he can. Didn't he hear me? Sticking together isn't smart. It'll make it easier for them to run us down, and they have ATVs.

This time, I can't count on Dr. Perry pulling me into his hunting blind, and there's no tree house to hide in either, just an endless stretch of trees. Dry branches snatch at the tatters of my suit, but it doesn't matter if it rips further. I'll leave slashes of plastic all along my path and call it a good sacrifice, as long as I get away.

"Jackson, don't! I'll be fine. You should save yourself."

Maybe he's not sticking with me to help; possibly we chose the same direction and he's dodging bullets, same as me. I note movement in my peripheral vision, an ATV tracking us through the trees, about twenty meters behind, gaining fast. Soon they'll be able to peg us like the assholes who shoot "hunting" videos, taking down deer from a moving vehicle. I never wondered what a fleeing animal feels like. Now I know.

"Stand down! You will be taken alive if you don't resist."

Sure we will.

I'm sure Dr. Bruner has questions, and she won't kill us until she gets satisfactory answers. She'll want us to name who we're working with, for starters. She suspects Dr. Perry, but she doesn't know for a fact that he's behind our actions today. There might be other moles or dissenters to root out.

We can't let them take us.

None of us can withstand a painful interrogation. We're not spies or soldiers. I wanted to do this, and I convinced everyone else, and now—I can't breathe, the fear is so intense. I snatch glimpses of the guards getting closer, closer. Their ATVs are too damn fast, and they're confident on them.

My heart thunders in my ears as more bullets spray the area. I get stung on a ricochet and a sharp pain slices across my calf. Shit, it hurts. My speed drops, and I wave Jackson on. He hesitates, and in that split second, they unload with another furious burst. He takes a shot to the gut, presses his hand to his stomach, and stares at it openmouthed when it comes away red.

I know it's too late—I know that—but I can't leave him. Limping toward him at top speed, I try to catch him when his knees buckle, but I'm not strong enough. The momentum of his body topples me backward, and we go tumbling down a wooded slope, slamming against hidden rocks and fallen branches. I come to a stop at the bottom of a crevice too big to be called a ditch, smaller than a ravine, and spot a small opening, overhung with roots and leafy weeds. With all my might, I haul Jackson toward the grotto, likely some animal's burrow, and then hide us with a pile of sticks, dirt, and fallen leaves.

There's no way I can carry him to safety with the guards nearby. They'll come looking, and the best I can do is keep us safe until they give up. Or find us. Shivers wrack me from head to toe, and this narrow space reeks of copper: my blood and his. Jackson reaches for me with bloodstained hands—wait, no, he's trying to get his helmet off. I yank the tape that seals the suit together, and he gulps in deep, gurgling breaths. That sounds bad. He needs a hospital, now, but we won't make it unless I'm clever and careful.

"Araceli . . ."

This time, I'm not mistaken. He reaches for my hand, and his is so cold, scary cold. The light's dim in here, shaded by the underside of a great tree growing into the hillside, but I can tell he's far too pale. Hiding won't help. I have to make a move, or I'll lose him, but my mind is blank. What am I supposed to do against trained guards equipped with automatic rifles? I won't get lucky again like I did in the swamp, and besides, Derek has the sledge, my weapon of choice.

I hear them now. They must've ridden the ATVs down, and they're scouring the area for us. Footsteps crunch over dead leaves, the heavy tread of those who have no doubt they've got you outnumbered and outgunned.

"I know they came this way." German accent, curt delivery.

"I'm looking." Local help, impatient with being bossed around.

Did we leave a blood trail? Maybe I can ambush them from behind, grab a weapon and take out the other one, then load Jackson on the vehicle. If we get out of the woods quick enough, maybe a doctor can save him. I can even picture myself doing those things, action-movie style, but I'm quivering when I crawl toward the exit.

I'm probably going to die.

A weak hand snags my ankle just as I'm about to exit the overhang. I try to pull free, but Jackson has me in a death grip. Literally. "Don't do it," he breathes. "They'll kill you."

"You'll die if I don't try!" Keeping my voice soft doesn't diminish any of my anguish. First Logan, now Jackson? No. I can't just hide if there's any chance of saving him.

His fingers tighten, digging into my ankle bone. "This is a bad risk. Stay still. You can make it out if . . ." Jackson releases me on a sudden intake of breath, and he bites down on a stick to muffle his cries.

"Please don't ask me to watch you die." I'm begging.

This can't be real. None of it is. Please let this be an uncommonly vivid dream. I want to wake up in my bed.

I even try pinching myself, but it doesn't help. The scene remains static—dying boy collapsing in my arms. Jackson's head falls against my shoulder, so to leave, I'd have to drop him, and I can't do that either.

I'm in hell. This is hell.

His voice comes out liquid with blood and breathy from his struggle for air. "When you find Eunsoo . . . tell her that I was thinking of her at the end."

"Don't talk like that. You'll be fine." Even I don't believe what I'm saying.

Jackson gives me a sad smile, his teeth stained with blood. "Funny, my grandma's here. I really . . . didn't expect to die like this."

He goes limp in my arms then, and I try, I try my best, but I'm only playing at CPR. I don't know what I'm doing. His heartbeat doesn't return when I press on his chest, and my mouth on his is only a heartbreaking goodbye kiss as the last of his breath trickles out. I tilt my head against his, silent tears scalding my scratched cheeks.

Jackson's blood is all over the soil and the stones, staining my hands and the suits he made to protect us.

48

I don't know how long I crouch in that cave.

The men are still scouring the area, but I don't hear them right outside anymore. This might be my only chance to escape. I hate leaving Jackson's body here, but I can't transport him. Not now. I'll have to come back later, once I make it out.

That's what I'll do.

It still doesn't feel right, but my choices are bad and terrible. With a heavy heart, I crawl toward the front of the overhang and peer out through the detritus I raked up, checking for the guards. I don't see anyone, but there's an ATV right in front of me. I've never driven one, but it can't be too much different than a car.

Before I make a conscious decision, I take off, running toward the vehicle as fast as I can, considering my injured calf. Okay, it's different than a car, no pedals, but it has a throttle like a motorcycle, and I'm not sure where the brakes are. I don't have time to study the controls. The guards will be back soon. I start it up, and the engine noise draws the guards, who are searching the trees behind me.

"There's one of them! Stop her, any means necessary!" The raw fury of that command sends a chill down my spine.

They bring up their weapons as I take off, lurching into motion, and it's purely terrifying. The two guards jump on the remaining ATV, but they're better at driving. No, I can't think about that. Trees whip past me, and I'm bouncing all over the place. Any minute I expect to feel a bullet slam into my back.

I don't have a plan. I don't even know how to leave the woods; running like mad has got me completely turned around. For all I know, I'm headed toward the lab now, but with them gunning the engine behind me, I have to keep pushing forward. There's no chance for me to check my direction or figure out which way leads to home.

Shit, even if I knew, I probably shouldn't head straight there. Not with these assholes on my tail. I need to lose them. I push my ATV for greater speed, going full-out, and the whine of the engine tells me I'm being rough on the machine. I zip over a small rise and go airborne briefly and barely turn fast enough to avoid a tree that's suddenly right in front of me, and now I'm careening down a hill, the trees thinning until there's only scrubby bushes and tall grass.

They snap shots at me as they can, but it's not as easy from the back of an ATV, firing at a moving vehicle. I might do this. Hope rises a bit, like dough left in a bowl to rest, and I wrench the steering handle as a road rises to meet me. Oh shit, this might not be good. When the ATV hits the pavement, I can't control the spin. It loops out on me, and I hit the road hard, pinned by the dying grind of the broken machine.

It feels like my back is bleeding, and I can't pull free. My only hope is a car will come upon the accident before—no, they're here. I stare up at the blue sky as tears trickle from the corner of my eyes. The guards cut the engine and pull the ATV off me, but this isn't a rescue.

"Check for weapons," German Accent snaps.

They rummage through my backpack and I can hardly breathe for fear they're going to realize I'm carrying one of the

Project Paradox prototypes, but they don't seem to notice the symbol. Relief trickles through me when they shove it back in the bag. The treasure box looks intact, thank God. I haven't warned Oliver about the battle in the Argonne forest yet. Before, I couldn't figure out how to offer the intel, and possibly I shouldn't worry about him when I'm in so much deep shit, but I can't stop caring.

When they find my cell phone, they pull out the SIM and pointedly grind it against the asphalt. Then German Accent makes a call on the radio. "We caught a girl. What are your orders?"

The unit crackles and pops, then the same voice I heard talking to Sheriff Reed replies, "Transport her to the lab. We only need one person alive for questioning. When you hunt down the others, liquidate them."

High-octane terror spikes in my bloodstream, prompting tremors that rock me all over. They have to make it out. It's bad enough that Jackson didn't. If something happens to Kimala, Derek, or Tamsyn, I don't know what I'll do. I can't live with myself—well, I may not be able to live, period. Funny, I'm not really scared for myself anymore, now that the worst has come to pass. I feel bad for my parents, who thought America was safer than Venezuela, and I'm worried about my great-aunt. Based on the position of the sun in the sky, it must be about time for her to get up. She'll be so worried when she finds me missing.

"Understood."

German Accent twists my arms behind me and binds my wrists with what feels like a zip tie, then drags me out of sight while his partner moves the ATVs off the road. I open my mouth to scream—like that will do any good—and a balled fist slams into my mouth. I taste blood from where my lips split against my teeth.

"If I had my way, I would kill you," he snarls, right in my ear, then he gags me with a strip of cloth.

What kind of monster has gags ready to go in his pocket, anyway? He kicks my legs out from under me, so I fall into the tall grass growing along the road, hiding me from any potential good Samaritans. A few cars do pass, but they don't see me since I'm prone with a heavy boot on my back.

A truck arrives then, white and unmarked, but the guards recognize it. They toss me in the back like a rack of beef and throw my backpack in after me. I need to keep this with me, somehow. I hope everyone else got away.

The truck moves with a jolt, throwing me against the side. I can't brace myself since my arms are tied behind my back, and I roll around, trying not to slam my head into the sides. Right now I'm helpless but still determined.

I have to stop them. Somehow.

49

The goons don't bother to blindfold me when they drag me out of the back of the truck. I snag my backpack with one hand as I'm pulled out, and it's awkward holding it like this, but I hope the guards are more interested in getting credit for capturing me.

I blink against the bright, sudden sunlight, stumbling when German Accent shoves me toward the building. Finally, I've made it to the Fairhaven facility, but none of this has gone according to plan.

Let's face it, I have no plan.

From the outside, you'd never know what goes on here. The buildings are more than thirty years old, basic and blocky, connected by second-story walkways. The number of cars in the parking lot is frankly astonishing. I have no idea what Dr. Bruner is trying to accomplish with the field generators we destroyed, but the scope of it is mind-boggling. She also doesn't seem to care that she's majorly screwing up people's lives and destroying families on her path to . . . whatever the endgame is.

"Move it," the guard snaps.

Inside, the facility is cool and more modern than I expected. It's all white tile and fluorescent lights, long hallways with secure doors at the end that require both DNA and card clearance. They're not joking around. Now that I've seen their internal security, getting captured was probably my only way inside. We couldn't have done this with optimism and bolt cutters.

GA drags me into an elevator, and I nearly drop my backpack. It's straining my wrists, but damned if I leave it behind. We go down two levels; something tells me this isn't the research section.

No, this is grim and gloomy, unpainted cement block, and it smells like damp basement even before I get shoved out of the lift. I stumble and nearly fall, catch myself with my shoulder on the wall. My left leg burns from the bullet graze, but the bleeding has stopped at least.

We walk a little farther, then the guard opens a heavy metal door and shoves me through it, then slams it shut. This time I do fall, but at least I keep my bag. I'm surprised the guards were that careless, but I suspect it's because I'm a teenage girl.

Men always underestimate us. I remember Ma telling me the story of Truus and Freddie Oversteegen, who took advantage of this fact during their time in the Dutch Resistance. They'd invite Nazis to "go for a stroll in the forest" and then shoot them or have them shot. The girls also blew up bridges, and they were so good at it that they both lived past ninety. I need to channel the Oversteegen sisters now.

I think I have a notebook and pen, but it will be hard for me to write this way. That's the first obstacle to overcome. I've seen this done in videos, never tried it myself, but I'm desperate. I need to get my hands in front of me . . . there are two ways this can happen. I can roll my shoulders over or roll backward and push my legs through the loop of my arms. I can't risk popping a shoulder out of socket, and I think maybe my dance flexibility will help with the latter, so I'm trying that first.

I rock onto my back while sweeping my arms forward and

thrust my tucked legs upward. The first time I fall over. Same with the second time, but the third, I thread the needle just right and pull my arms up over my legs.

Better.

Carefully but quickly, I unzip my bag and pull out the box, checking it with careful hands. There's a crack in the side, likely from the ATV accident, but I won't know if that impacts functionality unless I try. Notebook, notebook, here we go. This is just an idea pad really, but it will work. Two of my three pens are broken and spilling ink, but I still have a marker. Thank you, Sharpie.

This might be the last letter I ever write to Oliver, and I don't have time to reflect on my words, because I need to get two messages off before they come for me. Hurry, hurry.

My Dearest Oliver,

You said you wanted answers, so let me be clear. I know so much about what you're going through because I'm writing to you from the future. In my world, the first World War is long ended. That's why I could tell you with certainty that it doesn't last forever—that there is life and happiness waiting for you.

Which brings me to my next point. Don't wait for me. Don't watch for me. You should meet someone else, fall in love, lead a good life, and be happy. I want that for you. Really, I do.

This will likely be my last message, as things have taken a dark turn in my time. I wish I could accept the ring you wanted to give me, but more than distance separates us. Know that you will live on in my heart for as long as I draw breath.

One final word of warning—dire times are coming to your unit. I'm not sure when, exactly, but you'll receive orders to push. Your officers will not listen if you tell them to disobey, but when all hope seems lost, tell your commander he must choose the carrier pigeon Cher Ami to send a message to Allied Forces. He must do this. It's your only hope of coming out of the forest alive.

Yours at heart,
Araceli

P.S. I remember how you said the guys teased you for having a soft heart. Please raise your sons to be good people rather than "real men." That's how we can make the world a better place, one where there's no need for war.

I fold the note, check the date setting, and then tuck it in the box. Waiting is so hard, it feels like I could peel my own skin off, but after counting to five hundred, I open the box with shaking hands.

My message is gone. Thank God.

Outside in the hallway, I hear footfalls coming toward me. Nearly out of time. I do the math quickly, then adjust the date dial and rip out a sheet of paper for my next letter.

Dr. Winslow,

When you die, your son will sell all your equipment and research to Sofia Bruner. She does TERRIBLE things with your well-intentioned work. Please stop it. Prevent this by any means necessary. Prohibit it in your will or burn everything before you pass away. Please help us. The fact that I'm using the prototype means I'm telling the truth.

Araceli Flores Harper

As someone unlocks the door, I shove the page into the box, shut it, and hide it in my backpack, which I slide behind me into the shadows near the wall. The lights flicker in dire portent as the door groans open and a slender, blond woman steps in. Her face holds the intense pallor of someone who works indoors beneath artificial lights. I'm startled to see Dr. Perry step in with her, but I don't react. She must have only suspicions at this point, no solid evidence, but that's not enough to keep her from murder for hire.

"What's this about?" he asks.

She strides over to me, giving me a view of her black-clad legs. "Do you recognize her, Edward?"

He raises a puzzled brow, the picture of confusion. Wow, he's good. "Why would I? Are you in the habit of abducting children now, Sofia? I'm worried about you, truly."

"Only those who interfere with my work," she says coldly.

I'm glad Sheriff Reed hasn't acted on her order to take Dr. Perry out. She kneels next to me and brushes the hair out of my face. I want to bite her hand, but Dr. Perry gives an infinitesimal shake of his head.

"You will tell me who gave you the coordinates to the field generators. If not now, soon. If you cooperate, I'll send you home. Your family must be worried."

Yeah, bullshit. I don't buy this offer for a second. If I talk, once I roll on Dr. Perry, we're both done for.

"Pity," she says, straightening. "The girl in the next cell will probably prove more . . . malleable."

50

Wait, what?

Does that mean Bruner has Kimala or Tamsyn? I open my mouth, but Dr. Perry catches my eye. Another tiny headshake. It's a bluff, then, one designed to make me spill my guts in a panic. I also remember her saying that they only need one person to interrogate when she was talking to that guard on the radio.

Breathing deep, I steady myself. Don't let her play you.

I decide defiance is the way to go. "Then kill me, because I have nothing to say. You don't need two hostages."

Her thin mouth tightens, fury pulling her brows together, and she raises a hand. I brace for the strike, but her radio crackles. "Dr. Bruner, we have a situation."

"What is it?" she snaps.

"It's kind of hard to explain, but . . . the front gates are kind of . . . under siege."

What the hell?

Dr. Perry widens his eyes, and I think he's asking me silently if this is my doing. Definitely not. I mean, I got someone killed today. I'm desperately hoping my message to the past can change . . . something, but so far, nothing. Maybe Dr. Winslow was stoned when he got my note, laughed and rolled a joint with it.

"Explain," she demands.

Even through the radio, the guard's voice takes on a plaintive note. "You need to come out. There's no protocol for what we're supposed to do with . . . dancers."

"Excuse me?" Dr. Bruner could not sound more astonished, and I'm right there with her.

"I don't know what's going on. There are thirty high school girls in uniforms, and they're prancing all over the front gates. A girl with a ponytail is screaming about animal rights, and I think they're filming—shit, a news truck just showed up. I tried to tell them we don't do any experiments on live animals, but . . ."

Music tinkles through the radio, and holy shit, I recognize this song. This is the number we did at the game on Friday night. Did Kimala bring the freaking *dance team* to save me? I could cry, seriously.

Lana's voice is audible, shouting her perkiest battle cry. "Animals are people too! Heck no, we won't go! Dance for feline freedom! Dance like puppy and kitty lives depend on you! Because they do!"

This . . . this is genius. How do you take punitive action against girls protesting to save fluffy pet store pals? Kimala is a mastermind. And this is the kind of story that catches fire on a slow news day. Plus, the dance team is mostly white girls, which means any hostile action the lab takes, the country will condemn it fiercely. I wish America cared the same about Black and Brown girls, but there's a lot of work to do yet.

Dr. Bruner growls a curse and beckons to Dr. Perry. "We'll continue this conversation later. Come with me, Edward."

He follows for a few steps, and I see him pluck something from her coat pocket. The door shuts behind them, and I can barely make out the panicked guard saying to Dr. Bruner, "I'm telling you, we're on the air right now. What should I do?"

More cursing from her, then she orders the pair of guards

to watch Dr. Perry. I can't see what's going on, but the radio crackles, then I hear the sound of a taser discharging and the impact of a fist hitting flesh. Hopefully I wasn't overhearing Dr. Perry get beaten up but the security team. I'm so scared that I can't even breathe right.

Then my cell door swings open, revealing Dr. Perry, who's twirling the keys on a finger. Damn, the way these guards are laid out, that's some special-forces shit. What did Dr. Perry do before he became a scientist?

He motions for me to get moving. "We don't have much time."

Grabbing my backpack, I hurry into the hall, where Dr. Perry uses a pair of small, sharp scissors to cut the plastic ties on my wrists, then I help him haul the bodies into the room where I was locked up. It's the fastest way to hide our escape and he duct-tapes their wrists, ankles, and mouths to be sure they'll stay quiet long enough to give us a head start. When the door shuts behind us and I'm on the right side of freedom, I let out a slow breath in relief.

"Let's go," he says.

"Do you have a plan?" I shoulder my bag and rush after him.

"I'll overload the system and see if I can start a chain reaction. I have an idea of how to do that, but we need to get to the archives."

"For what?" I ask, limping as fast as I can.

"That's where they've stored the first prototype. I've run the simulations, and if I overcharge the connected computer, then toss the prototype through one of the portals . . ." He launches into a complicated technical explanation and loses me a third of the way in.

"Back up, I don't need to know how. I just need to understand what the endgame is."

Still moving, he sighs a little, but he breaks it down for me in layman's terms. "We start a chain reaction that leads to a complete implosion of all portals and timeslips. Kind of a time vacuum that devours itself."

"Okay, I'm with you."

He glances back at me with a worried expression. "It would be better if I had both prototypes for maximum particle agitation. According to the sim, that's the only way to be sure of the desired outcome."

Oh wow. I take a breath, knowing once I say this, I'm closing the door on Oliver. I already said goodbye when I thought I might die here. I still could, of course, but this will be it, if I give the box to Dr. Perry so he can hurl it through a portal and seal all the timeslips for good.

"We do have the other one," I say.

"What?" Dr. Perry gapes me, stumbling over his steps.

"It's in my backpack."

He clears his throat, so shocked that I sort of enjoy it. "When we're out of danger, you need to tell me who you work for, Ms. Flores Harper. Their resources are extraordinary. I wonder if they're hiring . . ." he muses, leading the way into the elevator.

He'll be so disappointed to find out that I really am just a high school senior who happened to find this box in my great-aunt's junk room, but I'm proud of how far I've come. I start humming "Run the World" by Beyoncé, earning an amused glance from Dr. Perry. I loved this song when I was younger.

On the third floor, he gets out, running now. We pass a few guards, but they're not high-ranking enough to question Dr. Perry. I do see one of them get on his walkie, though, so he may be reporting this sighting.

"This is it," Dr. Perry says. "Once I use my credentials to steal the prototype, the clock is ticking. No going back for either of us. Are you ready?"

"As I'll ever be. There's only a cell waiting for me here any-way, so we either finish the job and stop Dr. Bruner or . . . well, there is no option B. Let's do this."

He scans his pass card and his eyeball to get into the vault, which is clinically clean. The air even smells sharp and pun-gent with chemical agents. Shelf upon shelf of interesting giz-mos are lined up, but he knows right where he's headed. To the third row, second shelf—and that's where we find the other half of my heartwood box. This one looks newer, thanks to better care and painstaking preservation. No scratches, no crack.

"Hide it in your bag," he instructs. "They won't know I've taken this right away. I'm not sure how long we have, but we need to get to the control room, where the computer and the first portal are located."

"The prisoner has escaped," comes a booming announce-ment, facility-wide. "Dr. Edward Perry was last seen in her company and is suspected as an accomplice. There is no need to take either of them alive. Anyone else caught aiding and abetting the intruders will be terminated."

"Guessing they don't mean a pink slip?" I try to joke, but he's not feeling it.

Dr. Perry rushes toward the archives as security measures activate. We barely make it out before bars slam down. I stuff the other heartwood box in my bag and follow him, not to-ward the lift but the stairs. Probably safer; they'll spot us on camera and lock the elevator down.

"This way. We may have to fight to get to the control room."

"Weapons?" That might be too much to ask, but I can't go hand-to-hand with trained combatants.

"I've been preparing for this," he answers. "Though I wasn't sure how or when the moment would arrive, I trusted that it would." He opens a closet full of cleaning supplies just outside the stairwell and digs two sidearms out of a stack of paper towels. "I have small caches all over the facility."

"Why are you so determined to stop this? I mean, I know it's right, but you're risking so much. Your life, even."

His dark eyes contain an ocean of sorrow as he switches the safety off, going weapons hot. "I think I mentioned her in passing before, but my wife worked here with me, until two years ago. There was a mishap, and . . . she is now among the lost. And I would do anything to bring her home."

I take solace in his resolve. There are so many souls counting on us now. Great-Uncle Archibald, Tamsyn's brother, Eunsoo and her father, and now Dr. Perry's wife. I don't let myself wonder about Logan.

We've come too far to let fear or doubt cloud our path. Hell, even Lana is outside being a heroine in her own way.

Dr. Perry hands me a pistol. "Do you know how to use this?"

"Not well," I hedge.

He raises his brows at me, but it's too late for him to question my background. Though I've never held a gun in my life, I get a quick crash course from Dr. Perry. I *have* played shooter video games before. Let's see how well that translates to real life.

"Time to turn back time," I say.

51

"Great," Dr. Perry mutters. "I'm headed off to possible doom, and you've got a Cher song stuck in my head."

"What?" I barely know who Cher is, and I've never heard any of her music.

"Never mind. Stay close to me. We need to get to the first level and through three checkpoints to reach the control room."

"Understood."

So far, the dance team is keeping the bulk of security busy outside. I can imagine the dance team threatening to rush the fences to liberate the bunnies they imagine are being held hostage inside. Per the historical overview, they did use animals for portal testing in the early days of the project. Maybe not anymore.

"Dr. Perry . . ."

"Yes, what is it?" he asks, stepping out of the stairwell.

Three checkpoints to go.

"Did you perfect the portals? I mean, have you been sending people back?"

He cuts me a sharp, assessing look before nodding. "Bruner calls them observers. They stay for precisely twenty-four hours and return."

"Do you know why she's doing this?"

"I do, but let's focus on getting the job done. Later, once

we're safe, I'll explain everything, answer any questions you might have."

"What if we succeed, and you don't remember the answers? What if we fail and die, and I never get to ask?"

He sighs at me. "Best- and worst-case scenarios, eh? Fine. Then . . . in brief. Dr. Bruner is descended from a legendary German spy. Early in her life, she found her great-grandmother's papers and she began to nurse a fanatical conviction that if Germany had won the First World War, the entire world would be better off. Hitler would never have risen to power. There would have been no atrocities from the Second World War, and instead of spending most of the twentieth century divided and impoverished, Germany could have led the world to greater prosperity."

"Damn," I say.

"She's quite mad, of course. Her plans would have a devastating effect on the timeline and might actually unravel the framework of reality as we know it."

Oh shit. Now I'm worried about the warning I sent to Dr. Winslow.

"How bad is it? Meddling in the past, I mean."

"It depends on the scale of the intervention, but people can cease to exist, as if they were never born. Certain events that once came to pass might never happen."

"I see." Well, it's too late to worry about it now. I'm going to assume Dr. Winslow ignored my message since we're still sneaking along this white-tiled hallway, creeping up on the first checkpoint.

It's a set of heavy double doors. I don't see any guards, but Dr. Perry's pass card doesn't work. And when he swipes it, an alarm goes off. Awesome, now they know exactly where we are, and if Bruner has any sense left at all, she can probably guess where we're headed.

Now, she's aware the dance team is the least of her problems.

"Stand back and shield your eyes."

Dr. Perry fires two rounds at the reinforced glass, one to crack, the next to penetrate, then he strips off his lab coat and wraps his hand to bash the glass until he makes an opening large enough for me to slip through. He boosts me, and I open the door for him from the other side, but I'm conscious that time is ticking.

He sets off at a pace I can't match, but that's good since he slams into three guards coming around the corner. His weapon flies out of his hand, clattering to the floor, and the guards draw on him. I catch up in time to shoot one of them.

There's more kick than I expect, so I hit him in the belly when I was aiming for the leg. The guard screams and topples over while the other two show signs of fear in the sweat trickling down their faces.

Both have their guns on me, giving Dr. Perry the chance to dive for his weapon. He shoots one in the foot from the floor, and the other one squeezes the trigger just as I drop. The bullet slams into the wall behind me.

On my knees, I fire another round, shoulder. Dammit, I cannot aim. Good thing we're at close range. When we push past, none of them give any sign they want to chase us, too busy rolling and screaming.

"Messy but we're still alive," Dr. Perry says.

I think that's a compliment, not sure.

The next checkpoint is manned with two guards screening visitors in and out. There's a metal-and-wire cage on the other side of the doors, and I have no idea how we're getting past here.

Then it comes to me like magic. I knew my obsession with superhero movies would pay off. "We're doing 'Get Help.'"

"What?"

Thor would be so proud of me right now. "There's no time to explain. Just give me your lab coat and lie down."

This has to work. His lab coat makes me look halfway official, and I use spit to clean my face as best I can, and I tie up my hair using one of my shoestrings. Voila, I'm a scientist. If they don't check the badge before opening the door, we're golden.

I slam against the door with both palms and scream hysterically. "Help, please help me! I think they shot him. Please, the intruders are going to kill me. Please save me! Please!"

It's an Oscar-worthy performance, and the two guards are moved enough that they open the cage door and then pop the security doors to see who's threatening me. Which is when Dr. Perry shoots them neatly, two chest shots, two clean kills.

"Former military," he says with a touch of pride. "I'd feel guilty if I didn't know these two are Sofia's most brutal enforcers."

I take the credentials from one of them. "Then they should still have clearance for the last checkpoint, right?"

"Good thinking. Johann's badge will get us in the control room too, which is the last stop on this crazy train. Dammit. Now I ear-wormed myself." He sighs. "Ah well, at least Cher is gone, and Ozzy is a better mental soundtrack for the big finish."

"If you say so."

Sirens are still blaring, and I hear booted feet moving our way. "Lock the door and the cage," Dr. Perry orders. "That will buy us some time."

We get that done just as forces appear on the wrong side of the checkpoint. They bring out the big guns, more automatics like they used to murder Jackson in the woods. Rage surges through me like nothing I've ever felt, but Dr. Perry pulls me on.

My leg hurts like hell, and I'm so tired. Every part of my body throbs, but I have no time to feel sorry for myself. We round the last corner and find four men waiting for us at the checkpoint. Bullets spray the whole zone, and I dive backward, landing hard on the far side of the corner wall.

Slugs slam into the blocks, shaking the cement. I can't tell how Dr. Perry is doing, but there's no cover. When I peek out, he's down, bleeding from several wounds. Oh shit. He'll never make it.

Still, he manages to shoot three of the four, and I fire on the last one while he's reloading. I crawl toward Dr. Perry through a mess of blood streaks and plaster dust.

"It doesn't matter if I . . . make it. You can get there. Control room . . . not far. Command for overload . . ." He whispers a series of letters and numbers.

With tears streaming down my face, I memorize them. I don't stay to wait for him to take his last breath. Instead, I use Johann's pass card to open the final checkpoint, and I can see CONTROL ROOM clearly marked at the end of the hall.

With grim determination, I limp the last few steps and unlock the door, the command sequence burning in my head. The portal is a metal framework with a ghost light dancing in the center of it. My breath catches when I realize this one seems to be linked to 1915 or thereabouts. I *could* go find Oliver; it is possible for me to be with him. An ache surges through me, longing so intense that I take a step.

He could give me that ring he promised when he comes home from the war. When he found me waiting, he'd kiss me, twirl me around like they do in black-and-white movies. I can picture our reunion, and I shiver a little. I'd learn about life in the early twentieth century, and while it'd be hard, we'd be together, our own happy ending. It would be so easy to step through and live a new life. I imagine candlelight dinners and long walks hand in hand. I could learn jazz dancing with him, figure out how to cook on an old-timey stove, and—

In that time, I'd also have to anglicize my name, drop Flores, and pass for the rest of my life, pretending my family in Monterrey don't make me who I am. It would mean abandoning everyone here and now, letting all these sacrifices go for nothing. I can't. I must finish Dr. Perry's mission.

More tears, as I input the command string. The computer immediately locks, and a clock appears on the screen, counting down from ten.

"What are you doing?" Sofia Bruner screams from the other side of the door, more men behind her.

I can't let her stop me. With all my might, I hurl my backpack through the portal.

And the world goes white.

52

My eyes are too heavy to open.

A cool breeze blows over me, tickling my lashes, and I become aware that every part of me aches. I manage to lift one eyelid and recognize my room at Tía's house. There are subtle differences, of course. The room no longer radiates benign neglect, and all of the furniture is beautifully polished, complemented by modern touches here and there.

What the hell happened exactly? How did I get here?

A man I don't recognize comes in, holding a tray. I start to hide beneath the covers, but something tells me that if he's here in this house, he belongs here. And as he gets closer, I see a resemblance to an old photo I saw of Ottilie with her missing husband.

"Tío," I say, testing my theory.

"Oh, you're awake, are you, darling?" What a sweet smile.

Archibald's quite distinguished, tall and slim, and wearing a blazer, though most people would be lounging in sweats. Silver spectacles perch on a long nose, and he has snow-white hair, brushed back from a lined forehead.

"What happened?"

I know what went down in my reality, but Dr. Perry's plan worked—it must have—and things are different now. The reset made it so the lost ones never slid into the timeslips? If he had been missing for twenty years and just returned, Ottilie wouldn't let him out of her sight.

"Don't you remember? You went for a hike with your friends and took a nasty spill. The doctor says there's no permanent damage, but you may feel fuzzy for a while."

That's handy for someone piecing together their new reality.

He sets the tray on my bedside table, and it's so adorable, a cup of tea and tiny sandwiches with the crusts cut off. "Eat something, please. Your auntie is so worried. She's been threatening to call your mother."

"How long was I out?"

"Overnight. That nice Reed boy carried you home on his back, and I called a retired doctor friend over to have a look at you. He said there was no cause for alarm."

Nice Reed boy . . . oh my God.

"Logan brought me?" Is he back? Did we save him too? Those are questions I can't ask aloud without them calling a psychiatrist.

"That's what I just said. Are you having trouble concentrating? Perhaps I should call Dr. Lee again . . ."

"No, I'm fine. Or I will be. I'm still a bit sore. It must've been quite a fall."

"All the way down the hill, I'm told. You'll likely have a scar on your left leg, where a branch . . ." Archibald stops, but I can well imagine the impalement he's trying not to describe.

Left leg, though? That's where the bullet grazed me—in the time that never was. Or ceased to be? I'm not clear on the verbiage.

"It's fine. I heal fast. And thank you for lunch. I'll rest for a while and come down later, if that's okay."

"Of course. I'm sorry this happened while you're staying

with us." He tsks. "Your parents trusted us as your legal guard-
ians too. I feel terrible."

"Accidents happen. It's nobody's fault."

What else has changed? I check my phone, scraped from
my misadventure, but not destroyed as it was on the road when
I was captured. I have messages from my parents waiting;
they're doing well . . . in Antarctica? There wouldn't be a rev-
olution or corruption to report on there, so is this a vacation
for them, a peaceful penguin interest piece?

Okay, timeline, I have some serious catching up to do.

I respond to their texts, then I check my phone further. A
group chat exists, and I'm part of it, along with the crew from
before, but there are new additions too. Lana and Miguel. I
don't recall meeting anyone with that name at Central, no
matter how I search my brain.

It's cool to have friends, I guess. Awkward in that I don't
know all of them. Dr. Perry's name isn't in my contacts anywhere, and I don't have the Telegram app downloaded. Does
that mean I'm the only one who remembers?

Even now, the details are fading. Maybe that's the nature
of paradox. Your brain finds it impossible to hold onto things
that never happened, so the details slip away bit by bit. Soon,
I might start thinking I had a psychotic break or that I dreamed
everything due to this head injury.

I hope Oliver's okay. I'm scared to death that I'll forget him
and it will be like none of this ever happened.

Even if he's gone, forever beyond my reach, I still want to
find out what happened to him. I'd be lucky to find his grave,
and that . . . that is killing me. If the reset took his letters too,
I'm not sure how I'll cope. Shivering, I open the shoebox I hid
in my dresser.

I find a neat bundle of letters, tied with a green ribbon. It happened; I didn't dream any of it. Somewhere in the world, assuming my notes weren't destroyed, my words are now over a hundred years old.

That realization bolsters me so I can go on. I eat the food and struggle out of bed, checking myself over. As Archibald mentioned, my left leg is bandaged, and I'm covered in scrapes and bruises consistent with a serious fall. My head aches too, so I hang on to the banister on my way down.

"You shouldn't be up," Ottilie chides, coming to help me.

First thing I notice? The downstairs is different. No more sad Victorian style to show she's locked in the past. The furniture is clean and modern, and the walls are painted in warm and cheerful hues, a pretty contrast to the original woodwork. Her style is different too. She's wearing slacks instead of a long skirt, matched with a pretty twinset and a gleaming strand of pearls, less Miss Havisham and more timeless New England elegance. The lines beside her mouth come from smiling, no frown lines etched from sorrow.

She helps me to the sofa, a cushy white sectional, and I sprawl, propping up my left leg. "Sorry to worry you like this."

That's an apology for what she must've gone through the day I went missing, taken by Sofia Bruner. She doesn't remember, but I do. For now.

I have so many questions, but nobody can answer them.

"I'm calling Logan. He was over first thing this morning to check on you. Someone has a crush," she teases.

Huh. I think that was true before, but I never gave him the chance to tell me. Really, I'm not ready to hear it now. Oliver is still an open wound, a love that feels as inevitable as it is impossible.

He wanted to give me a ring.

That sounds faintly ridiculous because people don't marry this young in my time, but in his day, they did. And he was ready to propose and live every day with me for the rest of his life.

"Araceli? Is that all right with you?" Tía prompts.

"Oh, sure." I'm kind of a mess, but that doesn't matter. I wonder if Logan remembers my lice story, or if I haven't told him that in this life.

No idea what my aunt said to him, but he's knocking on the door in less than five minutes. She lets him in, and the moment he strides into the room, I still, because he's Logan, but also . . . not Logan.

His features are the same, but his hair is shorter, and he carries himself with a confidence he lacked before. There's no hint of the clown in his bearing, and his eyes are so direct. Damn. His expression . . . it's like Oliver's the night we met in his camp.

When he sits on the cushion where my leg is propped and gazes at me with intense dark eyes, my heart flutters. That has never happened before. At best, he was a puppy I might snuggle.

"I'm so glad to see you're all right," he says.

"Me too," I whisper.

He cocks his head, questioning, and I know he's baffled when I hug him, but I wasn't sure I'd ever see him again.

Logan is back. The lost ones have come home—no, it's more that they never left.

I think it's understandable if I'm feeling a little smug right now. Everyone dreams of making the world a better place, but I did it.

Too bad nobody will ever know.

53

Logan hugs me for a few seconds, then he sits back with a quizzical look. "Are you okay? You're acting odd."

"Yeah, I'm fine. It just feels like it's been a while."

His brows shoot up. "It was yesterday."

"Whatever," I snap. "You can go home."

"I was planning to, now that I've seen that you're awake and relatively recovered." He gets up and heads toward the door with his new, easy confidence.

I watch him through the window and he waves at me before jogging across the street. Damn, I have so much to figure out. I check for Jackson's contact information in my phone and find it, thankfully. I send a simple message—What's up? My heart's in my throat. He should be fine, right? But I can't erase the memory of him dying in my arms.

You feeling any better? he sends back.

Was he on the hike or not? I don't have any memory of the trip we supposedly took, and maybe I should have said that earlier, but then there would be awkward questions and maybe brain scans. I need to get a handle on things without worrying anyone.

About as well as you'd expect, I answer.

Ah, well, take it easy. I guess I should I have gone with to keep you out of trouble. What was Logan doing anyway? Fairhaven

National Park is like his backyard. He should've taken better care of you.

I read the text a couple of times before it sinks in. There's no lab here? Quickly I switch to the browser on my phone and do a search for Fairhaven Lab. Before, there wasn't a lot online about them; now there is nothing. I search Fairhaven National Park and find a complete website about camping and fun activities for the whole family.

It's not a big deal, I send to Jackson. Don't blame Logan.

Jackson is alive. He didn't go on the hike, but he's fine. Does that mean Dr. Perry is healthy and whole too? Probably the man I killed with a hammer and the ones I shot, they're all restored too. It's a weight off my conscience that I'm not a killer in this timeline, but I have the potential in me. I'll never be able to forget that.

Chill for a bit, use this to skip school if at all possible. I'm headed over to Eunsoo's.

Are they together now? Before, Jackson died thinking of her. Then it hits me. Oh my God, she's back. Quickly I check my phone for private chat records, but to my dismay, I don't find any. So Eunsoo has become someone I met recently, rather than a friend I chatted with online for years? Sighing, I try to adapt. I can get to know her better slowly so it's not weird. She can be my best friend again, as long as she's here and safe.

Taking it a step further, I look up Sofia Bruner. There are several of them, but when I switch to the images tab, I identify her in the fifth row, third over, and then backtrack to the page where she's mentioned. It seems like she's participating in a symposium in Geneva soon, where she will be presenting a paper on recombinant DNA. From what I can tell by skimming the article, she became a biomolecular engineer in this timeline, nothing to do with her ancestor, the spy, at all.

Did she not find the first Sofia's papers? Or did she give up when Lawrence Winslow wouldn't sell his father's legacy? I check for Frederick Winslow online, but I don't find anything. Same with Hans Weber. I suppose if their work dwindled to nothing in the eighties or before, there wouldn't be much on the internet about it.

Ottilie and Archibald come in from the kitchen together, adorably holding hands. I wonder if they sense on some level that being together like this is kind of a miracle. Whatever it was like for Archibald, I'm glad he doesn't remember all those years of lonely exile. I imagine it was like living in a ghost town, where you can interact with all the objects, but there's nobody else around. Maybe as other people got lost in the timeslips, they might have popped into his reality, but there's no way to be sure of that. Worst-case scenario, he spent twenty years utterly alone, roving a town with no other inhabitants.

I would have had a breakdown.

My great-aunt and uncle win top marks for cutest elderly couple, as their hands linger even after they sit in armchairs across from me. Ottilie asks, "Will you be up to school tomorrow? It's all right if you aren't. You need the rest."

"I should be fine."

"If you're sure," Archibald says.

I'm not used to having him here, but there's no doubt that Ottilie is happier. Though they've probably been married for forty years—or longer—they give off a honeymooner vibe. Feeling like they need some privacy, I slide off the couch and make for the stairs.

"I'll rest up tonight, no worries."

"Call me if you need anything," Ottilie offers.

I mumble something in response and struggle to my room. The leg I wasn't shot in hurts a lot, which is so confusing. It was a stick, a stick I don't recall falling on. A groan escapes me as I let sleep take me.

When I wake, I can't remember dreaming anything, which underscores the fact that Oliver is lost to me. I only know his first name and the unit he served in; even a skilled historian couldn't figure out what happened to him with such scant information. My failure to follow up means I can't look for him now, like I never found out about Lester and Lucy.

My heart aches as I roll out of bed.

No regrets—I did the right thing, but I do wonder what would have happened if I had chosen differently. Would I be wandering around 1915, trying to contact Oliver? It would have been a Herculean task to find one GI in a time without computers or cell phones. Hell, I might have spent years searching, even assuming he came home from the war safe and sound.

I gather up my clothes and take them to the bathroom. Showering is a pain, but I manage not to get my bandage wet through some impressive feats of agility. As I get dressed, a delicious smell drifts in—pastry and bacon? Curious, I hurry to the kitchen and find Archibald in a blue gingham apron. The bacon is perfectly crisp and he's finishing up a short stack of French toast.

"Good morning, my dearest," he says cheerfully. "I hope you brought your appetite."

Okay, I love him already. No wonder my great-aunt waited for him in sorrow and silence. No wonder she never considered moving on or marrying someone else. There's just something so lovely and sweet about this man that I'm tearing up over breakfast.

"Thank you."

His food tastes delicious, made even better when he offers me a glass of fresh-squeezed orange juice. Then he packs me a lunch while I'm eating, and I have such a happy glow as I'm leaving the house that I can't believe this is real life. The Victorian house is warm and charming, and the entire neighborhood glows like a jewel. Well-kept houses with fresh paint and emerald-green lawns as far as the eye can see, and people seem friendly as I walk down the street. The neighbors aren't all white either.

A squad car rolls up beside me, and I tense when I recognize Sheriff Reed. But this isn't the same man I knew before. For one thing, his hair isn't buzzed with military precision, and he's grown an ugly mustache. He's smiling as he rolls down the window.

"How are you today, Miss Araceli?"

"Fine," I say cautiously. "And you, sir?"

"Excellent! Do you want a lift to school?"

That seems . . . uncharacteristic. "No, it's okay. It's not that far."

"I heard about your accident, and I saw you're favoring your left leg. Are you sure I can't take you? It's the least I can do for one of Logan's friends."

54

That's how I end up going to school in a squad car.

It's only four blocks, but I expect things to go wrong almost as soon as I get in the car. Except Sheriff Reed is warm and friendly, joking with me about school. He's so unlike the scary, angry man I knew before that I pinch myself once to make sure I'm awake.

There's no hidden twist, though. He doesn't suddenly say, *ha ha, fooled you,* and then drag me off. Sheriff Reed drops me at the door, as promised, and offers a wave as I get out of the vehicle. Logan's bike is already locked out front—so strange that he'd own the same model when so much else has changed.

School is strange and surreal. My classes are a little different than I remember, and I finally have to get a new schedule printed at the office. I guess stories about my epic pratfall are making the rounds because the secretary gives me a sympathetic look as she hooks me up and doesn't ask any awkward questions.

At lunch, our table is crowded. Lana and Kimala seem to be dating, and Lana has lost that indefinable quality that made me think she was pretending to be nice. Now she radiates sincerity, still painfully cheerful, but it feels authentic, not as if she'll start bad-mouthing you the minute your back is turned. I'm glad to see Derek, Tamsyn, and Jackson, all alive and unharmed. Eunsoo is sitting close to Jackson, which makes me think they're a couple, and Miguel, I don't remember at all.

He's a handsome boy whose parents came from Guatemala, dark hair, light brown eyes, medium-brown skin. And he seems to know me better than Eunsoo. Wait, have I been chatting with him online? Is Miguel my current best friend? I check my phone and find that that seems to be the case.

Apparently, he went hiking with us. "You look way better than you did yesterday."

"That's not saying much," I joke.

Derek nods. "Got that right. Your leg was bleeding so much."

"Sorry for scaring everyone." Not sure if an apology is the proper response, but I don't know how I fell or why. I glance at Kimala. "I think I'll need to skip dance team practice for a few days."

Kimala glances at Lana, who shrugs. Then she asks, "Uh, are you confused? You didn't make the cut, remember?"

Damn, I auditioned and failed in this timeline? Ouch. I wonder what went wrong. Well, overall, things are better, right? This is no big deal, though I'll miss being part of the team and performing at halftime. The dance team saved my ass, though they don't remember doing it.

I put a hand to my head, pretending to experience a painful twinge. "Oh, right. Sorry. I dreamt that I made the squad last night, and I guess my head is still fuzzy."

Logan reaches over without hesitation and grabs my chin, tilting my face so he can look deeply into my eyes. "Your pupils are fine. It's probably not a concussion."

"Reality is just a bit twisted for me right now," I say, pulling his hand away. "Don't worry about it. I'll adapt."

From the looks they're giving me, everyone at the table thinks I'm being weird. Nothing I can do about that, but I don't feel like eating anymore. How am I supposed to figure out what activities I'm involved in? There's no manual for a situation like this.

"You don't look good," Lana says gently. "Want me to take you to the nurse?"

I give up. "Sure, maybe I should have rested more before coming back."

That won't solve anything, though. Hiding in my room won't help me adjust. I let Lana escort me to the nurse's office, where the nurse takes my temperature. "It's a little elevated. Do you want to rest in here for a while?"

"Yeah, thanks."

I kill the rest of lunch hour and one whole class on a cot, but I can't milk a mild fever any longer, or she'll call Ottilie and Archibald. After thanking the nurse, I finish my classes in a daze, and I'm about to leave when Tamsyn calls, "Aren't you coming to show choir?"

"What?"

"Damn, you're really not okay. Show choir," she repeats the words slowly. "We have practice tonight. Mrs. Beard will understand if you sit out the dance aspect, but you need to be working on your solo."

She won't be amused if I say, Hold up, I need to find out what show choir is, so I follow her quietly to the music room. As it turns out, this group sings and dances, and their sets include both vocal performance and choreographed dance routines. I've never had any formal training, but I do like singing along when the right song is on.

It's past four when practice lets out. I'm dying to ask how I ended up as part of this group, but people are already questioning my behavior. That can't lead anywhere good.

"Need a ride?" Tamsyn asks. "If you give me ten minutes to talk to Mrs. Beard, I can drop you off."

"No, it's fine. I'll take it slow. Thanks, though." Really, I just want some time on my own to process, but when I leave school, I find someone I never would've expected waiting for me.

Dr. Edward Perry.

He's leaning on his car, a nondescript white Buick, and I can't believe he's here. There's no reason he would be; he can't possibly remember me. I limp toward him cautiously, half expecting him to wave at someone else. Maybe he's here to pick up his kid? We never talked about his family, other than his missing wife.

"Araceli," he greets me, as I'm about to walk past. "We need to talk."

"Yeah, sure." I'm operating on automatic, mind racing.

Maybe he's a bad guy in this timeline. Even as I think that, though, I still get in the car when he opens the passenger door for me. The look in his eyes seems the same, so I'll risk this conversation, mostly because I'm dying to talk to someone about all this. The only way he'd be here is if he recalls some part of what we did together.

He drives for a while in silence, eventually parking at a rest area off the highway, far enough out of the way that we shouldn't run into anyone I know. I shift in my seat and ask, "What's this about?"

"First, I want to thank you. Ivette is back . . . and safe. I told her I had to attend a conference and drove nearly five hours to see you. We're living near Baltimore, it seems. Never moved to New York, I suppose, and I can't say I'm sorry."

"How do you remember me?"

He shakes his head. "I don't know. There's so much I don't understand . . . and maybe never will, because the memories are fading. I had to get to you before every scrap of cognition from the prior timeline leaves my head. Even now, it feels like a dream, or something that happened to someone else. I mean, I remember dying, bleeding out on the floor . . . and the next thing I knew, I was eating breakfast with Ivette."

"Maybe it's a defense mechanism," I suggest. "Like, our brains can't cope, so they overwrite the old reality to protect us?"

"Possible. The way things have unfolded . . . it doesn't match the simulation. The missing people were supposed to return from phase when we closed the timeslips, but I don't understand why nobody recalls they were missing."

"This was a . . . shift," I say, because I don't really know how to answer. "Something else happened. I'm just not sure what."

"Do you have any suspicions? It took all my mental discipline to hold you in my head on the way here. It's like new memories are trying to superimpose themselves over the old, events that never happened, but my mind is trying to convince me that they did. I won't have the wherewithal to discuss this with you in a week, so the debrief has to be now."

55

My memories are blurry, but not in the same way. I wonder why I can hold the old timeline easier than Dr. Perry can. But I'll admit the past is becoming hazy. Only Oliver remains bright and shining and indelible, but he's starting to feel like someone I made up, a fictional hero who won my heart.

No, he was real. He was.

I'm torn on whether I should admit this or not, but since he drove all this way to get closure, I should be honest. "I may have . . . meddled in the timeline."

"What?" Shock and horror are apparent in Dr. Perry's widened eyes and gaping mouth.

"So many people died or disappeared. I wasn't sure if closing the timeslips would be enough, so I wrote a letter warning Dr. Winslow not to let his son dispose of his life's work. I think maybe it had some effect? I don't know if I changed the past, or if I started a new timeline. I'm not clear on how any of that works."

Dr. Perry is speechless, gazing at me with dark eyes that burn like embers. "Even Dr. Bruner was careful in the beginning, Araceli. She spent years observing, making meticulous notes, and trying to decide the right point to intervene—and you just *scrawled off* a letter?"

"Uh. Yes." In fuchsia Sharpie, I might add.

He starts laughing and doesn't stop until I fear he's having a psychotic break. Finally, he scrubs his palms over his face and shakes his head. "Did you do anything else I should know about?"

Maybe this isn't important, but . . . "I also wrote some letters to a soldier who owned my box in 1917. Nothing I said to him changed anything, though." Not on a grand scale. I just did my best to make sure he survived the grueling horror of the war to end all wars. If only I could find out if he lived and whether he was happy. "I don't understand something, though. Everything else is different, but I still have those letters. You weren't in my contacts, but in this timeline, I still wrote to Oliver?"

Dr. Perry thinks about that, offering a joke as he ponders. "Well, it was called Project Paradox for a reason. But my best guess—the lab never existed in this timeline, but the prototypes did. So when history diverged after Dr. Winslow's death, you still had the chance to acquire the box, and you wrote to your soldier, even though everything else has changed. Does that make sense?"

"Oh. Yeah, it does. But . . . I don't have the box anymore. I threw it through the portal to close the timeslip."

"Are you sure? Have you searched for it?"

Oh, damn. Of course I haven't. "Would it still work?"

Jubilation goes off like fireworks. I could change the date and write to Oliver after the war, find out how he is. But maybe that's unfair and unkind. I already said goodbye and told him to move on. For him, there's no telling how long it's been. I could never figure out how our timestreams differed. Though it's only been a couple of days for me and the wound is fresh, for him, I might be a forgotten scar.

"Unless it's been damaged somehow, it should. But . . ." He hesitates.

"No, tell me."

"As long as those prototypes exist, there remains a chance for another Sofia Bruner to come along. This could start all over again, and it might not be stopped next time."

"You think I should destroy the box if I find it."

Dr. Perry nods. "I would. I'm heading to Pennsylvania after this. To see what became of Dr. Winslow's prototype, the box that we took from the archives. If I must, I'll leave myself notes like dementia patients do, so I can hold these memories long enough to be sure the threat is ended."

"I'll do the right thing," I promise.

"Then I think our debrief is done, unless you have further questions?"

When I shake my head, he starts the car. As he drives back toward my house, he says, "You don't work for anyone, do you?"

"I never said I did," I mumble.

"Strongly implied it."

"Listen, that was your assumption. I just let you believe whatever made you feel more comfortable."

"Then how the hell did you take out all those field generators?" His tone is all reluctant respect, laced with perplexity.

"Never underrate the power of determined teenagers," I say.

It's easy for me to talk now, but the price of that mission was so high. I'm not sorry I wrote that letter to Dr. Winslow. If I hadn't, the people might be back from phase, but they'd all be traumatized from their time in exile, and the people who died during our run on the facility would still be gone. Thanks to me, Dr. Bruner is doing important work, not on her way to becoming a supervillain.

"I feel like I got took," he says.

Which makes me laugh because Dr. Perry doesn't do slang, at least not that I've heard before. I'm a little sorry this is the last time I'll see him. After this, he probably won't remember me, and maybe I'll lose my memories of him too. In a month or two, this may feel like the only life I've ever known.

"Here we are." He parks in front of the updated Victorian.

My great-aunt and uncle are sitting on the porch, waiting for me with cookies and lemonade. This is so idyllic that I can't stand it.

"Thanks for everything," I say.

"That's my line. Look for the box, all right? And take care of yourself."

I hop out of the car and wave as Dr. Perry drives away. Great-Uncle Archibald comes down the stairs toward me, dapper in a pressed shirt and bow tie. Really, how is he so relentlessly adorable? He frowns at the back of the departing Buick.

"Who was that? I don't approve of you riding in cars with people we don't know," he chides.

"Just a friend."

"He looked rather old to be described as such." Now Ottilie is in on the parenting action, but it doesn't feel bad. "Is there something you need to tell us? We won't judge you. Grown men who entice young girls should be ashamed."

Oh Lord. Poor Dr. Perry.

"It's not like that. He's Papi's friend who bought me pizza while passing through town." Hope they don't check with Papi on that, but good luck getting a hold of him in the Antarctic.

They both relax visibly, and their obvious care is sweet. "Oh, I see. Sorry for jumping to conclusions," Archibald says.

I smile at them. "No worries."

"Well, if you had pizza, you probably don't want a snack." Great-Aunt Ottilie casts a woebegone look at the platter of cookies.

"Hey, cookies are always welcome." I grab a couple on my way into the house. "Homework calls. I'll see you for dinner."

I limp up the stairs, but instead of getting down to work, I open the drawer where I kept the heartwood box—and as Dr. Perry predicted, it's here. Because the lab never existed, I never threw it through a portal.

Even if I remember doing that.

I check it over. There's no crack from the ATV accident, and it's been polished until it shines, maybe by me? I remember how the tree sigil glowed when it got close to the field generators. What's inside this thing, anyway? Putting on a hazmat suit to break it doesn't seem like a bad idea.

The urge to write Oliver swells in a drowning wave, and I even open the box with a wistful sigh.

To find a shiny gold ring.

Here it is, the band he promised in his last letter. I don't know how it's here or why, but Oliver sent it. I slip it on; it's a little loose, but not so much that it will fall off.

Tears slip down my cheeks. I said farewell to him and let him go once already. How can I do it again?

56

No, this is a parting gift. It can't be anything else.

Dr. Perry trusts me to do the right thing, or he would have insisted on destroying the box himself. Some things are too dangerous to exist. This is one of them. Oliver has my necklace; I have his ring. That's all we can ever give one another.

This is the end.

Still, I can't stop crying as I pick up the box. There's a chance this is dangerous, so I can't just smash it on the floor of my room. Before I can lose my nerve, I call Logan. "Can you take me somewhere?"

"You don't feel up to driving yourself?" he asks.

Do I have my license already? Maybe just a permit. No matter, I can use my sore leg as an excuse. "My injury might make it hard."

"But you drive with your right."

The other Logan was much more eager to please, but I like the steel in this version, even if he's using it to block me. "Are you taking me or not? I can call someone else."

He sighs at my avoidance of the issue. "It's fine. I'll pick you up."

With the box hidden in my backpack, I tell the greats I'm heading out with Logan, and they must like him because I get beaming nods of approval in response. He has a car, apparently, a cute blue hatchback. I slide in, shut the door, and buckle my seat belt.

"Don't ask me any questions, okay? Just take me to the nearest junkyard."

"Excuse me?"

"That's a question. I'm not kidding, Logan. If you care about me at all, do this for me and don't make it harder."

My tone must penetrate because he puts the car in drive, and we take off. It's about ten miles on the highway, neither of us saying a word. He turns onto the dirt road flanked by two rusty gates, and yeah, this is a junkyard, rusty appliances and wrecked cars lined up in rows. He parks in front of a trailer with a dirty OFFICE sign posted on it.

I'm doing this.

Ignoring the throb in my leg and the ache of my heart, I step out and rap on the open door.

"Come!" someone shouts, a little old lady wearing a ball cap and too much lipstick. "How can I help you?"

I pull the box out of my bag. "I want this crushed. How much will that cost?"

Logan stares at me like I've lost it, but I ignore him.

The old woman gets up with a grunt and comes over. "That little thing? Why bother? Just hit it with a hammer, honey. It'll be way more personally satisfying." From her expression, she thinks this is a teen-girl breakup ritual.

"It's really important," I say.

She sighs. "Don't tell anyone I did this for you. I don't want to see a steady stream of angsty youngsters in here. Come with me."

At her instruction, I drop the box into a big metal container, and I can see a car suspended above it. There's a hammer-like thing that will mash the car. I think she's going to drop a car on the box, then crush it. Yeah, that should do the job.

Dr. Perry would be proud.

"Ralph is on break, but I worked this thing for years. I'll do this for you, so cheer up and stop thinking about the rotten shit who broke your heart."

I sniffle and try to smile as she climbs into the machine and starts moving levers around, getting the car in perfect position, then she lets it fall. The junked vehicle smashes down, then she activates the compressor, smashing the metal into a cube. There's no way a wooden box survived that. There's no explosion, no leaking of chemicals as far as I can tell.

"Thank you," I whisper.

"No problem." She pats me on the shoulder on her way back to the office.

Logan leads me to the car, and I don't realize until I get in that I'm crying uncontrollably. That was my last link to Oliver. I did the right thing. Again. It's best for both of us, and the sooner I accept that, the better.

"Hey, stop," Logan says, alarm in his tone. "You're freaking me out."

"S-sorry. Just drive. I'll . . . be fine."

Eventually.

By the time we get back, I have myself together enough that I hope I won't terrify my great-aunt and uncle when I come in. Logan stops me as I'm about to climb out, a gentle hand on my arm. "Are you ever going to tell me what this was about?"

"Probably not." It's best to be candid.

"That's not fair."

"Such is life."

"If you go in now, they're going to ask you a lot of awkward questions. And I doubt they'll let you deflect like I did. Why don't you come to my place for dinner?"

That's an unexpected invitation, but I could use the recovery time. "Won't your parents ask what's wrong with my face?"

"If they do, I'll say you have allergies. I'll also get you a cold compress. Deal?"

Reluctantly, I smile, because he seems committed to making this dinner happen. "Let me call the greats. They'll worry if I don't keep them posted."

"You're so sweet to them," he says. "It's one of the many things I like about you."

Wow, he just came right out and said it. He's not the Logan I knew before. I get on the phone and notify the elder relations that I'll be dining across the road. Honestly, they seem delighted, so I guess they ship me with Logan.

"All set. Let's go in."

He rushes around to get my door and help me out, as if this suddenly became a date. I'm not ready for this, not at all. His parents are inside already, and his mom is cooking. The house is nothing like before. Though the house is small, it's painted in light colors to make it feel more spacious, and I love the cozy cottage style she's chosen.

"Glad to finally meet you," Mrs. Reed says, waving a spatula at me. "I've heard so much about you from Logan that I feel like I already know you."

"Nice to meet you," I reply.

"Shoes off," Logan says. "My maternal grandmother is Japanese, so it's a habit."

Ah, that's why he did that at my place. I slip into the slippers he offers me and spot Sheriff Reed lounging in his recliner. He gets up to welcome me with a two-handed shake, cupping my hand warmly. "So happy you're here. How's the leg?"

Okay, why is Logan's family so different? His dad has the same face, but that's about it. He used to be such a hard-ass who was never satisfied. I'm glad for Logan, but this is so damn confusing.

"We'll be in my room until dinner's ready," Logan says.

His mom nods, busy frying something. "Keep the door open!"

He sighs, but when we retreat to his room, he does leave it cracked, gesturing at the bed. "Have a seat. I promised you a cold pack. Be right back."

Since this is the only place to sit, I curl up on a corner of his bed. When he brings me the ice, I put it on my eyes and tilt my head against the wall. "Thanks."

"Good, keep your eyes closed. It'll make it easier for me to say this. I *really* like you, Araceli. In fact, I fell for you almost from the start, as soon as I heard your name."

"I . . . what? Why?" That's such a strange way for a crush to begin that I can't help asking. I did suspect he was into me, but that was in the other timeline, and I haven't been living in this timeline long enough to be sure how he feels.

Logan plucks the ice pack from my face and gazes into my eyes. "I tried to tell you this story once before, but I got cut off. Will you listen now?"

57

"Sure," I say.

"When you told me your name is Araceli Flores Harper, I started to tell you my name is Logan Oliver Reed. I was named after my great-grandfather."

My heart can't take this. I'm frozen, staring at him in wonder. Are those Oliver's eyebrows? Oliver's dark eyes?

"Oh?" I manage.

"And here's where it gets really interesting. When I first saw you, I thought you were pretty, but later I found out your name, and I swear it's destiny. See, my family has this . . . legend, I guess you'd call it. My great-grandfather fought in the First World War, and somehow, I was never clear on how . . . he met this lady named Araceli. Nobody in the family ever met her, so some of them think he made her up to keep from going insane in the trenches. He never spoke about her, except when he'd had a little to drink, but according to my great-uncle Lester, she was the love of his life, the one who got away."

"That must have made your great-grandmother sad," I whisper.

He lifts a shoulder. "I don't know. I think she lost her first love too, so she understood a little how he felt."

Logan is Oliver's great-grandson? I can't believe what I'm hearing, but at the same time, I desperately want this to be true because it means Oliver survived the war, lived through being lost in the Argonne, and came home to start a family.

"Do you have any pictures of him?" I ask.

"What?" He blinks, likely surprised at how seriously I'm taking this story. "Sure, let me get the album."

I sit, staring at the gold ring on my finger. It's not on my left hand; I chose to wear it on my right because this couldn't be my wedding ring. Oliver grew old with someone else, but more importantly, he *lived*. Maybe because of me, and that's why Logan—

Oh shit.

When Logan faded, when he was erased, that wasn't because of the timeslip. That was *my* doing. I remember how Oliver said he'd wait for me, that he'd look as long as it took. If he had done that, he wouldn't have married or had children. Logan and his father would have ceased to exist. I wonder if it was faster for Logan because of his brush with the ghost lights? Most likely, Sheriff Reed would have vanished at some point too.

Logan returns with an old photo album, one that I feel like I need to be careful touching. That's how old the pictures are. Logan opens it to show me a somber young man in military uniform, and oh my God, it is Oliver, my Oliver. With trembling hands, I touch the photo through the protective cellophane. I don't wait for him to start flipping pages. I do it myself, turning slowly through a visual progression of my first love's life. I watch him age and change, until I see him at the end, as a very old man.

My eyes are wet when I look up at Logan, who is so worried. That's Oliver's sweetness, Oliver's gentleness. It hits me then, how I asked him to raise his sons to be good people instead of "real men." Is that why his dad turned out better in this reality? I hope that's true. I want to have left more than hopeless longing behind.

"I had no idea you'd find this story so touching," he whispers, wiping up my tears with his fingertips.

Maybe it's strange and wrong, but I let him. My heart is on fire with wonder and gratitude. "You said some of your family doesn't believe she existed. What about you?"

"I think she did. He loved her so much, and I have this." He tugs on a necklace hidden beneath his shirt, revealing an incredibly old-looking leather strap adorned with a green agate amulet.

It was new when I sent it.

"Where did you get it?" I almost can't get the words out. It's so hard not to curl up and sob, hearing all this.

"It was a legacy from my grandfather. Well, he left it to my dad, but according to the story, it's supposed to protect the person who wears it, so my dad said he wanted *me* to have it." Logan tips his head, sheepish, but his smile reveals how much he appreciates his dad's gesture.

"It's pretty," I say softly. "I hope you never take it off."

"Only to shower. Anyway, when I found out that your name is Araceli, I just knew."

"Knew what?"

"That you're meant for me. It must be fate that you came halfway around the world to meet me. I've never known anyone with that name before, so it's like . . ." He struggles for words, leaning closer to me instead. "This will sound cheesy, but I'm positive we're supposed to be together. Don't laugh."

"Maybe you're right."

"Logan!" Mrs. Reed calls. "Can you come help me make the salad? We're almost ready to eat."

"On my way. Feel free to look more at the album. I'll get

you when the food is on the table. We'll . . . talk more about us later?" Such a hopeful smile.

"Sure. Yeah."

I'm back to staring at Oliver's pictures in the album, touching each one like it can transport me across the years. Wow, if I'd chosen to step through that portal, would I be in these pictures as Logan's great-grandmother? Or maybe Logan wouldn't exist. There would be some other boy sitting here, or who knows, possibly we wouldn't have had kids at all. I don't even know if I want them. In my time, I'm way too young to think about that.

The portrait of Oliver as a stately elder gentleman, probably taken in the early sixties, draws my eye, mostly because it feels thicker than the rest. Curious, I peel back the cellophane and find a small, folded page tucked behind the picture. When I spread it out, I recognize the handwriting immediately, though it's somewhat crimped with age.

My darling Araceli,

I believe what you wrote. It's true that I struggled with it at first, but it explains so much. Once I accepted it, everything made sense. And since that is true, I'm leaving this behind in the hopes that you may come looking for me some day, long after I'm gone.

I missed you every moment of my life. I tried not to look for you in crowded places, but I never stopped. You remain the love of my life, even now. My family owns part of my heart, but I cannot give them what you took, so long ago. The year is 1963. And I am still pining for you. I've done my best to do as you asked—to raise my boys to be good people. Only time will tell if I succeeded.

I don't know if you got my ring. After that last letter, I don't know what became of you, but I hope wherever, *whenever you are, that you are safe and happy. I'm also selfish enough to hope you remember me.*

This may be nothing more than an old man's fancy, but I will pretend that my words have reached you, somehow. That's the only way I can die in peace.

Please be well and live your life like I'm there with you. Maybe some way, somehow, I will be. You were my life's saving grace, and I carry you with me from this world into the next, and I hope if there is another life for us, we'll meet again. Until then.

My love always,
Oliver Wendell Reed

I bite down on my hand to stop the sobs. How am I supposed to act like nothing's happened when this is the last time I'll ever hear from someone I love this much? I can't breathe but somehow, I hold it in, because I hear Logan coming down the hall. He pops his head in the doorway, smiling so brightly that I feel guilty for the ambivalence roaring through me.

Is this what you meant, Oliver? Is this how you're with me?

"Dinner's done," he says. "Are you hungry?"

Mustering a smile, I tuck the note into my pocket, to be filed under impossible love, and I take Logan's hand when he offers it. I chose already, after all. First, when I said farewell to Oliver at the lab, and again, when I destroyed the prototype, my only link to him.

With each step I put the past behind me and step into a future that is wide open, shining like the sun.

ACKNOWLEDGMENTS

First, let me cite some of the sources that I used in research-ing this novel. I read a lot about World War I before I started writing. Check out *Finding the Lost Battalion* by Robert J. Laplander. It's a long book, so if movies are more your speed, you could watch *The Lost Battalion* instead. For a more per-sonal look at what life was like then, try *Love Letters of the Great War*, edited by Mandy Kirkby. I used the love letters I read to craft Oliver's correspondence to Araceli. I also read up on slang of that time, but I tried not to use too much. If you're interested in World War I, ask a librarian for some other rec-ommendations, because there are many unsung heroes whose stories should live on.

The town that Araceli lives in goes unnamed in the story, but it's inspired by a real place in upstate New York. I won't say more than that, but if you're curious, input "New York town with Nazi street names" and start reading. You may be shocked by what you learn. America has a lot of secret history that you won't learn in any classroom. As a fun side note, I made up 7TOG, which is a nod at GOT7. Give yourself a good-job pat if you noticed. K-pop forever!

Moving on, I'll give credit where it's due. Thanks to Luci-enne Diver for her great ideas. She's the best agent I could ask for and I'm so grateful for her help and experience. Next, thanks to Melissa Frain who partnered with me to take this project from a flicker of an idea to a fully executed and beautiful book. I also thank my copyeditor, Christa Soulé Désir, whose every suggestion was brilliant and impeccable. I truly appreciate the whole team at Tor for their hard work and exceptional expertise in polishing my words to a diamond-bright shine. This is a job for many hands, and I couldn't do it without them.

Thanks to Rachel Caine for always listening when I need her. Thanks to Bree Bridges, Donna J. Herren, Alyssa Cole, and Lilith Saintcrow. I couldn't do this job without their support. I also appreciate Kate Elliott for sharing her wisdom. Thanks to Beverly Jenkins, Kate Kessler, Suleikha Snyder, Victoria Helen Stone, and Melissa Blue for inspiring me with their work. I am surrounded by greatness and constantly aspiring to the level of my gifted colleagues.

I send hugs to my beta readers, who have been field-testing my stories for many years—Karen Alderman, Fedora Chen, and Pamela Webb-Elliott. You ladies deserve all the cookies. Last but not least, I send love and gratitude to my family for putting up with me, especially Alek, who loves bouncing ideas around with me.

Finally, I couldn't do this without readers who are still eager for my stories. Thank you for your support and please keep letting me build new worlds for you to explore.